THE WEREWOLF'S KISS

CHERI SCOTCH

D1007568

DIAMOND BOOKS, NEW YORK

MAGICAL DISCLAIMER
This book harms none and is for the good and enjoyment of all.
So Mote It Be.

This book is a Diamond original edition, and has never
been previously published.

THE WEREWOLF'S KISS

A Diamond Book / published by arrangement with
the author

PRINTING HISTORY
Diamond edition / October 1992

ISBN: 1-55773-801-7

Diamond Books are published by The Berkley Publishing Group,
200 Madison Avenue, New York, New York 10016.
The name "DIAMOND" and its logo are trademarks
belonging to Charter Communications, Inc.

PRINTED IN THE UNITED STATES OF AMERICA

10 9 8 7 6 5 4 3 2 1

On stormy nights, at the dark of the moon, when sensible people seek the comfort of strong doors and reassuring lights, there exists a company of people who welcome the ferocious dark. They glory in the lightning; they have union with the night; they find excitement and the joy of life in the touch of the unknown. They are the people who seek out books like this, because they know that life without the electrifying frisson of fear is no life at all.

They share with the author the sure and certain knowledge that It is always out there, lurking in the moonshadows. And in a world made dull by too much common sense and too little imagination, they thank the gods that It is.

Keep imagining. Keep dreaming. Keep watching at the gates of night. It was for you that I did this.

ACKNOWLEDGMENTS

Bruce Laing, for support and Godiva chocolates

Lori Perkins, for dead-on instincts and sheer stamina

Andrew Zack, for impeccable literary taste

Laurie Cabot, for wit, wisdom and witchcraft

Diana, Selene, Hecate, Cernunnos and Pan; and the Temple of Diana

Jerry and Vicki Sawyer, for all sorts of things including the pumpkins

And thanks to the masters, Lyle Saxon and Robert Tallant, the twin wellsprings to whom so many writers on Louisiana folklore have come

PART ONE

†

The Loup-garou

1

"Aw, John . . . I'm having me a big ol' muffaletta, drippin' with oil and vinegar and the whole works. I don't want to hear about no corpse with his heart torn out, no."

Achille Broussard alternately frowned at the phone and wistfully looked back toward the counter, where the counterman was putting together an enormous, garlicky sandwich. His beeper had gone off at just about the same time he'd placed his order.

"Look here, John, and remember this so I don't have to tell you no more. This guy dead, right?"

"Lieutenant Broussard," John said, a little offended, "I can tell when somebody's dead."

John Sullivan, the young cop on the other end of the line, sounded nervous. Achille knew the kid had just been promoted, wasn't sure of the established procedure, and had the disadvantage of having lived most of his life in Shreveport. *Shreveport*, for God's sake . . . that was practically Texas. Considering all the handicaps, Achille figured he'd give the kid a break. Educate him a little in the way things were done in New Orleans.

"Well, he still gonna be dead twenty minutes from now, which gives me time to sit in Jackson Square, eat this masterpiece of a sandwich, have me a cold one, and watch them pretty girls pass by. You not from the bayou, John, so you don't understand. It's sacrilegious to interrupt a man while he's contemplatin' nature in Jackson Square. So you tell them forensic suits to just do their jobs and hold their dicks till I get there."

"Yes, sir, I'll tell them."

"And don't nobody touch nothin', you hear me?"

3

"I hear you." The young cop's voice sounded a little amused now. He was beginning to get into the rhythm of the way things obviously were at the N.O.P.D.

"This your first homicide?" Achille said.

"Yes, sir."

"You just wait, boy. We gonna have us a party. Ooo-*wee*!"

Sullivan put down the mike in the police cruiser and turned around to the uniformed cop standing a few feet away at the crime scene. "Don't nobody touch nothin'," he told the cop. "The Ragin' Cajun's on his way."

"Where's he at?" the cop wanted to know. "Knockin' off a piece over by the Voodoo queen's?"

"He says he's studyin' nature in Jackson Square."

The cop laughed, shaking his head. " 'Ooo-*wee*!' " the cop said.

Less than a half hour later Lieutenant Broussard, outfitted in a pair of oversize mirrored sunglasses, was out in City Park doing his job. A lot was going on: John Sullivan was there; a whole fleet of uniforms, including Joe Ed Landry, an experienced cop who'd worked with Broussard for twenty years; and more forensic suits than Achille could remember seeing at one crime scene. In one hand, Achille carried the half-eaten muffaletta in wrinkled, messy butcher's paper.

"Hey, Achille!" Landry called. "I like the shades. Who you think you are, Cool Hand Luke?"

Achille shot him the finger and lifted the sheet to look at the body.

Sullivan was standing by the corpse and looking a little shaky. Achille knew that they didn't get nasty murders like this in Shreveport.

"This is a mean one," Landry told him. "Poor bastard. Very bad way to die."

"Um, um, um," Achille said sympathetically, "this boy done pissed somebody off bad, yeah. When'd they find him?"

"Early this morning. About six-thirty," Landry said. "Some joggers almost tripped over him; lady 'bout had a hemorrhage when she looked down and seen this sweet thang. Now, don't he look familiar to you, Lieutenant?"

Achille bent down to peer at the corpse. "I'll be damned! Floyd Thibideaux! He's not looking his best, no."

This was true. The body lay on its back, its mouth still trying to scream. The eyes were wide open in horror and frosted with a film of death. The hands were frozen in a clawlike position in front of the chest, as if Floyd had been fighting off something inexorable.

"Ain't he cute?" Landry asked Achille.

"Looks better than the last time we seen him, huh, Joe Ed?" Achille looked around. "So where's the missing body parts?"

Landry shrugged. "Don't know. What you see is what we got."

John Sullivan tried to look at the corpse—which was his job—and to do it without actually looking at it—which was his preference. This effort wasn't lost on Achille.

"You know, Joe Ed," Achille said loudly to Landry, "in New Orleans heat, a body starts to fill up with maggots in six to eight hours. The medical examiner told me."

Joe Ed loudly expressed his surprise. "No shit? I guess this old boy's about to bust open. We better stand back."

Achille held out the remains of the dripping muffaletta to Sullivan. "I can't finish this. You want it?"

Sullivan turned a delicate shade of green and ran to the bushes.

Achille turned to Joe Ed with a satisfied grin. "Jesus save me, but I love doin' that."

"You real bad," Landry said, shaking his head.

One of the forensic suits came over. "You're gonna love this, Achille. The guy's throat is completely torn out, just ripped apart like a wild animal did it. And you'll notice that his chest cavity is opened up, but nothing inside is touched or missing—except his heart. It's like the killer started to rummage around in there, but got interrupted."

"Most likely had to stop to barf," Landry observed.

"But here's the good part." The forensic guy held up a little plastic bag.

Achille squinted at the contents. "Hairs?"

"Yeah, you right. Animal hairs. And guess where they were? Under the fingernails."

"So some killer comes out here in City Park, waits for Floyd Thibideaux, the scumbag's scumbag, and sics his pit bull on him? I like it. Landry, put out an all-points: if Rin-Tin-Tin's in the area, pick him up and haul his furry ass in."

The forensics guy shrugged. "Yeah. Make fun. Remember: forensics wins in the end, bro. The mobile lab's still doin' their stuff here." He waved a hand vaguely toward the huge van parked at the scene.

Achille regarded the body thoughtfully. "You know, if we'd been able to get a conviction on this guy three months ago, he woulda been in Angola right now, safe as church," he said.

Sullivan, back from the bushes, hadn't heard the story. "What happened? What'd he do?"

"The worst you can do, yeah. Child abuse. Repeat offender. Beat up his girlfriend's four-year-old boy so bad the kid was in the hospital three times. The last time, the emergency room wankers, who're not real bright sometimes, figured that *just maybe* the kid couldn't have gotten two broken ribs, a head wound, and third-degree burns from a fall down the stairs. This time it's so bad that the kid has convulsions and is in a coma. The girlfriend is having second thoughts about how much she loves Floyd, and it looks like she's gonna make a statement. But by the time we get to court, she's decided to stand by her man and claims she lied when she turned him in. That he wasn't even in town when her kid bought it. Just perjures her fine white ass all over the stand. The D.A. tries her damnedest to make a case against Mom, but that falls through, too. So the whole case gets thrown out, since we no longer have a credible witness. Now, don't that just knock your dick in the dirt?"

"Jesus," Sullivan breathed, looking at the deceased with less sympathy than before.

"Oh, no, *cher ami*, you ain't heard the sweet part. We know, or we're pretty sure we know, that a couple of other kids got beat up, and one eventually died. And ain't it a coincidence that old loverboy Floyd here was bangin' their mamas when it happened?"

Sullivan looked like he was going to be sick again. He retched, but fought it down.

Achille observed this. "Uh huh," he said quietly.

"You know what this looks like?" Landry said. "Voodoo. Them Voodoos got their own justice. Hey, Achille, you still seein' that Voodoo queen? Maybe you better ax her does she know any of them black-magic Voodoos."

"Yeah, she'll be happy to tell me anything, her," Achille said, smiling. He took off the big mirrored sunglasses.

"Holy shit!" Landry said, astonished. "That's some black eye, Lieutenant!"

"Yeah, you right," Achille agreed.

"The Voodoo queen give you that? That's some temper she got, that lady of yours. What you been doin', Achille? Hangin' out in the French Quarters with them horny tourist babies or what?"

"I can't help it if the ladies like what they see, *cher ami*."

Sullivan, his good manners suddenly overwhelmed by curiosity, blurted out, "Who in hell is this Voodoo queen you guys keep talking about?"

Landry laughed. "Son, the lieutenant here keeps company with the most powerful Voodoo woman since Marie Laveau, Mae Charteris. And Mae thinks he's too good-lookin' to be honest."

Talk like that made Achille uncomfortable. If there was one thing he didn't need, it was trouble with women; he had enough problems just keeping Mae happy. One night, under a waning moon, Mae had pierced one of Achille's ears and placed a small gold hoop through it. He wasn't sure whether that was just one of Mae's whims or if it was a gris-gris to keep him from straying, but the hoop, shining gold against his long black hair, was the final little touch that made Achille look just like one of New Orleans's pirate legends. He was already a romantic-looking man: tall and still muscular at forty, dark eyed, with a mysterious, smoky look. All this had a devastating effect on women. It had gotten him in big trouble with the Voodoo queen more than once, although Mae knew her stuff: there hadn't been another woman for him since she had put that ring through his ear.

"Yeah," Achille said, putting his sunglasses back on, "Madame Mae. She put gris-gris on you that dry your blood to dust, she got spells that turn your eyes back in your head and make you crawl on all fours and howl. And if that don't work, she throw stuff. Girl's got an arm, ooo-*wee*!"

The forensic guy came back to Achille.

"You're gonna love this, Lieutenant," he said again.

"Aw, man!" Achille moaned. "You still givin' me this 'killer dog' stuff?"

"Nuh uh. One of the guys did a quick test. These are wolf hairs."

Achille ran his hand through his own hair in impatience. "Wolf hairs. Well, that lets Old Yeller off the hook."

Achille paced around the body, searching the ground, looking in the flower beds and the bushes. He ran his hands over the grass.

He called back to Sullivan and Landry. "You guys find any prints, animal, human . . . anything?"

Landry shook his head. "Nothing. Just the deceased's. The grass ain't even torn up. Now that's strange: you'd think there'd been a hell of a fight."

Achille bent down to touch a patch of ground, still sticky with blood. He looked up. City Park had some old trees, tall trees with thick trunks. Floyd Thibideaux's body lay in a grove of those trees.

On one tree, very high up, almost twelve feet off the ground, the bark had been freshly torn off. And on the white, exposed tree pulp was a bright smear of drying blood. It looked as if Floyd had been picked up and thrown against the tree, so hard that the back of his head split.

Achille wondered if the forensic guys and the medical examiner would be able to find out that Floyd hadn't died of his wounds, terrible as they were. Instead, he had died of heart failure, of sheer terror, even before he had been touched. His killer, in a fury at being cheated of his vengeance, had flung Floyd against that tree before he tore him apart. The killer knew what Floyd had done to that little child, and what he had done to other kids before.

No matter. Floyd wouldn't do it again.

Achille admired the forensic guys. They were right on the money with that wolf-hair diagnosis. There'd be a full-scale investigation, of course, and a lot of noise, but the forensics' and the medical examiner's reports would all contain information so weird that it made an arrest impossible. Either they had a killer wolf who could perform precise chest surgery, or a psycho who wore a wolf's fur coat to do his killing in. But nothing would ever come of it, mainly because nobody had the imagination to carry it one step further. No one would ever officially mention the old Cajun term: *loup-garou*.

The state of Louisiana, in all its baroque legal wisdom, may not have executed Floyd Thibideaux, but the loup-garou did. The *Acadien* werewolf of the bayous was as much a part of Louisiana legends as the ghosts in the ruined plantation houses, a law unto himself, a force of nature and magic, making his own judgments on who was to live and who to die.

The police were to be forgiven for not recognizing the signs. A killing by the loup-garou was common, but actually finding a body was rare, very rare. The werewolf, with an animal's cunning and a human's intelligence, was ingenious at covering his tracks. This particular body was left as a gruesome valentine to the district attorney and all the good cops who had busted ass trying to put Floyd away.

Very few men had seen evidence of the presence of the loup-garou. Achille Broussard had seen it many times.

One of the first things that had brought Achille and Mae together was her understanding of the loup-garou, an ancient knowledge that Mae had acquired both by tradition and by instinct. The loup-garou was very much a creature of the Louisiana Voodoos, not enslaved by them, but voluntarily serving as the Voodoos' justice. Whatever Achille knew— and it was more than any man in New Orleans knew about the loup-garou—would never have been learned without the Voodoo queen.

Inadvertently, as he did every time he thought of Mae, Achille touched the gold hoop, as if drawing on some secret power she had given him, some gift of sight beyond what could be seen.

"Okay, let's get this stiff outta here, yeah," Achille told the forensic crews, "he ain't gonna tell us nothing we don't know while he's out here."

He wouldn't tell them anything more when they got him in the lab, either. No more than Achille knew now. And certainly no more than could ever be explained. If the police wanted a full accounting, only one person could give it to them: the loup-garou who had carried out the death sentence.

Only Achille knew who that was. He would live with it, as he lived with the full moon that swept his soul away on the steamy Louisiana nights when he danced on Bayou Goula with the werewolves, when they deferred to him, and paid him respect, and called him—simply, as one would call a king— Achille the loup-garou.

2

Andrew Marley wasn't quite sure what it was that woke him up. One moment he was sound asleep and the next his eyes were wide open.

Instinctively, he looked over to see that his wife was safe. He'd acquired this habit from the first dangerous days of their marriage, when he was in constant terror that he would inadvertently hurt her during the night. He knew it was irrational, but some remnant of that fear stayed in the dusty back corner of his mind. Even now, twenty years later, the first thing he did every morning was to check on his family.

His wife, Angela, was asleep.

He looked at the clock as he felt around for his slippers. Three-fifteen in the morning. And he could tell he wouldn't be back to sleep again: he was as awake as if he'd had a full night's rest.

The breeze blew the lace curtains in through the bedroom windows. Andrew loved this time of year. In Louisiana, spring came early and softly. The winds blew off the river, carrying cool currents of slightly crisp air that felt good against Andrew's skin. It was the kind of weather that made you sleep well, nestled under the covers against someone warm.

So what was the problem? he was thinking. What is it that feels so wrong?

He could see the round moon through the lace. There was a time when the sight of a full moon only presaged sorrow for him. It had taken so long to get over that terrifying, confusing part of his life. Perhaps he had been dreaming; dreams sometimes unlocked those doors that he had so carefully closed behind him.

He was just about to get up and look in on his kids when he heard a voice outside. A light, summery voice, a young woman's laughter. He leaned out the window to look.

"Sweet Jesus!" he breathed.

He didn't even stop to put on his robe. He ran down the stairs completely unaware that he was only in his pajama bottoms. He lost one of his slippers on the stairs, the other on the veranda steps leading out to the broad lawn.

She was a fairy queen standing on the wet grass, her gauzy gown floating out around her as the breeze lifted it, her long red hair the color of dark embers glowing under the moonlight. Her bare feet hardly seemed to touch the ground. Every so often she'd reach up toward the moon, as if she fully expected to catch it.

"Sylvie!" Andrew called.

She turned, smiling as she saw him. "Isn't it beautiful!"

"Sylvie, what are you doing out here?"

"Enjoying the moon," she explained. "Actually, I'm not quite sure. I couldn't sleep, so I got up and sat by the window, just looking out, thinking. And then I started watching the moon and I just felt so . . . strange. But a good kind of strange. I got this big surge of energy, like I could do anything. I guess I wandered out here without really thinking about it."

Andrew felt a cold band of horror grip his chest. He tried to fight down the panic. "I want you to come inside. Right now."

She laughed delightedly and jumped in the air, turning her body as she took a swipe at the moon. "One of these nights, I'll catch it."

"Sylvie . . ."

"Dad, it's fine. It really is a gorgeous night. How many perfect nights does anybody get in a lifetime? Let's sit for a minute and enjoy it."

"You shouldn't even be awake now. It's three in the morning. Come inside."

She stared at him, puzzled. "Three in the morning? But . . . that's not possible. I looked at the clock before I went out and it was only ten. I couldn't have been out here that long. I've just been sitting."

She held up the hem of her gown as if she'd never seen it before. It was ripped and ragged; filthy, as if she'd walked miles in it.

"I don't understand . . . ," she murmured distractedly, "how could I have gotten so dirty?"

Her father put his hands on her shoulders and turned her to him. Those eyes of hers, those innocent eyes; their deep turquoise marked her clearly as his daughter. They were his eyes, his father's, the eyes of all the Marleys before, passed to Sylvie along with . . . what? He felt the shudder start, but fought it down. "Sylvie, where have you been?"

She looked vaguely disturbed. "I haven't been anywhere. I don't *think* I've been anywhere. I just came out to enjoy the night."

She let him take her hand and lead her across the lawn. "Do people change under the moon, Dad?"

Andrew was sure his heart had stopped. Everything in him seemed to go cold. "What do you mean?"

"When I was a kid I used to think that they did. I was sure that the moon worked magic on people so they could do wonderful, magical things. And, you know, sitting out here on a night like this, I can almost believe that it's true."

Wonderful things, he thought, horrible things. Things that drive you screaming into the dawn. But to his daughter, seventeen and about to cross the borders into adult life, he only lied. "Well, you're no kid now, Sylvie, and I'm sure you know that everything's the same at night as it is during the day. Come inside."

She linked her arm through his and he led her into the house, gripping her tightly as if, by holding on to her, he could keep trouble away from his firstborn child.

3

Andrew was making breakfast when his wife came downstairs.

"What's all this?" Angela asked.

"I'm saying early Mass. As long as I had to be up before everyone else, I figured I'd make myself useful before I leave. Louise is sleeping in." Louise was the cook.

Angela sat down, still a little groggy. For some reason, she hadn't slept well: she kept falling into a restless half-sleep. She'd been glad to wake up, but she'd felt disoriented to find that Andrew wasn't beside her.

"I thought when you made the big leagues that you wouldn't have to pull hard duty anymore. Since when does a bishop have to take a curate's Mass?"

"Since the curate's so young that he's got measles, that's when."

Angela threw back her head and laughed that slightly bawdy laugh that Andrew loved. He had always thought that Angela's laugh had been what seduced him when he first saw her. That, he remembered, and the sexy cleavage. After twenty-two years of marriage and three kids, the laugh and the cleavage were still intoxicating.

"Are you kidding me?" Angela said. "That cute li'l Father Deslisle? How old is that sweet thing, anyway?"

"Just about the age I was when you seduced me at that party, so you keep away from him."

She laughed again. "*I* seduced *you*? You put your hand on my ass. Twice. And when we were dancing, you stuck your tongue in my ear and said, 'Wanna fuck?' I *could not* believe it . . . a young stalwart of the Anglican faith like you."

14

He smiled. This was old and familiar territory to them, something they never got tired of reinventing. "Please. You know perfectly well I would never have said any such thing," he said patiently, pouring milk into pancake batter. "I asked politely if you didn't want to leave the party. I escorted you home like a gentleman. I saw you safe inside."

"Then you said 'Wanna fuck?' "

"Then I *politely asked* 'Wanna fuck?' " He shrugged. "I was twenty years old. You were wearing that dress and those tits. What did you expect me to say? Besides, you were ten years older than me. I saw you as a mother figure; morally upright, mature judgment and all that."

Angela reached over and pinched his cheek. "You Oedipal little sweet talker, you."

He shrugged. "Well, I was counting on you to be the sensible one." He looked over at her and smiled. "I still do."

Their two youngest children, Walter and Georgiana, ten and twelve, came barreling down the stairs, arguing, teasing, Walter only half-dressed for school.

Angela gave Andrew an I-told-you-so triumphant glance. "And look where it's gotten you. Hi, kids," she said as they sat down.

"Mom, Geo's got a date!" Walt announced.

"A what?" Andrew said.

"It's not a date," Georgiana said with a hard look at Walt.

"Twelve-year-olds don't have dates, Geo," Angela said. "If they did, your father would have gotten married sooner."

"It's not a date," Geo repeated, "we're just having this dance after school and Mark Henry asked me if I'd dance with him."

"George*eee* loves Mark*eee*!" Walt chanted.

Geo rolled her eyes to heaven. "Get a life, Walt," she said, picking up a piece of toast.

"Where's your sister?" Angela said.

"Sleeping," Walt said. "She's tired because she was up all night."

Walter was the family radar system. Nothing ever escaped him.

"She couldn't sleep," Andrew said. "It's okay, I talked to her. She's not sick or anything."

"Probably excitement," Angela said. "Honestly, I've never seen a girl so busy at being social. Her coming-out party, her *friends'* parties, then she was queen of Mardi Gras. Before I married you, honey, I never knew being rich was such hard work."

"Pul*eeze*, Ma," Geo moaned, "you were a debutante."

"Yeah, but I was a debutante in Texas, where it wasn't so polite and a lot more fun. Tell you what, Geo, why don't you elope with this Mark kid, so I don't have to go through this again in six years?"

"Forget it, Ma. I want a big party; not just a presentation tea like Sylvie. This 'quiet good taste' thing of hers is too boring."

Sylvie came downstairs just in time to catch this.

Andrew looked around and his face lit up to see his daughter. All his children were a marvel to him, but Sylvie looked so much like her mother and had so much of her grandfather's curiosity that it almost broke his heart. His father, Walter, would have adored Sylvie. Sylvie never knew Walter, but she shared his passion for uncovering facts, for staying doggedly at a problem until she solved it. Of her long and illustrious family history, Sylvie was most proud of her grandfather's Nobel prize. She often said that one day, she'd hang hers right next to his. Walter's obsession had been anthropology. Sylvie's was psychiatry.

"You are so ostentatious, Geo," Sylvie said.

"Greedy, too," Geo agreed. "I want to collect big debutante presents. Dad, will you give me a Lamborghini when I come out?"

"Yeah. No problem," he said. "A black one. Just perfect for a bishop's daughter. You'll get a discreet pearl necklace and that's it."

Angela touched Sylvie's hand. "Why couldn't you sleep, honey?"

Sylvie and Andrew shared a look that was not lost on Angela, but Angela let it pass.

"I don't know. Just the pressure of everything. And I have a killer chemistry final coming up."

"That's your best subject," Andrew said.

"Yeah, but there's so much riding on it." She took a drink of orange juice, then studied the carton as if it were the most fascinating object she'd seen all week. "I didn't tell you this before, but if I graduate with honors and it's okay with you guys, Uncle Simon says I can work as his research assistant this summer before I start at Tulane."

"Simon never mentioned this," Andrew said.

"I asked him to let me tell you."

"Honey," Angela said, "isn't that going to be a little too much? You've got a lot on your plate right now."

"Mom," she said patiently, "I can't believe you'd think social life was more important than my career. What's the real problem?"

Angela laughed. "Jeez, your kids can read you like a book. I'm just worried about you working with Simon's patients. You're so sympathetic, baby, I don't want you eating your heart out. You know his patients are difficult cases. I just worry that you're too young for this. You're brilliant, but you haven't had time to get tough."

"But I won't be working with them. Just in the neurobiology lab with the other drones, doing scut work for the technicians and stuff."

"Yeah, Mom," Geo said. "And maybe Sylvie can figure out a cure for Walt. Some anti-dork vaccine."

"That's it," Angela said, "everybody out. Walt and Geo, get your books and get out to the car. Sylvie, eat. Andrew, go talk to God. Ask Him if He can fix it so that when we wake up tomorrow morning, all our kids are twenty-one and have their own apartments."

In a few minutes, Andrew was left alone with Sylvie.

"Honey," he said, "what made you go outside last night?"

She frowned as she buttered a piece of toast. "I don't know. I don't remember. It was just a pretty night, that's all. And I was restless."

Did she know? Was she lying? Did she have the same feelings Andrew had on nights like that, the nights when he lay awake and ached for something he should never want, should never even think about?

It's like being an ex-addict, he thought. You don't want it, you know it's wrong, it's killing you, and you're glad you're over it. But your body knows. You still have to have it.

It had begun early for him, too. He was just a child when he first felt the moon pull him outside. He'd found himself on the lawn as if he'd just woken from a dream, not sure how he had gotten there, not sure what he had wanted. Even now, the memory was vivid enough to cause a faint physical sensation, a sudden flutter of the heart.

He had to know if it was the same with his daughter. If it was, it was still no indication that she'd go the way he had. He had to have time to save her, to help her.

It's not true! he thought in a sudden flare of panic. It won't happen to Sylvie, to any of my kids, never! Good God, didn't I make sure of that years ago? Didn't I go through hell to save them, long before they were born? If I hadn't been sure—absolutely certain—I wouldn't even have had them!

"It's like Mother says," Sylvie told him, "I'm just stressed out from the deb season and finals and everything. I'll get over it."

That sounded reasonable. But Andrew noticed that she didn't even look up at him when she said it. She didn't want him to see her eyes.

4

For sixty years the Reverend Mother Pauline had commanded the shadows and spirits of the dead. Now she was going to join them.

Word spread that the queen was dying, and the entire Louisiana Voodoo community gathered in New Orleans to attend at her deathbed.

Mae Charteris stared out the bedroom window at the quiet, respectful crowd, both black and white, waiting in front of Mother Pauline's house on Rampart Street. Some of them cried. Some prayed. Some only waited in silence. They were there to show their love and respect and, more importantly, to hear whom Mother Pauline would name as the new successor.

Mae inhaled the incense burning in a small brass bowl, a special mixture sacred to the Orisha, the Seven Powers of Africa. The sweet scents of verbena, ginger, and snakeroot sharpened the memories of work she had done with Pauline over the years.

I'm going to miss her forever, Mae thought. I'll dream she's dead, then in that first confusion of waking up, feel relief that it was only a dream. Then I'll remember, and the loss will be new all over again. There'll be a hundred things I want to tell her, and she won't be there.

In Mae's religion there was no death, only a passage from the World of Form to the Invisible World. No one was ever really lost to the Voodoos, and especially to Mae and Pauline, whose rapport with the spirits was as strong as with the living. But it was *different,* Mae was thinking; we love someone for the spark of life in them, the flash of personality, the way they

19

turn a phrase, or furrow their brow when they read, or the smile they give you when you walk into the room. I'll always have her guidance and her spirit, but oh my soul, how I'll miss the woman.

Mae turned away from the window. She would see enough of grief in the next few days.

The title of "Mother" wasn't just a formality. The Voodoos did look upon Pauline as a mother, an earth goddess who led them through the complexities of life with a sure hand. Her power came from her being perfectly attuned to the *loa,* the traditional Voodoo name for the spirits, and the Invisible World, perfectly aligned with the Higher Powers. Pauline didn't manipulate the *loa;* she let them work through her and, in return, they did as she asked. They gave her the power, the magical arts, the ability to see that which is unseen.

Unlike some of her predecessors in New Orleans, who corrupted the power for personal advantage and intimidation, Pauline took Voodoo as her faith. Hers was a fervent blend of the old religions of Africa, the Caribbean, and the New Orleans of slave times. "White people don't understand what Voodoo means to us," she often told Mae. "That it was always our root religion, as o'd and dear to us as their Catholicism or Protestantism. As long as there have been black people on the earth, there has been Voodoo." Still, Pauline had many white followers devoted to the faith and to the *loa,* and always welcomed them.

Voodoo in New Orleans was a permutation: like most things in Louisiana and most traditions imported there, Voodoo had undergone many changes through the centuries and through the various queens. Pauline's mother, herself a great queen, had mixed the traditional rites with a little practical witchcraft that she had learned from her sister. The Witches taught Pauline's mother the primary rule of doing good without ever doing harm. She learned to manipulate natural law and her own psychic powers to accomplish her work, something that fit well with the Voodoo traditions in New Orleans. This was how she trained Pauline, and how Pauline had trained Mae.

Where former queens had no compunctions about conjuring bad gris-gris, Mother Pauline preferred to stay away from harmful spells. That wasn't to say that she couldn't do it; she simply used the same power to turn bad situations to good.

The first time Mae had watched Pauline do this, she had been amazed at its simplicity and at Mother Pauline's understanding of the human heart.

A man came to Pauline wanting her to put a curse on his wife, whom he suspected of "running around."

"Do you love your wife?" Pauline asked.

"No!" the man fumed. "She broke my heart!"

"If you don't love her, why are you here?" Pauline said. "Get rid of her. Let her go. Kick her out."

"She's shamed me," the man said stubbornly, hanging his head.

"Ah. That's quite another thing, then." Mother got up from her chair, selected a bottle from a shelf, and brought it back to the table. The light glinted off the old bottle, the pitted glass so ancient it was iridescent.

Mother turned the bottle in her hands. "This is what you want. Vengeance. Gris-gris to reclaim your pride. Give this to her in her coffee. It will turn her old before your eyes, it will turn her blood to black bile. She'll die at your feet, admitting her sins and begging your forgiveness."

She pushed the bottle toward the man.

He drew back, staring at it in horror.

"Here's your vengeance. Go on, take it. When things are bad, it's the only way."

"But . . . things used to be good," he said plaintively. "She used to love me."

Mother Pauline clucked her tongue and put down the bottle. "I'll tell you something, my dear," she said kindly. "You don't want revenge. You want things to be the way they used to be between you, isn't that right? You want it to be good again."

The man hung his head, his voice heavy with unshed tears. "I guess so. But that can't be, Mother. Too much has passed. I don't think she loves me anymore."

Pauline drew herself up to her full, commanding, awe-inspiring height. "You doubt my power, and the power of the *loa*?" she demanded.

He looked up, his eyes flashing fear. "No, Mother, never!"

"Well, you listen to me. I'm going to give you gris-gris, all right, and we'll do some magic. You want to be back with your wife, you want things to be right, you want to be happy together, making love together. So let's get started."

She sat down and took both his hands in hers across the table. "Mae," she called, "bring me that jar of pink powder and that little vial of red oil and a pink candle and that large crystal of rose quartz. Now," she said to the man, "we'll let the spirits do their work and we'll do ours. We'll call on Mistress Erzulie to restore your love. Just close your eyes now and relax."

Erzulie, the powerful, graceful goddess of love, was Pauline's closest ally. Many times, Mae watched and listened respectfully as Erzulie possessed Pauline and passed her the power. Sometimes Erzulie spoke to Mae, instructing her on her life and her future.

Twenty minutes later the man left, happy, optimistic, certain that the love of his wife was restored. A few days later Mae saw the man and his wife down by the river, sharing a big poor-boy sandwich, laughing and kissing like young lovers.

Mae was impressed and told Mother Pauline so.

"Most people who'll ask you for bad work don't really want it, my dear," Pauline said. "It only makes them unhappier, and makes the world unhappier. All that bad energy flying around gathers more of the same and comes back to you. If someone is in a bad situation, change it to a good one. Now, instead of two people being miserable, both of them are happy. Good perpetuates good, and evil perpetuates evil; never forget that."

Mae never did.

She had been under Pauline's wing ever since she was seven years old. Her mother, a minor Voodoo woman with a small following, recognized that her daughter had extraordinary gifts. From an early age, Mae had the sight, the power. She could foretell certain events, she could see into the soul, she could talk with the spirits. Mrs. Charteris knew that Mae would be a great queen someday, if she had the right training and the right contacts, so she took the girl to visit the legendary Reverend Mother Pauline.

Pauline was indeed impressed with Mae, so every day after school and on weekends, Mae spent her afternoons with Mother Pauline, learning the old ways and wisdom. When Mae's mother died of tuberculosis and there was no family to take the girl, Pauline took Mae in and raised her like a daughter.

As much as she missed her mother, Mae was glad to be with Pauline. Mae's gifts sometimes frightened her; she felt that they were leading rather than guiding her. Pauline taught her to direct her energies, to tune herself to the spirits, to take control. She taught Mae a new respect for the Invisible World, and how the world of the spirits and the world of the living interact for the good of both.

Now Mae wasn't sure what she'd do without Pauline. It wasn't just the Voodoo work—for a long time now, Pauline had been too sick to do the work herself and had relegated most of it to Mae. No, it was the affection she'd miss, the woman's warm wisdom and kind heart. With Pauline's passing, something good was going out of the world. And for Mae, it was like losing her mother for the second time.

"Mae." Pauline's commanding, musical voice was weak now. It broke Mae's heart to hear it. "Come over here, my dear."

Mae pulled a chair close to the bed. "How do you feel, Mother Pauline?"

Pauline made an impatient face. "I'm eager to have done with it, if you really want to know, my dear. The shadows are waiting to claim me, and I'm happy to go to them."

"If there was anything I could do to hold you, Pauline!" Mae said bleakly.

"If there was, I wouldn't let you do it. It's my time, Mae, and I'm not unhappy. You've done what you were supposed to do; I wouldn't have lasted this long without you. Now, who's here?"

"The people have been gathering all week. The most important are here: Sister Layla, Sister Delphine, Brother Oliver . . ."

"Antoine?"

Mae sighed only briefly before she caught herself. Pauline's grandson, Antoine, was taking her death with very bad grace. Half the time he was drunk with despair, the rest of the time he was talking arrogantly to Pauline's followers, as if he were already their leader. Then, at other times he was charm itself, calming people's grief, recalling old friendships and better times. When Antoine wanted to show it, he had a lovely manner.

"He's here, Pauline," she said smoothly. And thank God he's sober and in one of his better moments, she thought.

Pauline's hand, weak and feverish, closed over Mae's. "Bring me the *asson*." She noted Mae's slight hesitation. "No, my dear, don't be afraid to touch it."

Mae handled the *asson* with reverence. To an outsider, it would have looked unprepossessing: simply a medium-sized calabash with the stem used as a handle, webbed with strings of beads whose brilliant colors had faded long ago. The beads rattled when the *asson* moved. Sealed inside were several snake vertebrae that gave the *asson* a special resonance when shaken. But it was the significance of the *asson,* the power given to it by Pauline and by generations of Voodoo queens that made the *asson* sacred. It was the instrument used to invoke the *loa,* to initiate the ceremonies; in Pauline's hands, the rhythm of the *asson* became the rhythm of the rites. No one ever touched it but the queen, so that the energies that came from the *loa* into Pauline and out again through the *asson* would be pure, and it was never relinquished until the time came for the power to pass to another.

"Antoine wants to be my successor, the *houngan.* He wants me to pass the *asson* to him."

"That's his right, Mother. He's your closest relative. I'll be proud to work with Antoine. Although," she smiled, "I don't know where we'll find a replacement bamboula dancer as sexy as Antoine. The women at the meetings go wild when he dances in all those beads and feathers and that tiny strip of red cloth he wears."

A shadow of pain passed over Pauline's face. "Antoine is a handsome man, yes. He can be sweet and charming. But there's a dark streak in him, something renegade in his heart. The power would ruin him, Mae, as surely as it made you strong. No, my dear, you're the one. You know it can't be anyone else."

Mae sighed. "I was afraid you'd say that, Mother. And when the time came, I didn't know what I'd say. I still don't."

Pauline patted Mae's hand and smiled. "Just another reason why it's you, Mae. The people love you, they trust you. They think of you as Queen already. The choice doesn't come from me, it comes from the spirits. Why do you think your mother brought you here so long ago? That was no accident, my dear, it was meant to happen."

So long ago, Mae thought. Thirty-one years. Almost my entire life has been dedicated to the Voodoo ways, and I've never looked back on any of it with anything but satisfaction.

"You're frightened," Pauline said.

"Of course, Mother Pauline. It's an enormous responsibility."

"But one you're able to handle, my dear."

A swift pass of pain wrinkled Pauline's eyes, and she sighed as she sank back onto the pillows. "I should have done it before, Mae," she said sadly, "when I still had the strength to preside over a fine ceremony and a great feast for the people and the *loa*. It would have been such a festival, my passing the *asson* to you. But I wanted"—she cradled the *asson* to her chest, her eyes looking beyond the room—"I suppose I wanted to hold on to it. As if giving up the authority was giving up my life."

"I don't care about a ceremony," Mae said, "and I'm glad you held it. I want you to, up until the very end." She could no longer control the rush of tears and pain. She held Pauline's hand, so terribly light now that it was free of its strength, to her cheek.

"No, my dear, you take it now," Pauline said. "Use it to free the *ti bon Ange* when the time comes." Mae knew what she meant. One of the gravest responsibilities of a Voodoo queen was to conduct the ceremonies for the dead, formally parting the soul from the body. The *ti bon Ange*, that part of the soul that was the last to leave the body, must be freed with the proper rituals.

"Just think, Mae," Pauline whispered with a smile, "Baron Samedi will take my hand; he'll lead me lightly into death like a gentleman leads a lady to a dance. I'll see Erzulie clearly and plainly, not in my mind's eye, but in my own. I'll be free, Mae; but you, my little one, it will be you who is bound. A great queen is never free, never her own person. The responsibility sits heavily on her. But you were born for it. Erzulie loves you, Mae, and she will never fail you."

Pauline passed her hand over the *asson*, making the beads and bones answer lightly, but with authority. It was a sound no longer for Pauline, no longer reminding her of the burden she carried, but a sound that now called for Mae, for the anticipation of a greater power yet to come.

Pauline took Mae's hand. "Remember, Mae. You are no one's guru. You are no one's messiah. You are the servant of the *loa* and the guide of the people, and you must see that they are all served well." She took a deep breath and released it slowly. Mae could see the weight leave Pauline's chest, as she prepared to travel, weightless and free, joyously, into the Invisible World, to soar with the spirits. "Not long now, Mae. The *ti bon Ange* even now struggles to fly. Now, call in the sisters and brothers, and call Antoine. We'll announce the joyous news."

Afterward, back at his apartment on Decatur Street, Antoine didn't even stop to take off his jacket. He closed the door behind him, took a glass and a bottle of bourbon out on the terrace, and let his mind seethe as he watched the boats go down the river.

He replayed the scene over and over in his memory. In time, he would alter the details, ever so slightly, to justify his later actions, but right now the scene was fresh and accurate.

He'd been stricken when his grandmother announced Mae as the new Queen. He supposed it showed in his face; he just couldn't summon up the cool to hide it.

"Antoine," Pauline had said, taking his hand, "I love you more than anything in the world. But this is how it has to be, according to the old traditions. The Voodoos must be led by a Queen; the true power always resides in women, in their roots to the earth and the moon, in their regenerative nature. Men are not sensitive enough to channel the power, they have no true capacity for humility. There is always something in the male ego that gets in the way of the work, that sees the power as a tool to manipulate others. No matter how well Voodoo men start out, they end up badly. The power corrupts them. Sometimes, it kills them."

"But that can't be true, Grandma," Antoine said, his mind still numb. "Doctor Jim was a great Voodoo, a great healer."

"Yes, as long as he was still working with Marie Laveau. But remember what happened to him when he broke with her. His lust for money and power and women ruined him and did the entire Voodoo community great harm. He died in violence and poverty. You feel I've slighted you, but I'm protecting you from something that would be completely against your nature. No, Antoine; carry on with your work. Lead the dancing and let Mae teach you, follow her and gain strength from her. Live your life in harmony with the spirits and you'll always be happy and safe."

Antoine had recovered himself enough to make his face a placid mask. He kissed his grandmother and agreed with her. He turned to Mae and, with a pretty, touching gesture, kissed her hands, but he could tell that she wasn't fooled. No matter. He knew that Mae would give him the benefit of the doubt, that she would make allowances for him. She didn't want her reign to start with discord in the ranks.

He *did* love his grandmother, that was the thing. He knew that she wanted what was best for him, but damn it! This time she was wrong! She was mired in the old ideas of matriarchy. Well, times change, the old ways change.

He flung himself in a chair and seethed. All his life he had waited for the day when the power and the glory would pass to him. He had never doubted that it would. Even when Mae came to his grandmother, even when it was obvious that Mae was extraordinarily gifted, he simply assumed that he would lead and she would follow, lending her gifts to his service. It might not be the Voodoo way, but it was the way the world worked. Men led. Women followed. How many women billionaires were there, how many female captains of industry? How many women led Fortune 500 companies? You could count them on one hand and have fingers left over.

What good was power if you couldn't make people do what you wanted? If they don't quake when you thunder, if they don't look at you as if you were a god, if they don't take every word you say as gospel wisdom?

Antoine refilled his glass and watched a tugboat guiding an enormous white ship down the river.

He slammed his glass down, the bourbon and ice splashing over the filigreed iron balcony.

He didn't have to settle for this. He wouldn't. Power? He had power that his grandmother and Mae never dreamed of, that they never suspected existed. He had hoarded it all these years, a precious, dangerous secret that he kept locked away.

Stalking into the living room, he pulled up the corner of the Oriental rug and, on his hands and knees, felt for the loose floorboard. It had been so long since he had looked for it, so long since he had dared to touch what was under it.

One of the boards moved. He pulled it away from the floor and plunged his hand into the darkness. The lockbox was there, as it had been for years and years.

His fingers shook slighty and he made a couple of false starts finding the key among the larger ones on his key ring. But once into the lock, even after all this time, it turned like a hot knife through wax.

He lifted out a little bottle of strange dust, dust that looked alive, that held a slight sheen, a dark glitter as it lay caught under the glass. Antoine's breath held as he looked at it.

Next was a carved rosewood box with gold fittings, about ten inches square and two inches deep. It didn't lock, but the little gold latch had to be turned to open it.

His hands were shaking so much that he had to stop for a minute.

I should have taken another drink, he thought.

He turned the latch and lifted the lid. Coddled in burgundy velvet were several small bones. Human finger bones. And next to them, a huge crystal of shining obsidian, large as a small woman's fist, smooth and deep black, glinting with dark lights.

How long had it been since he had looked at them? Ten years? Twelve? Fifteen?

They had belonged to the most evil woman in Voodoo history, *la Reine Blanche,* the White Queen, who had braided a dark skein of black magic into Voodoo and had terrified the entire city. They called her the White Queen partly because of the unprecedented rise of any white so high in the Voodoo world, and partly because of her silvery blond hair.

Reine Blanche's magic had little to do with the true faith. Her *loa* were not the *loa* of the Voodoo. The spirits she dealt with were untrustworthy at best, evil at worst, and it was said that she danced with demons. She cursed her enemies so that they lived in suffering and died in frenzies, but according to her whims and to how much money changed hands, a repentant supplicant might find his curse lifted. Sometimes the price wasn't money; the White Queen knew the value of a little well-placed blackmail. It was rumored that she was a master poisoner, and there was no reason to doubt it.

It was hard to sort out the truth from the fiction about her, but one story kept cropping up in every recounting of her history. While she was very young, even before she was a Voodoo, she had conceived a passion for a young sea captain. Though she was a very beautiful girl, he left her for another woman. She never forgot it, and years later, when she was becoming infamous, she cursed his family. The stories were never specific about what the curse was, but it was said to be so awful that *la Reine Blanche* had to sell her soul for the power to place it. She had called a spirit so powerful and so evil that he demanded her heart and soul, and she gave them— without hesitation.

She had died while still in the lush bloom of her beauty, and on one evil night under a malevolent dark moon, *la Reine Blanche* walked out of the trees at Bayou St. John, back from the dead.

She reigned over her renegade cult for years after that, never speaking, barely moving, her eyes flashing with life. Through the years, she never aged; she was as beautiful as she was when she had died. It was rumored that she was the Devil's paramour, that she ate little children, that she was a vampire, that she had seen Hell and that her escape from it had driven her mad. No one knew which story was true or if all of them were.

No one knew, even now, whether she was dead or alive.

Of all the Voodoos, only Antoine knew. He had seen her destroyed. He had seen her body crumble into dust around her bones. Only fifteen years old, hiding among the tombs of St. Louis Cemetery, he had watched her die and had waited, horror-struck, as her murderers left her there. He had the foolish bravado at fifteen that he'd never have now—he had crept over to *la Reine Blanche,* not much more than a memory by that time, and had gathered her dust, her bones, and this obsidian.

The obsidian. He was still reluctant to touch it. Of all the stories about the Voodoo queen, this was the only one he knew was true. *La Reine Blanche* had embraced forces more evil and more powerful than any the Voodoos had known. Some say it was the Devil himself.

Antoine had put the dust in the bottle, the bones and the stone into a jewel box left to him by his mother, and had never spoken of them. From time to time over the years, he lifted the lid on the box and peered inside, but every time he did, something bad happened to him shortly afterward. Nothing catastrophic. Just little things, unnatural things. He tripped over nothing and sprained his wrist. His pet cat died from no apparent cause. A swarm of bees invaded his city apartment—in the winter.

In time, he simply sealed everything in the lockbox and stashed it under the floorboard. But he always knew it was down there, brewing trouble, gathering strength. Sometimes he thought about it at night and wondered why he just didn't toss it all into the river or turn it over to his grandmother, who would undoubtedly know how to neutralize it.

But he couldn't. He always thought that someday he'd have learned enough to handle what was in that box. That when the time came, he would harness its magic and make it his.

What clearer time than this? He was the grandson of the great Mother Pauline, herself the seventh daughter of a seventh daughter. The power was his by right and he was going to take it!

He lifted the crystal heart.

It had a strange look, flat and opaque, as if the light in the stone had been put out.

He cupped the stone in his hand, then almost dropped it; it was so cold!

You're being stupid, my man, he told himself. The thing's been lying under the floor. Did you expect it to radiate heat?

But it was just *so* cold, unnatural, as if it had been refrigerated.

As if it were a body without a soul, he thought suddenly.

His hand shivered. The White Queen's power was legendary, yes, but so was her curse. A great Voodoo must have the true gifts, and only the strongest of them, the most fearless, could control *la Reine Blanche*'s magic.

Think about what you're doing, boy, he told himself, there's no stopping this once you've started. You'd better be good at what you do, you'd better be the best, you'd better have all the spirits on your side if you're going to do this.

They say that at the dark of the moon, out where Bayou St. John joins the lake waters, *la Reine Blanche* can still be heard screaming in Hell, trying to claw her way back to the cool air aboveground.

He shook his head at his own nervousness. Dumb. He was letting the old stories get the better of him.

But when you open the door, what are you inviting in? It had taken years to wipe out *la Reine Blanche*'s murderous cult. What if it wasn't the woman who had controlled the power in the stone, but the stone using the woman?

No, he decided, that was pure rot. Foolish folktales, stories kids told to scare each other on Halloween night.

If the power was in the stone, he would master it. The stone belonged to him now, and he was entitled to what it offered him. This was his chance, his moment.

His fist shut around the stone. He closed his eyes and took a deep breath, centering his thoughts, concentrating on his single goal.

Mine! he thought. The power, the adulation, the respect. It should have been given to me, but now I'll take it like a conqueror takes a sacked city. I don't care what it costs me. I want it!

He opened his hand and looked at the stone resting there.

He could swear it was clearing, losing that dead opacity.

As he stared, the coldness of the stone ran up his arm, down his back, freezing his body. His heart pumped faster, the fear paralyzing his mind.

The crystal was dazzling in its clarity now, the black depths almost endless. A tiny stream of vapor rose from it, curling toward the ceiling, spreading into a cloud. It rose higher, spread wider, moving and taking form.

A spirit hovered over him, a lovely woman, elusive as smoke but perfectly formed in every detail; a pale pastel sculpture of a woman.

Her lips moved but her voice came from a distance.

"You want the power, Antoine?" she asked. "But what will you give me for it?"

He had never been so completely terrified, but he realized that he had already set in motion something that he was unable to stop.

"Anything!" he whispered.

"Anything?" her voice sounded amused. "Even that which you thought you couldn't live without?"

Antoine was blown on a hot wind of madness, of delirium that screamed in his ears and burned his heart. "Yes. Oh, *yes*! Please!"

She undulated, hanging there above him, gathering substance. Her vaporish form solidified into flesh as she lightly floated to the floor. She stood in front of Antoine, her hair tumbling over her shoulders like a silver waterfall.

"Do you know who I am?" she asked him. Her voice was light and sweet.

Antoine nodded. Of course he knew. How could he forget? He saw her die.

"I suffer so," she said in that lovely, lost voice. "I suffer hourly, daily. From moment to moment my life is a torment. Don't think I haven't paid for my sins!" She said this last with resignation. "And the loneliness . . . I never dreamed how desolate it would be."

She turned her head slightly, but Antoine could see the first tear glimmer in her eyes.

"I saw you, you know," she said, almost shyly. "Dancing at the Voodoo meetings. Oh, don't think the dead can't see!" she said, with some bitterness. "It's part of our punishment, to be able to watch the living, but not to feel, to touch life. Our curse is that we can remember the joy of being alive, but we can no longer feel it. I watched you; I watched the way your body moved and I saw the vitality in your face. I thought, 'Ah, if only I was still Queen! What wouldn't I give to this man!' And I wanted so much—just one more time—to feel the warm, living touch of a man's arms around me."

The despair in her voice was more than Antoine could bear. His fear had completely deserted him, and in its place was the beginning of a lust so strong that it overpowered reason. He had never seen a woman so beautiful, so vulnerable. And she wanted him! Women had always come easily to Antoine, but never anyone like this. The very paradox of the situation was what maddened him, the touch of the forbidden, the dangerous.

"You've called me back, Antoine, and for only this moment, this sliver in the glass of time, I can be real again. Will you . . . ," she asked, turning her face up to his, her eyes shining with quicksilver tears, "will you be my lover? If you will, I'll give you all you ever wanted. The power. The magic. Everything I know, everything I was, will pass to you. If you'll only love me. If you'll only let me, for one minute, recapture the life I've lost forever. For afterward, I have nothing but eternal death."

He was intensely aware of her body, draped in translucent veils, her skin glowing through the fabric. She stood there, waiting for him to move.

In a sudden impulsive wave of heat, Antoine circled her waist with his arm, drawing her against him. She closed her eyes and took a deep breath as he buried his face in her throat, his free hand stroking her body. He was amazed at how warm she was, her skin hot and soft, as his hands explored her body. He plunged his hand between her legs, the silken silver hair brushing his fingers, her responsive warmth as fiercely hungry as a human lover's.

She twined her arms around his neck. "Will you give me what I want?" she whispered against his hair.

"Yes," he said raggedly, "anything."

He caught a glimpse of her face just before she kissed him. She was still beautiful, oh yes, but her eyes! Good God, he thought, her eyes are mad! They were filled with such malevolence that the sudden transformation terrified him and he pulled back.

But she had him in a grip too strong to be broken. Her arms were like steel chains.

"My perfect lover," she said, with such mocking irony and such pure hatred that he was panicked. He tried to break free, but she held his head between her hands and, suffocating him with suddenly fetid breath, kissed him.

Antoine thought he was going to scream. The tongue she thrust in his mouth was cold, scaly, serpentine. It slithered down his throat. Overwhelmed with horror, he tried to scream, but the sound was swallowed by that glacial snake, freezing his nerves and blood as the cold spread through him. He could feel his stomach begin to heave.

He began to lose his mind, as slowly as a man freezing to death. She's killing me! he thought in terror.

She suddenly pulled away and laughed at him, her voice no longer ethereal, but the laugh of the dead, of the damned, boiling up from Hell to scald him.

Her color was rapidly changing to an unpleasant greenish gray, the color of grave clothes left to rot in the ground. The room grew unbearably cold. A putrid smell rose around them, a miasma of the stink from rotting garbage and stagnant swamp water, of gangrenous wounds exposed in foul air. The thick stench of it made Antoine stagger back, but it only grew stronger.

He turned and groped for the door, but it seemed to have disappeared. In terror, he looked for a window, an opening, *something* to get him out of that room, but the walls had turned blank.

A booming laugh filled the room, the voice hoarse and grating on the nerves. "You enjoy my perfume, eh? An ethereal aroma to delight the senses!"

Antoine's eyes stung, the tainted atmosphere choked his lungs. He screamed and dropped to his knees.

She stood over him, vastly amused. "Ah," she said, picking up the black obsidian, "my heart. How good to see it again!" She glanced at Antoine. "You're such a fool, Antoine, for thinking that you had the power to control this. Don't you know what it is?"

Antoine realized it all of a sudden. When the legends said that she would never die, he made the mistake of taking it literally. What it meant, he now understood, was that her evil, her influence, would live as long as that stone existed. He had made a disastrous mistake. That stone was the key to the very gates of Hell.

She knew exactly what he was thinking. "You're simply fulfilling your destiny—and mine," she said. "You saw what happened when I died, Antoine. How my body became dust and only my heart was left. But the power of evil never dies, it only changes form. And mine changed into that heart, trapped in those black depths with my soul. The thought of evil frightens you, perhaps repulses you, but if you want to be great, if you want the respect and the power, you must accept the fear. You can have the power, Antoine, like I had it, if you're only willing to give up your soul for it. You'll soon find that the evil will seduce you and melt itself around you like liquid gold, and it will be more than a means, it will be the end itself."

Antoine realized that he was losing his last chance at backing out, at ever again being a human man. He was being asked to pay too much—nothing was worth losing his soul. "No!" he gasped. "I don't want it! Go back to Hell, where you belong!"

"Oh, but you're too late," she taunted. "You've already agreed. I asked you twice, and you said yes. Too late, Voodoo man, much too late. You have what you wanted. The stone is yours and everything that goes with it. And I'll be free at last."

Antoine covered his face and sobbed in despair, and waited to relinquish his life.

"Take some comfort, Antoine," she said, "the very existence of pure evil makes possible the existence of pure good. Giving up your soul will be the last completely moral act you'll ever perform."

She leaned over, all mocking gone from her face and her voice, and touched him lightly on the forehead.

"It's done," she whispered triumphantly.

It was an ice-cold spear piercing his brain. He screamed in torment, then fell over on his hands and knees, retching so hard his belly went into spasms. He felt his mind slipping away from him, receding further and further into some unknown void. He was vaguely aware of his own tears just before he went away.

When his mind cleared again, it was over. *La Reine Blanche* was gone. The room was restored. The temperature was normal. All that was left was a faintly nasty odor.

Crying, gasping, Antoine opened all the windows, gulping in the fresh air.

When he was somewhat calmed, he found the obsidian lying on the floor where he had dropped it.

How brilliant it had become, as if something was burning inside it, something living and glimmering in the heart of it. He knew immediately what it was that gave the stone its fire.

He picked up the heart, marveling at how warm it was. He cradled it in his hand, measuring its weight. He would wear it from now on, caged in gold as his own soul was caged, a symbol of honor like a Heidelberg scar, to convince the Voodoos that he had braved *la Reine Blanche* and won.

No one need know that he had actually lost, that she had bested him. Her soul was released, and his was locked into that black fire. Antoine was alone now, more alone than he had ever been. He no longer had a soul, or the conscience that went with it. What he had instead was the power: slightly distant, disconnected, but there. He got what he wanted, and in the days to come, until the last of his humanity faded, he would be only vaguely aware of how dearly he paid for it. Eventually, he would forget entirely that he had ever been a good man.

5

The distinguished gentleman had been bent over the worktable for some time, examining some sea blue pottery figures. The strong worktable light reflected off the silver streaks in his thick black hair.

One of the men, waiting nervously for him to finish, couldn't contain himself much longer. "Well," he asked in a fluttery, nervous burst, "are they real or are they fakes?"

The gentleman straightened up, drew an immaculate handkerchief from his pocket and wiped his magnifying glass with exaggerated leisure. "They're fakes," he said in his slightly accented English, "but they're valuable fakes."

"What you mean, Dr. Endore," another man said, "is that we're being asked to pay a great deal of money for what are, essentially, useless items."

"I'd advise you to buy them anyway, if you renegotiate the price," Endore said. "They're only useless if you present them as Middle Kingdom. However, they do date from only a century later, so I'd say they were a good addition to a collection from that period. Surely the museum has a place to fit them? They're excellent work, and by a master glazer, too. It looks almost exactly like Middle Kingdom pottery, but the blue is just a tiny shade off, because the clay base isn't exactly the same. Look at this."

He handed the magnifying glass to the man. "Look at the bottom of the piece we know is real, and then compare it to the fake. The clay of the fake is coarser and darker; it discolors the glaze." He chuckled and tapped one of the figures lightly. "I'll bet this drove the potter crazy. They experimented with all kinds of combinations of glaze, of clays, of firing temperatures

37

and times, trying to get this look. And whoever did this came so close it must have infuriated him not to get it exactly. But by the time this piece was done, the region that produced the clay for the earlier pieces was politically inaccessible. You know how this particular glaze has always had a slight variation that we couldn't account for, some little chemical oddity that's been difficult to pin down? Well, the makers of the real stuff had a little secret to assure the uniqueness of their color. As they mixed it, they pissed in it. That's how they got that lightness in the blue. It was considered an uproarious thing to do, although the glaze differed slightly, depending on who was mixing that batch and how much he'd drunk the night before."

"Dr. Endore," the curator said in fascination, "how do you *know* these things?"

Endore looked at the man matter-of-factly, his dark eyes innocently frank. "I was there. Don't I look it?" He ran his hand through his curly silver-and-black hair, and everyone laughed. Endore couldn't have been more than forty-five.

"Well, you've just saved the museum several thousand dollars, plus the possible embarrassment of having displayed these things as authentic. Certainly worth the fee."

Endore left the museum with a fat check in his pocket. He maintained bank accounts in most major cities of the world, since he did so much traveling, and his bank in Los Angeles was only a few blocks away. He loved Los Angeles; he was one of the few people he knew who admitted it. It had a wonderfully tacky, flashy atmosphere in which anything could happen. San Francisco, while sublimely beautiful, was just too polite. You'd never find a hot dog stand actually shaped like a hot dog in San Francisco. New York was too neurotically conformist and desperately pretentious. But Los Angeles still had a pretty good grip on childish naivete and, in a world where things were getting entirely too serious, Endore thought that was an excellent thing.

He cashed the check at the bank, taking the money in large bills. Then he visited three charitable institutions, all three carefully chosen for the fact that the money they collected went primarily for the charity, not for the administrative costs or some secret slush fund.

The amounts he donated exactly equaled—divided by three—the amount he'd just been paid.

Tomorrow morning he was going to be on a plane headed for Rome, on his way back to his home on the Palatine Hill, but for the rest of the afternoon he was going to enjoy himself.

He'd gone to National Car Rental and rented one of their classic cars, a bright red '51 Olds 98 convertible with red-and-white rolled and pleated seats. The one he'd wanted, the pink T-Bird, was already out. The Buick was absolutely a tank to drive without power steering, but Endore loved it. Distant galaxies in chrome glittered under a plastic dome in the center of the steering wheel. He stopped and bought a pair of Ray-Bans, knowing that not wearing sunglasses in L.A. violated one of the several California State Coolness Statutes. All he had with him were Vuarnets, and those were last year's thing.

He'd do Spago and the nouvelle pizzas later. Right now, he was cruising to Venice Beach.

Of all the places that do Southern California Crazy, none of them do it as consistently well as Venice. Endore liked it there: the people were so full of life and so varied. Some things were predictable, such as the exhibitionists on Muscle Beach, who always seemed to be the same boring guys, but other things were complete surprises, the traveling show hitting the beach for one day only.

This time it was the Hell's Angels. The Angels had decided to raise a few bucks the easy way, that is to say, without actually breaking any heads or federal laws. They'd set up a table piled with Angel T-shirts and paraphernalia. Two Angels, a middle-aged biker who'd done it all and had the face to prove it, and a younger, brasher version whose tattoos hadn't even begun to stretch out yet, stalked back and forth behind the table, glaring at passersby, swigging beer and belching loudly, trying to figure who was tough enough to negotiate a deal and take home some authentic Angelwear.

Endore picked up a T-shirt and took a second look at the insignia emblazoned on the front.

The older Angel stopped dead in his tracks to get a good look at Endore; he blinked and pulled back a little in surprise.

"Iowa City chapter?" Endore said, as if he couldn't believe it. "You've got a Hell's Angels chapter in Iowa City?"

"You got a fuckin' *problem* with that, man?" The young Angel leaned forward as if he hadn't hit anybody all day and was hurting.

The older Angel stopped him. "Wait a minute, kid; you know who this *is*?" He whispered in the young Angel's ear.

A dramatic change came over the young Angel's face, a look of respect. It took him a minute, since that particular look wasn't one he had to use very often. "Oh, *wow,* man; I had no idea! I'm really sorry. . . ."

Endore smiled. "No problem. You're a young one, aren't you?"

"He's mine," the older Angel said.

"Welcome," Endore said to the young one. "Just try to use a little restraint, will you? For my sake? As a favor."

"Oh, *wow*!" the kid said again, overwhelmed. "*You* askin' *me* to do you a favor. . . ." He shook his head.

The older Angel regarded Endore warmly. "It's sure good to see you, man. Last time was . . . what? Lotta years ago, huh? So, what's the scam this trip? What name you using? You got a job?"

"Does it matter?"

The Angel shrugged and gave Endore a cynical smile. "Never does. I've been through so many of 'em myself that I lose track. I was even a history professor once, at Yale. Does that crack you up or what?"

Endore laughed. "Not as much as the time when you were at Vatican City."

The Angel shook his head. "That *was* a fuckin' trip. I might go back to that someday, the perks were so good. That was the first time around, wasn't it? I met you there when you authenticated some paintings. Remember?"

"I never forget people, John. You know that. I even remember that you were Giovanni then."

The young Angel respectfully took the T-shirt out of Endore's hands. "Here, dude," he said, "you don't want no T-shirt." The young Angel carefully shrugged off his own hand-painted, hand-studded sleeveless denim vest, folded it reverently, and presented it to Endore. "I'd appreciate it if you'd take it, man. I'd feel, you know, fuckin' *honored* to know you was wearin' my colors."

Endore smiled and slipped the vest over his white knit shirt. It fit perfectly. "Thank you"—he smiled at the young Angel—"I won't forget you for this, Tony. John, take care of yourself."

Endore started to turn away when the older Angel stopped him. "Don't go so fast, man," he said quietly. "There are lots of us here, lots of us who've never seen you or touched you. The young ones especially need to hear what you have to say; it's so hard these days to make them understand what their lives are about. Stay awhile."

The Angel's battered face was so wistful that Endore hurt to look at him. That alone was enough reason to go. "Teach them what I taught you, John. That's why there are a few like you all over the world; because I can't be everywhere."

The Angel nodded and reluctantly let go of Endore's arm. Endore turned back to him suddenly and, taking the Angel's face between each of his hands, kissed him warmly. "I'll always be with you, John," Endore said kindly.

The young Angel's eyes were the size of saucers.

As Endore walked down the beach, Tony seemed overwhelmed. "Oh, man! Did you *hear* that! He even knew my fuckin' name!"

The older Angel smiled. "You better believe he knows more than that, dude. Just by looking at you, he knows everything about you. And you heard what he said." He lightly batted Tony on the side of the head. "So shape up!"

Tony shook his head in wonder. "No problem, man! Oh, *wow*!" he said again, watching Endore retreat.

Back at the car, Endore looked up at the wide blue sky, stretching out to the sea, and felt the sun warm him. He felt good, satisfied with his life at just that moment.

Then it came: an unsettling cry, a weak sob like a plea for help. He knew it was useless to look around for the source: it was coming from inside his mind.

The signals were confused and weak, hardly a cry at all, more of a feeling of despair, but nothing definite.

He wondered if he should stay in Los Angeles for a couple of days, if the signals would get any clearer. No, he couldn't do that. He needed to take care of some details at home, then he was due in Japan and then in London. If anything really terrible was happening, someone would know how to get in touch with him in a more definite manner than this. His best course was to go back to Rome and wait to see who called.

He started the car and drove away from Venice Beach, but the whole day—the meeting with the Angels, the vague fear—bothered him much more than it should have.

6

Umbrellas in pastel stripes shaded the twenty white wrought-iron tables set up on a green lawn sloping down to the lake. It was late afternoon and the sun was starting to go down, so the host switched on the many strings of white twinkle lights strung through the trees. A small band was just setting up their equipment on the patio.

Huge galvanized iron washtubs simmered on Coleman stoves, the mouth-watering steam carrying the scent of crawfish boiling in spices and halved lemons.

Sylvie and Quentin sat in front of a huge pile of crawfish heaped on a big plastic garbage bag.

"Now, this is what I call elegant dining," Sylvie said.

"Anything that involves a cold Dixie beer and a pile of hot crawfish is elegant to me," Quentin said.

Sylvie pushed the mass of her red hair back and let the wind off Lake Pontchartrain cool her face. She'd been dating Quentin off and on for three months, and he was a nice guy, but she just couldn't work up any real enthusiasm for him. She should break it off and let him find some girl who'd appreciate him, but lately she just hadn't had the energy to do even the least little thing with any decisiveness. What was it that was bothering her? She couldn't come up with a definite answer to that, either, only the flimsy feeling that something was wrong.

She felt that her life was in transition, but it had nothing to do with her social or academic lives. All that was set in stone, it was regular and ordered. No, it was something else. More and more often now, she'd find herself stopping in the middle of something and thinking "What is it I'm supposed to do?" It

would stop her for several minutes. But there was no decision
to be made, nothing looming on the horizon waiting for her
answer.

She couldn't figure it out. Nothing like this had even happened to her before. If any girl knew where her life was going,
it was Sylvie. She was graduating, she was starting college, she
was set with a summer job that meant a lot to her future. As
far as she could see, nothing was missing.

So what was this odd feeling of potential loss? Of having to
take control *right now* or let something important slip through
her fingers?

She was hoping this party would take her mind off things.
Nothing lifted the spirits, she found, like being surrounded by
friends. They were all about the same age, had the same back-
grounds and common experiences, had gone through school
together, and most of the girls had come out this season when
Sylvie did.

Nothing threatening about this crowd, Sylvie thought.

"So," one of the girls at her table was saying, "this jerk
rear-ended my car and he's got the nerve to get out, walk
over to my window, and say 'Hey, lady, where you learn to
drive? Schwegmann's or what?' "

"Somebody rear-ended your Porsche, Elaine?" Quentin said
in alarm.

"No, thank God, I was in Dad's Mercedes," Elaine said.

"Jeez, Elaine," Sylvie said, "a good thing you weren't driving anything serious."

Paul, Elaine's boyfriend, shook his head. "Last time I was
making groceries at Schwegmann's, I was standing in line and
I felt somebody pat my ass; I mean a real *fondle*. No shit!
I couldn't believe it! Right there in the checkout line where
anybody could see. I figured it was somebody I knew, so I
turned around and there was this little old lady, prim as a pin.
She all of a sudden started looking at the *National Enquirer,*
but she had this teeny little grin." He shook his head again.
"I tell ya, it's all this afternoon sex on the soap operas. These
ladies are losing touch with reality."

"I don't know," Quentin said. "I'd say she had a pretty good
grip on it."

A tiny, distracted-looking blond, balancing a pile of craw-fish, sat down at the table.

"Please, please, please tell me you're all coming to my party next weekend," the blond said, "and bringing everybody you know."

"That depends, Mary Beth," Sam said. "You didn't let your mother pick the band, like at your birthday party, did you? I've heard better bands at funerals."

"No fucking way," Mary Beth said. "From eight to one A.M. we've got Zachary Richard, and from two till dawn we've got Queen Latifah. I wanted a little of everything. Do you love it or what?"

"Holy shit, put your dancin' shoes *on*! I'll be there," Sam told her.

Quentin looked at his mounting pile of crawfish heads with resignation. "I feel like I've eaten every crawfish from here to Baton Rouge. Anybody want to dance?" He nudged Sylvie.

She looked up, surprised. "Oh. What?"

"Honey, I think that Dixie's put you to sleep, you've been so quiet. I asked if you want to dance."

"Oh . . . I guess not. I feel a little tired."

"*I* want to dance," Mary Beth said, getting up. "They've got four big plastic pails full of Sno-Balls from Hansen's over there, and I had two helpings of chocolate creme. I need to work some of it off."

"You're on, babes," Quentin said, taking her hand. "Sylvie, you feel all right? We can leave if you want."

"No, are you kidding?" Sylvie said. "Have you ever known me to leave anything before two in the morning? I'll get my second wind in a minute. Go dance."

Quentin and Mary Beth danced through three numbers and came back still hot to party.

"Where's Sylvie?" Quentin asked.

"She's up at the house," Elaine said. "Bathroom. She said the crawfish were okay, but the hot sauce did her in."

"It'll kill ya," Quentin agreed. "Maybe I should take her home. She really isn't herself tonight. I don't think she feels well."

"The flu," Mary Beth said. "It's going around."

"Quentin, want to dance until Sylvie gets back?" Elaine asked.

"Let's do it, toots."

When Elaine and Quentin returned to the table, Sylvie still wasn't back.

"Elaine, do me a favor?" Quentin said. "Come up to the house with me and see if she's still in the bathroom. I'm getting a little worried. She must really be sick."

Sylvie wasn't in the bathroom. She wasn't in any of the other rooms, either.

"This is weird," Quentin said. "You think she went back outside?"

"Why don't you go look, and I'll stay here in case we missed her?" Elaine said.

But nobody outside had seen her. Quentin felt a frantic knot start in his stomach.

"Look, this is crazy," Sam told him. "Maybe she went home but she just didn't want to ruin the party for you."

"No, we came in her car. She wouldn't just leave me without telling me." Quentin ran a hand through his hair. "I really don't like this, Sam."

Quentin and his friends searched the house, the grounds, everywhere they could think of. Mary Beth found Sylvie's purse, with her house and car keys inside, in the bedroom where they'd all left their things. Her car was still parked outside.

Almost two hours had passed since any of them had seen her. Quentin was terrified. He finally called Sylvie's parents and told them what happened, then they called the police.

Falling. She was falling so slowly, so gracefully, the way a lily floats on a pond. Her head was arched back, and she saw the moon, full and magnificent, hanging in the sky. She smiled as if seeing an old friend in an unfamiliar place. But how odd it looked! It was upside down. Now, why was that?

She realized she was being carried. Her arm was around someone's neck, someone's arms held her, someone's delicious scent warmed her. Quentin.

No. Quentin didn't have such hypnotic green eyes, such

thick blond hair. His arms weren't this strong. Who was this?

Sylvie gave a soft little sigh and closed her eyes, burrowing her head into his hard chest, feeling like a tiny child being carried, half-asleep, to bed.

How wonderful it was, she thought, that he was here to take such good care of her, to watch over her.

She had never felt so safe.

The sun in her eyes woke her up. It took her several minutes to figure out where she was: in the gazebo behind her house, lying on one of the wicker chaise longues. She put a hand to her head and found that her hair was tangled with grass and small twigs. The white shorts she had worn to the party were filthy and there were scratches on her legs and arms. One shoe was gone.

Sylvie knew she looked awful. The weird part was that she felt great.

Wonderful, she thought, I look like a basket case, I don't know where I've been, I don't know what I did while I was there, and I don't have any idea how I got home. My parents are probably out of their minds. But I feel like dancing.

She took a deep breath and got ready to go in and face her family. Swinging her legs off the chaise, she felt a deep soreness in all her muscles, but it was a good kind of soreness, the kind that comes after invigorating exercise.

She crossed the lawn and pushed open the French doors to the living room, hoping to sneak upstairs and at least make herself presentable before her parents killed her. Unfortunately, her parents were sitting right there. And she had no words to tell them what she didn't know herself.

Angela saw her first. With a little cry, she rushed to Sylvie and held her. "Honey," she cried, "we were scared to *death*!"

She patted Sylvie's hair, then stopped in midmotion. She drew back to look at her: the tangled hair, the scratches, the blank look in her eyes.

What was it, Angela thought, that was so familiar about this, so terrifying?

"Sylvie," she said slowly, "what happened to you? Where were you?"

Sylvie made her way to one of the sofas and sank down into it. She wasn't feeling so great now, in fact she was exhausted.

"Mother, I wish I could explain."

"Honey," Angela said, taking her hand, "you know you can tell us anything. No matter how bad it is."

Sylvie closed her eyes and took a long, bone-tired breath. "I wasn't attacked or raped or anything. I know that much."

It suddenly struck Sylvie as odd that her father hadn't said a word. She opened her eyes to look at him.

He was standing with his back to the fireplace, directly in front of her, and was staring at her in absolute terror, his eyes stark and frightened, as if he'd been confronted with his worst nightmare. Mixed into that look, somehow, was a sorrow so raw and painful that it hurt Sylvie to look at it.

She had been ready to tell her parents some plausible, believable lie about going off with some other boy, sneaking away from the party and losing track of time. She'd be in terrible trouble, but at least it was something her parents could live with.

But looking at her father right then, she felt she owed him an honest explanation, as far as she could give it.

"I didn't mean to leave the party, all I wanted to do was just get away from everyone for a few minutes.

"I was sitting there, surrounded by friends I'd known forever. I should have felt comfortable, but there was just something so strange about them all of a sudden. One minute they were okay, and the next minute, it was like I didn't know them. They didn't look *real* to me. They seemed"—she groped for the word—"*abstract*, like mechanical dolls that couldn't really feel or see or hear.

"And I seemed to change, too. My own senses seemed sharper than ever before. Sights, sounds, smells; they were all clearer, more delineated. I've never felt anything like that before. I felt high, pumped up. Then I just sank into a black depression, like I had been given something valuable and was about to lose it if I didn't get up *right that minute* and leave those people.

"I said I was going to the bathroom and I just kept walking.

I only meant to go a little way down the road, to walk off some of those bizarre feelings, but I started to walk faster, then to run. I remember . . . I felt just *wonderful*, strong and free. . . ."

She broke off as Angela gave a sob and buried her face in her hands.

Sylvie didn't know what else to say. She couldn't remember what came next.

When her father spoke, his voice was tight and low. "And all this began just at moonrise."

Sylvie looked up. "Just about. Why? How do you know that?"

He turned away from her and she couldn't see his face, only the hopeless way his shoulders slowly began to slump.

"Quentin told us. Sylvie, we'll talk some more later. Just go to bed now."

"Dad, I'm sorry."

"Don't be sorry. Just go take a warm bath and get some sleep."

She walked over to kiss him, but he didn't turn around.

After he heard Sylvie quietly close the big sliding doors that separated the living room from the hallway, Andrew rested his forehead against the cool marble of the fireplace mantel. He felt boneless, every drop of life washed away in a flood of misery and guilt.

He heard Angela's footsteps behind him and turned to hold her.

But she stepped back, jerking away from him in fury.

As she stood there now, her face drenched in tears, her eyes huge with fear, he realized that the trust she'd always had in him was completely destroyed.

"What have you done to my baby?" she demanded.

He could think of nothing to say. He could only look at her, trying to make her understand.

She suddenly collapsed against him, her arms going around his neck as if she couldn't stand. With every sob, Andrew could feel her body rend itself into pieces.

"I'm so sorry," she murmured against his shoulder. "God help me, I don't know how I could have said such a thing."

"It's all right."

"God, Andrew, what are we going to do?"

"Angela, we don't know that it's . . ."

She drew back and looked at him, her face tearing his heart out. "Oh, Andrew, what else could it be? And what about Walt and Geo? What will happen to them?"

"Nothing. Nothing will happen to them, Angela."

"But how do you *know*? How can you be sure?"

"I just know."

She grabbed his shirt, her fingernails almost ripping the fabric, as she looked into his face. "Don't let this happen to her, Andrew! *Do something!* Help her!"

He held her very tightly. Old feelings were washing over him, horrible memories of feelings that should have been buried so long ago. Over twenty years ago he thought he had finished with this, had fought the battle and won what no man had won before. But he was wrong, and it took all of these years for it to become apparent, to manifest itself in the most awful way.

Once again, the child was paying for the sins of the father.

Sylvie sank into a steaming tub, the water's surface glimmering with fragrant oil. After a few minutes, the springs began to uncoil.

She had been honest with her father in all but one thing. She hadn't told him about the man who carried her, whose green eyes clear as seawater still mesmerized her. She could remember that fragment, and the feel of his broad chest, the silk of his hair. Where they had gone, what they had done, if they had talked . . . all that was a blank. But she knew she'd never forget the security she felt while she was with him.

She also remembered—and she wasn't sure whether she had said it or only thought it—the words *help me*. The meaning of the phrase was a mystery, but she was sure that, whoever he was, he could ease her confusion and end her terrible, dark longing.

PART TWO

†

Lucifer Rising

7

Antoine was pleased with his remodeled temple.

He had gutted most of the first floor of his grandmother's house and enclosed the courtyard to make one enormous room, with pillars spaced along where the interior walls used to be. Worshipers could enter the temple from the old front door, which took them into an anteroom. Two intimidating black matte double doors set with brass snakes for handles led directly onto a small platform, and down three wide steps to the main room. The grand processions of Papa Lucifer's meetings would begin through the double doors, down the platform, and through the room to the altar.

All Mother Pauline's gentle magic was gone, driven out under an assault of bloodred enameled walls and black ceilings and floors. Garish brass chandeliers with ruby glass shades made everything in the room lurid and evil. In the center of the room, beside the center post, was set a stained-glass pentagram with the goat-headed demon at its heart and the names and signs of the seven demons of Hell lettered into the perimeter. The whole thing lit up from below as if filled with the fires of the underworld.

In the main room, at the far end from the doors, was hung a ten-foot gilded wooden cross, suspended upside down, and a gilded pentagram, also upside down, with two points up and one down. By hanging the cross and pentagram upside down, Antoine had desecrated both the symbol of Christianity and the ancient symbol of the Witches. The altar, black and purple like a Victorian funeral catafalque, dressed with silver vessels and a silver dagger, sat between the symbols and the illuminated pentagram.

53

The people milling about, waiting for the entrance of Papa Lucifer, were there mostly out of curiosity.

"Look at all this," a man named Henry Roche said to the woman standing next to him, "looks like black magic to me."

"Don't look like proper Voodoo," the woman said doubtfully.

"It ain't proper. Where's the statue of St. Marron? Where's St. Jude? Where's the vevers for Mistress Erzulie and Damballah? And look at that cross hangin' upside down there! Where'd he get this stuff? Out of churches? Ask me, I think Antoine's makin' fun of the Church. Now, you know no good Voodoo makes fun of the Church, not here in New Orleans, he don't!"

"Me, I'm a good Cat'lic," the woman said, "and a good Voodoo. I don't hold wit' no ridiculin' the saints."

"And what's this name he's usin'—Papa Lucifer? That ain't no Voodoo name. I tell you, I'm here out of respect to Mother Pauline, him bein' her grandson, but I don't think this is right!"

"If Antoine's really got the power, anything he does is right. The *loa* gonna be with him. The question is, does he got the power?"

The people around Henry and the woman, hearing this exchange, nodded their heads in agreement. Everyone wanted to see what Antoine would do, and if he indeed had the power.

The lights slowly dimmed and the people grew silent, only a few murmurs breaking the quiet. Henry was one of these. "No drums?" he whispered to the woman. She shrugged.

The room was almost in darkness, lit only by the bloody light from the stained-glass pentagram.

Suddenly the glare of a spotlight crossed the room, and Antoine was standing in front of the altar.

He was dressed in billowing black silk robes, the wide sleeves lined in scarlet, so that with every movement of his arms the scarlet flashed. Several gold rings, one set with a large cabochon ruby, decorated his fingers. But the most spectacular object he wore was a fabulous gold chain with some kind of black stone imprisoned in a gold cage.

With a sudden gesture, he held up his arms and the black silk rippled around him.

"Do you want the power?" he demanded loudly.

His voice was clear, authoritative, commanding. The sound of it riveted the Voodoos' attention.

"Most of you follow Madame Mae. Now, I love Mae; you all know that I do. But Mae isn't strong enough. She's a good woman and, my friends, that's her downfall. We all know what happens to good people in today's world. It's the strong that make it, that get what they want. I'm sorry to say it, but it's the way of the world. And you have to deal with the world in its own way, you have to fight fire with fire, you have to pit strength against strength! Am I right?"

There was an affirmative murmur from the crowd.

"You can't just invoke the spirits and wait—you have to *take* what you deserve!"

The murmurs came louder.

"I can get you wealth! I can get you love! All you women—you want men crawling at your feet, ready to spend that money on you and buy you anything you want? You want marriage and babies? I can get it for you!

"And you men. You want to pick the right horse out at the fairgrounds? You want all the women you can handle and the virility to keep them happy? Do you want to get even with that boss who treats you like shit? Do you want an enemy out of the way for good? *I can do it for you!*"

The murmurs were much louder now, with some people becoming convinced, and some still waiting for proof.

"How can you do that, Papa?" one man called out.

Antoine smiled and lifted the gold chain from around his neck. He held it up before the crowd, the spotlight refracting light from its glittering links around the room. "Because of this," Antoine said. "You know what this is?"

There was a soft rustle of whispering in the crowd.

"You've all heard of the woman who gave me this, ever since you were little children. You've heard stories about her power, how she could make anything happen, how she ruled the Voodoos for years and came back from the dead. This"—

he thrust the chain forward—"is the black heart of *la Reine Blanche*!"

There was a concerted gasp from the crowd. Everyone knew the name, and everyone knew about her sorcery. If Antoine had anything of hers, and if it was the real thing, he had some potent magic working for him.

"*La Reine Blanche* came to me in a dream," Antoine said. "A dark, powerful vision. She told me that I would be the greatest Voodoo in the history of New Orleans, that she was going to give me the power. She held out her hand to me, and I tell you—I was afraid! Her eyes were like two burning coals, like the eyes of the Devil himself! She knew I was afraid, and she laughed at me. In her hand was this stone, this black stone. 'Go ahead and take what I give you,' she told me. 'You're the only person in this world who can touch it and still live.'

"She told me that she'd been watching me—watching from the very gates of Hell!—and she knew that I was the one to inherit her throne. 'This is the symbol of power!' she said to me. 'My heart, turned to black crystal so that no one can see its secrets. No one but the rightful King of the Voodoos!'

"I thought it was a fever, I thought it was a dream. But when I woke up, shaking and shivering, bathed in sweat, this"—he thrust the heart toward the crowd—"was around my neck. The White Queen had told me that the touch of it can kill you. But I put my hand around it, and I wasn't even afraid. I could feel the power course through me!"

He pointed to a woman in the crowd. Lurline had been a pretty girl but she'd been disfigured in a car accident six years before, and plastic surgery had only done so much. Her face was still twisted and scarred.

"Come up here to me, Lurline," Antoine said, holding out his hand to her.

Lurline was shaking in fear, but she let herself be led to the altar.

The hidden Voodoo drums began to beat, slowly and evenly. Holding the black heart, Antoine closed his eyes and put himself into a trance. The crowd, caught up in the familiar rhythms, the only familiar thing about this strange ceremony, began to sway and sing the old chants in low voices.

Antoine opened his eyes and motioned for two of his assistants. One opened a cage at the back of the altar and handed Antoine a black rooster. Holding it by the feet with one hand, Antoine decapitated the bird with a single flashing slice of his silver-handled knife. The assistants quickly pinned the screaming Lurline down over the altar as Antoine poured the steaming blood, pumping from the bird's neck, over her face and body.

Lurline gasped, and stopped screaming. Her body started to shake, to shiver and contort. Everyone knew what this was: Lurline was to be honored by being possessed by the *loa*. The people waited for the *loa* to make its identity known.

A woman's scream broke the expectant silence. "Oh my *God*! What *is* that?"

Hovering over Lurline's shaking body was an enormous, vaporous face, glowing evilly red as it hung in the air, a woman's face, beautiful but hideous. The eyes seemed to burn with a terrifying fire.

Many people in the crowd screamed, some cowered on the floor, some just stared, transfixed in horror. Never had they seen anything like this; things like this just didn't happen among the Voodoos. The *loa* were capricious, benevolent, sometimes tricksters, but never malevolent.

The luminescent red face shimmered briefly, then started to re-form itself into a thin stream of vapor, flowing into Lurline's gaping mouth, disappearing like a stream of water down a drainpipe.

The voice coming from Lurline's mouth was booming, nerve-wracking. "I am *la Reine Blanche*," it said. The sound was not female, not male, not human; it was like a synthesized recording of human speech, eerily playing at a strange speed. "This man is the one I have chosen for my successor. I gave him my heart as proof, and my power through my heart. To doubt him would be to incur my darkest anger!"

Lurline shivered and her body contorted, the blood obscuring her disfigured face. Suddenly, the red vapor erupted from her mouth in a great, shifting cloud that broke into particles and dissipated.

At a signal from Antoine, one of his henchmen poured a pitcher of water over Lurline's face, washing off the blood, then blotted her with a black towel. Smiling, Antoine gently took both her hands and helped her to her feet, turning her to face the crowd.

There was a great gasp as the Voodoos looked at her. Her face was as pretty, as smooth and unlined, as before the accident. The scars were gone, the tissues whole, the severed nerves reconnected.

"Black magic!" Henry Roche cried, unable to stop himself. "You haven't given us our religion, you've given us blasphemy and black magic! Just like *la Reine Blanche*—it's her evil all over again!"

"But how can you say it's evil," Antoine said reasonably, "when I've given this sweet girl her beauty back? Is that evil? Or is that doing good to help the people?"

"Where's it gonna lead us?" Henry demanded. "Madame Mae can heal the sick, and she ain't gonna lead us into Hell like you will! Everybody knows that *la Reine Blanche*'s magic was bad stuff!"

Henry jumped up near the altar and appealed to the crowd. "Madame Mae always took good care of us. You all remember when Marie Mercier was lyin' up at Charity Hospital and the doctors say she ain't gonna get no better? That she was gonna die? Remember Madame Mae went up there for seven days and seven nights, shakin' the *asson* over Marie, callin' on seven saints and the Seven Powers? And Baron Samedi was so moved by Madame Mae that he let Marie go, and she's back with her children and her grandchildren to this day, right as rain." He looked at Antoine contemptuously. "And Madame Mae didn't need no black heart to do it. She didn't need none of *la Reine Blanche*'s badness. She can talk with the saints and the Seven Gods of Africa. She's got Erzulie and Ghede Nimbo to do her work. She controls the power of the loup-garou, had that power since she was only sixteen!"

The crowd stirred a little, talking to each other. What Henry said was true: Mae had been good to them, and she *was* the rightful Queen.

Antoine fingered the black heart and regarded Henry impassively. "If you feel like that, you shouldn't be here. You aren't ready for the true power. You should go back to Mae."

"I will," Henry said emphatically. "I only came here out of respect for Mother Pauline. But you don't do her no respect. You shame her."

Antoine smiled. "I have a message for you to give Mae," he said carefully. He reached for Henry's hand, and quickly closed it around the obsidian heart.

Henry began to shiver, the same way Lurline did, only more violently. His eyes rolled back until only the whites showed, then the whites turned red as the delicate capillaries burst. Blood, mixed with mucus, began to flow from his nose and mouth; he gagged and choked on it, fighting for air. He fell slowly to his knees, struggling to stay upright, grabbing at the black-draped altar. The silver altar furnishings crashed to the floor as Henry fell, taking the black cloth with him. He was dead before he hit the floor.

It was stone silent in the room. Not a sound.

Antoine impassively regarded the crowd, but inside he was exultant. He could feel the fear of the crowd and it excited him, fed him. He signaled to his men. "Take him out," he told them. "Take him back to Mae. Show her what the real power can do."

He looked at the dazed crowd triumphantly, with a withering, condescending smile, and strode out of the room in a billow of black and scarlet silk.

When he was alone, Antoine gave vent to a jealous fury. He had let that stupid Henry go on for far too long. He'd reminded everyone of Mae's power, and only the mention of it was enough to trigger memories of her past successes in the minds of each one of the worshipers. He had no idea how many of the Voodoos would be back; he had staged this whole thing on the premise that most of them would be too scared *not* to come back. But even though it had been a decent crowd, it was nothing to the numbers Mae drew. And he hadn't noticed Mae's most devoted followers, her core group who carried power of their own, in the crowd tonight.

She was going to have to be dealt with, that was clear. But he couldn't just kill her through common murder. That would prove nothing. He could try a magical attack, but Mae would know how to protect herself from that; she had probably anticipated that very thing and was invulnerable right now.

No, there had to be another way to get rid of her. Something spectacular, something that would impress the people and establish Antoine unshakably as the unquestioned power in New Orleans.

Only one thought scared him, when he allowed himself to think about it. And then it was only a brief, flittering shadow across his mind: what if Mae was more powerful than *la Reine Blanche*?

8

After the last Mass, Andrew headed back to his office. He planned to skip the usual after-church coffee and beignets in the parish hall; he needed the time alone to think.

He was not prepared for the man sitting in his office. Obviously, the man had been waiting awhile: he was so deep into a book that he didn't notice Andrew at first.

Andrew cleared his throat.

The man looked up and smiled. As he tilted his head, the gold hoop in his ear caught the light. "Good morning, Bishop. Hey, you better sit down. You don't look so steady on your feets, no."

Andrew sat suddenly in the nearest chair.

The man regarded Andrew with genuine fondness. "I don't believe it. The last time I saw you, you had been ordained just a couple of months before, and now you're the Suffragan Bishop of the Episcopal Diocese of New Orleans. Married that pretty girl and"—he picked up a framed picture on Andrew's desk—"got you three beautiful *bébés*. This is a wonderful thing, *cher ami*."

Andrew wasn't sure his voice would work.

"Achille, why are you here?"

Achille looked delighted. "Ha! I knew you'd remember me! It's just like I done told you twenty years ago; you'll never forget Achille. And Bayou Goula, eh?"

"No," Andrew said, "how could I forget it?"

Achille's eyes grew serious, his voice quieter. "I told you then, and I still mean it now: it will stay with you forever."

"Achille, please!" Andrew said. "Don't make me remember these things."

61

"You're a loup-garou, Andrew; you always will be. You're one of us until the day you die."

"It isn't true. It hasn't been true for twenty years. That part of my life is over."

"I've always been regretful about that. That you never understood what it was, how it can enrich your life."

Andrew jumped out of his chair. "Are you insane? It was murder. *Murder!* How could you possibly think I could enjoy that?"

"That was all you saw of it. You never acknowledged our place in the world or our purpose. The loup-garou has a duty: justice. We aren't hampered by rules of evidence, we aren't fooled by professions of innocence. We can look right inside a man's conscience, look into his mind as if it were glass. There are no alibis a man can give us, because we know the truth. And if he is evil, he is going to die."

"How can you presume to judge who lives and dies?"

"Because, *cher ami*"—he leaned very close to Andrew— "we know who's guilty and who's not. We know who deserves to die."

Twenty years, Andrew thought, over twenty years since I've seen him, and we're in the middle of the same argument we were having then. And nothing has changed. Neither of us is going to bend, ever.

"That's blasphemy!" Andrew said, not wanting to have this conversation and yet not being able to stop himself. "Only God knows what's in a man's heart!"

Achille shrugged. "Perhaps. But *we* know what's in his mind."

"So you only kill bad guys. How noble of you. Murder is murder, whether you do it in the name of justice or not. What makes you better than a murderer? After all, you take human life—and on a regular basis. What is that?"

"I never said that we only kill bad guys. But as long as we have to kill, why not do some good? You're clouding your mind with hundreds of years of moralistic crap. Be pragmatic."

" 'Pragmatic'?" Andrew said, his eyebrows raised. "Excuse me, but what happened to the good ol' simple Cajun boy act?"

Achille smiled. "Yeah, you right. Education ruint many a good bayou boy, eh? It come poppin' out at the strangest times, yeah."

He leaned forward in his chair and folded his hands. "*Ami*, I didn't come here to make you uncomfortable or to open old wounds, but something's going on right now, that—" He stopped and ran his hands through his hair. "I don't know how else to say this. Andrew, which one of your children feels the call of the moon?"

Andrew darted out of his own chair. "What do you mean? How would you know anything about that?"

"Please, you know how I know. We all know. All of us are connected with a bond none of us can explain. For months we've been feeling it: the call of another loup-garou. And it's gotten stronger all the time. We know who is and who isn't one of us, and we can feel the unfulfilled passion, the confusion, the anguish. It has to be your family, Andrew. You're the only one outside the circle."

"It could be anyone!"

Achille shook his head with great patience. "No. The others may not know who it is, but I know you. We've always been linked, whether you liked it or not, and when we first began to feel the call, I knew in my blood it was your child."

Andrew knew there was no point in sparring with Achille. He remembered that Achille had an incredibly accurate psychic ability that made evasion useless.

"It's my oldest. My daughter, Sylvie," Andrew said. "But, Achille . . . she's just confused and restless. She's at that age. There's no way of knowing if she . . ."

"You want to believe that, *ami,* but you know the truth. Now, how about her? What does she know? Have you told her anything? Did you tell her about yourself?"

"Good God! No!"

"Denying the past won't make it go away. And it could make things very dangerous for your daughter. Who knows better than you what happens to a werewolf who is unprepared?"

"It won't happen," Andrew said through a clenched jaw.

"Don't try to make this decision for her," Achille said quietly. "In the first place, you can't. Nature will take its course, and what is supposed to happen will happen. Look, Andrew, I know what you went through all those years ago. I was there, you remember. But it isn't the same for her as it was for you—the girl is a true daughter of the moon, she was born to it, it runs in her blood. It was wrong for you, but it may be right for her. Bring her to Bayou Goula. Let her learn what she has to know to make her decision; you don't know that she might be repulsed and turn away from us. If you're worried about her, I guarantee her safety. She's one of us."

Achille leaned forward and took one of Andrew's hands. "And you, even after all these years and everything that's passed over and between us, you're still one of us, too, still our brother."

"That's all over. It's been over for more than twenty years."

"Yeah? Look at yourself in the mirror. How old are you? Forty-two, forty-three? And how old do you look? Twenty-nine, thirty if it's a bad day and you've been up late."

Andrew hesitated only long enough for Achille to catch the trapped look. "That's . . . I don't know . . . heredity."

"Yeah, right. Loups-garous just don't age much. One year to a human's ten. And sex? It's still good, right? You gotta have it—what? Two or three times a day when you have the time? And you never lost an erection in your life."

"I refuse to talk about this."

Achille shrugged. "I'm not trying to be nosy, *ami,* I'm just trying to make a point. You may be through with the loup-garou's life, but some of it always stays with you. And it might be what your daughter wants."

"You're wrong, Achille. It isn't right for her."

"I'm never wrong about this, *cher ami.*"

Achille's kind heart pitied Andrew. All these years, all the hopeless sorrow of his past, and he hadn't learned a thing. He had been given the gift and had rejected it, only able to see the horror and never allowing himself to see the purpose or the beauty of it.

But he knew that Andrew was a family man. He had chosen that life for himself, had wanted it as passionately as Achille had wanted his own. If Achille had made wrenching sacrifices to become what he was, Andrew's struggles had been worse, and more terrifying. Achille couldn't condemn him.

So why was it that whenever they met, Achille couldn't restrain himself from reminding Andrew that the life he could have led might have been more seductive than the life he'd chosen? Was it because Achille himself had had no choice? Or because Andrew had rejected everything that Achille believed was at the core of his own life?

Achille refused to think about it anymore.

"There's something else I came here to tell you," Achille said. "There's been a resurgence in black-magic Voodoo around town. Very scary stuff. I think the name *la Reine Blanche* means something to you?"

Andrew's face turned pale. Instinctively, he made the sign of the cross.

"Yes, I see it does," Achille said. "I want you to think about something: the Voodoo who has a loup-garou under his obligation is powerful and dangerous. A true loup-garou, one born to the moon, is even more effective. A loup-garou like you, Andrew. And your family has always been linked with the White Queen."

"That woman is dead, Achille," Andrew said, but his voice was shaky.

"Well, we always thought so, but that's been said about her on at least two occasions. And her brand of Voodoo is hard to miss, even harder to wipe out. You know better than I do what harm those people can do. Look, I don't mean to scare you, Andrew, but it's very important that you talk to your daughter. If you can't bring yourself to do it, I'll do it for you. I don't know what all this means: the black magic popping up again, people talking in low voices about a dead Voodoo queen and the things she can do . . . but I know that some scary things are going to happen, and soon."

He sighed and got to his feet, stretching his back, holding his arms out and stretching his hands and fingers.

"I'm easy to find," Achille said. "The New Orleans Police Department. Ask for Lieutenant Broussard. And, *cher ami*, please—this time—don't be too proud to ask for help. Remember what happened to you. Do you want her to go through that? It should be a beautiful experience, the first time, not an agony.

At least spare your daughter that much."

Achille was almost out the door when he hesitated and turned back to Andrew. "Tell me," he asked softly, "do you still feel it? The pull of the moon? Does it wake you in the night, when you feel the room close in on you and your skin feels like a prison? Does your body want to run, to fly? Your voice to howl with joy?"

Andrew turned away and stared for many moments at the crucifix on the wall, just behind his chair. Achille watched his shoulders slump slightly, could almost feel the reminiscent tingle of old excitements run through the bishop's nerves. Intellectual arguments, Achille knew, couldn't erase the remnants of so physical an experience. And he couldn't mistake Andrew's faint whisper: "Yes. God damn you, Achille, yes."

"Then you should understand what your daughter's feeling. Bring her to me, *cher ami*, let me teach her. Don't make her suffer for your past."

9

Lester Jackson was getting ready for his workday. Part of the reason for his success was that he was always at work so early, long before his competitors. Nobody could say Lester wasn't serious about his career.

He pulled on his gray sweats and his $120 Avias. He'd bought the shoes not from a status thing, like his peers, but because they encouraged his best performance.

He set out for work, passing the entrance to St. Louis Cemetery. The guard was just opening the gates and a few tourists were getting ready to amble in.

Lester shook his head. Despite warnings from the city officials about how dangerous the cemetery was, tourists still insisted on going there. Lester knew how people's minds worked: they figured nothing was going to happen to them because they were from Cincinnati or someplace. He eyed two people who were just asking for it. She was carrying a huge tote bag with her purse sticking out of it, and wearing a touristy T-shirt from one of those Vieux Carré joints. It had a crawfish on it and read "Eat The Tails . . . Suck The Heads." What good fuckin' taste. Her hubby had an expensive camera, complete with telephoto lens, and carried a camera bag, probably stuffed with more lenses and accessories. He had a matching T-shirt *plus* sandals worn with socks. White socks. Shit, if the fashion police gave tickets, Lester thought, this city'd be out of debt in one three-day weekend.

Why do people do it? Lester wondered, looking at the tote bag and the camera. They just encourage crime.

Lester made his way to the far side of the cemetery. Taking a deep breath, he looked up at the wall, surveying the chinks and crevices he knew so well. Time to do a dishonest day's work, he said to himself. He scaled the wall in a minute and landed like a jaguar on the other side.

He looked around quickly to make sure that no one had seen him. Nobody. Great. Now all he had to do was wait behind the tombs until Mr. and Mrs. Cincinnati came by. He checked his piece: for stuff like this he used a small, easily concealed .22. Muggers who used those big macho guns were asking for trouble. Any cop on the street could spot those things, no matter how many layers of clothes you had on. Besides, he'd never had to use it. Just the sight of a black man with a gun made most tourists very cooperative. Yes, sir, as long as you had to put up with racism, you might as well make it work for you.

Uh-oh. Here came the tourists. Lester kept his eye on them while he backed behind a tomb. They were only a few yards away. He stepped on something soft, almost falling over. Annoyed, he looked down.

Lester's scream startled the tourist couple, who dropped their bags and drew their .38 service revolvers. The woman covered her partner as he ran to the tomb and found Lester, still screaming, his Avia running shoes smeared with blood, staring down at the mutilated body with its heart cut out.

Joe Ed Landry, as usual, was at the murder scene before Achille.

"Hey, looka this," he said to Achille. "We got another one just like the other one."

Achille looked at the body, then frowned at Landry.

"Who's this?" Achille said.

Landry shrugged. "He ain't on my dance card. Just another John Doe for now. You make him?"

"Hell no. How am I supposed to know who he is?"

" 'Cause you got so many friends in low places. Since the last one was one of your cases, I just thought maybe you was tryin' to raise your conviction record."

Achille squatted down and examined the body. It looked just like the body in City Park: it was lying on its back, a look of terror on its face, and an ugly cavity where its heart should be.

This was no loup-garou killing, though. For one thing, Achille couldn't detect any familiar scents from the werewolf pack. For another, the job was very sloppily done.

The body was surrounded by a number of arcane objects. A ball of black wax, studded all over with black feathers and tied with a red cord with nine knots, was stuffed in the corpse's right hand. Nine silver coins were laid symmetrically around the body. Black candles pierced with black pins had burned down to the ground at its head and feet.

A black pin was stuck on each of the corpse's eyes. Three black pins sealed its mouth.

The murder weapon was there, too: a red-handled butcher's knife with dried chickens' feet tied to it with black cords and bits of red rags.

"Body was found by our own people," Joe Ed said. "Well, almost. We had two plainclothes cops on duty in the cemetery, doing the tourist number. They hear a scream and find a mugger so scared he'd shit his pants. He was the first one to see it."

"I'd about shit, too," Achille agreed. "So where's the mugger?"

"Over there, with Sullivan. You don't want to see him just now, though; I got a surprise for ya." Landry pointed to a tall black man kneeling a few yards from the corpse.

The man was unaware of the body, the police, or anything else. He rocked back and forth on his knees, wringing his bloody hands and repeating a strange chant. His eyes were glazed and blank.

Joe Ed nodded in the man's direction. "That's the perp, ain't he a prize? He's a John Doe, too."

"Ooo-*wee*!" Achille said softly. "He make any statement? Anybody read him his rights?"

"For all the good it did," Joe Ed said. "He don't hear nothin', he don't see nothin', he don't say nothin' except that stuff he's moaning, and we can't make it out. We got him cuffed, but he ain't going nowhere."

Achille and Joe Ed went over for a closer look. Achille squatted down to look the man in the face and recognized him.

"Hey," he said softly to the man, "LeRoy. Nobody's gonna hurt you, now. Hey, man, come on, you know me. Why don't you tell me about it?"

The man continued his rocking and chanting. He raised his handcuffed arms and one of his sleeves fell back.

Achille straightened up. "Look at his arm," he told Joe Ed. "Needle marks, some of 'em fresh. This old boy's not coming back anytime soon, no."

"You know him?"

"Yeah, LeRoy Dufresne. He used to be one of Mae's followers."

Joe Ed frowned. "Jesus, Achille . . . this ain't Mae's type of Voodoo, is it?"

"No, but I bet it's part of all that stuff we've been seeing lately: church desecrations, animal sacrifice. LeRoy stopped coming to Mae's Voodoo meetings about three months ago. He follows Papa Lucifer now."

"That nut again!"

"Yeah, you right." Achille glanced back at the body. "And I guess he's demanding more from his followers these days."

Mae Charteris had just finished a vigil at the deathbed of one of her people.

It had been a sad duty for Mae, but a blessed rest for old Miz Sadie, who had lived a marvelously long and adventurous life. In her youth, Miz Sadie had presided over one of the city's most exclusive brothels, catering to a clientele that had included a Louisiana governor—and his wife. Miz Sadie had always been a devout Voodoo, following first Mother Pauline, then Mae. It was said that Miz Sadie's mother had been the fabulous Storyville madam, Countess Willie Piazza.

Mae had seen Miz Sadie into the Invisible World with all the proper prayers, rituals, candles, and incense, and it had taken a long time. But it was best done quickly. For seven days the *ti bon Ange,* that part of the soul that is the essence of the living woman, the soul's own heart, would hover still attached to Miz Sadie, anxious for its flight. And until Mae released it, the *ti bon Ange* was prey to anything, even the control of an evil practitioner who would use the vulnerable soul to manipulate the body. Mae thought of Antoine, now lost inside his corruption of Voodoo with black magic, and shuddered. What would happen to those of his flock who died? What would he do with their souls? How would they suffer to feed his power?

Walking briskly under the streetlights on Chartres Street, Mae made a most unlikely picture of a Voodoo queen. She wore skintight jeans tucked into mid-heeled suede boots, with an oversize red sweater topping it off, and a paisley shawl shot with gold threads tied around her hips. Her gold hoop earrings against her mocha-colored skin and long, curly black hair gave her a Gypsyish look. A few too many gold and jeweled objects dangled around her neck, but very little of it was for vanity—they were amulets and charms that enhanced Mae's power. Mae was thirty-eight, but her lithe body and long hair made her look like a young girl.

But she was unmistakably the Voodoo queen. Most of the black people she passed and the knowledgeable whites nodded their heads to her in respect whenever she went out. Some spoke courteous greetings, a few approached her timidly and made whispered requests.

She carried a large wicker basket, gray with age, covered with a brightly patterned shawl. It had been passed on to her from Mother Pauline and served the same purpose as a doctor's bag: it carried herbs, powders, oils, and charms for the work.

Unlike some Voodoo women of the past who made the faithful come to them, Mae liked getting out, getting the feel of the town, seeing people, hearing the latest news and gossip. Maybe doctors wouldn't make house calls, but Mae did. Because of her psychic gifts, she was an excellent healer and regarded this as the most important of her duties. To Mae, the power to heal was something she gave back to the spirits for the guidance they gave her.

She crossed past the presbytère as the shadows lengthened, approaching the cathedral, when she became aware of footsteps following her.

She looked around. The square was almost deserted at this hour. Even the tourists were cosseted in their expensive beds. Strange how timeless the square could be this late, after the people were gone and the traffic faded. It could have been any century here, and you could almost touch the ghosts floating on the river breeze.

It wasn't ghosts who frightened Mae. She knew them. It was the unknown, those malevolent, angry entities jealous of mortal life, who looked for every opportunity to plague man. And it was man himself, warped beyond moral judgment, who was most dangerous.

She remembered the newspaper reports of the recent discoveries of mutilated bodies. A vile-tasting mixture of fear and sorrow flooded her throat. Antoine, she thought. My poor Antoine. How could you have been so foolish?

Mae could hear the sound of movement behind her, quick and furtive. She glanced at the cabildo, beside her now, with its tall, wide columns. Any nut could be hiding back there.

She stopped, standing very still, to hear better.

All there was was a slight rustling, then silence, the night holding its breath.

Mae slowly slipped her hand into her basket, feeling for the black-handled ritual dagger she carried. It would be sacrilege to attack someone with it, but she'd take care of that later.

A low, deep growl came from close behind her.

Before she could turn, Mae was swept up off her feet, lifted in the air. The knife scuttled across the pavement, into the shadows of the cabildo.

Mae's every muscle was tensed to fight, when a familiar voice growled in her ear, "Gotcha, baby!"

She sighed and relaxed.

"You do anything like this again, Achille," Mae said in disgust, "and I'm gonna kick you so hard, when you open your mouth, your balls gonna be on your tongue."

Achille set Mae back on her feet, and retrieved her knife for her. "Forgive me, daw'lin. I didn't think. What you doin' out so late all by yourself?" he asked. "Didn't your mama ever tell you there's scary things wandering around in the dark?"

Mae gave him a long, appraising stare. "Yeah, you right. She said if I wasn't good, the loup-garou gonna catch me and eat me."

"Your mama right about that, *chérie*," he laughed, swooping her up across his shoulder as she screamed with laughter.

He started toward Mae's house, her wiggling body dangling over his chest and back, her basket over his other arm.

They passed some late–Saturday night revelers, two sassy black girls, and their young men, who were astounded to see how the great Voodoo queen was being transported home.

Mae's slender fingers closed around the pillow and stuffed one corner of it in her mouth to stifle her screams.

Achille pulled the pillow away. "Make all the noise you want, daw'lin," he told her, his mouth against her skin. "It just makes me harder."

She grasped the pillow with one hand and reached down for Achille's hair with the other.

He laughed. "I'd never let you come this soon, you know."

She gasped again and smiled. Whatever psychic gifts Mae had, Achille's were stronger, more pronounced, clearer. He knew exactly how she felt, he anticipated every feeling she had. He knew exactly what to do, how hard, how gently, when to stop, and when to keep going. A loup-garou couldn't exactly read minds—it was more a matter of picking up on random thoughts and feelings. Mae didn't give a flying fuck *how* it worked, as long as it kept working.

A girl would sell her soul for a man like this, she had thought more than once.

It was the loup-garou way. Because of their animal natures, loups-garous were highly curious and experimental, with no sexual inhibitions at all. Once, during sex, something slightly kinky popped into Mae's mind, something she'd never done before. Achille had stopped what he was doing and asked, "You really want to do that?" She never said a word, she only thought, Why not? Achille had laughed indulgently, gotten out of bed, and dug in his coat pocket. He had looked back at her, still lying there. "You gotta know I trust you, yes, to let you do something like this to me." He had found his police handcuffs and handed them to her.

Now Achille raised up and ran his fingers lightly down the side of her body, starting at her breast and continuing all the way down her leg, a tiny flutter, a touch so light and barely there that it raised goose bumps everywhere he touched. Then his hand started back up, only the tips of his fingers trailing over her skin.

Suddenly, he got out of bed.

Mae grabbed the sheet and sat up, confused.

"Where the hell do you think you're going?" she demanded.

He pulled a chair over near the bed. "I'm gonna sit right here."

"And do what?"

"And I'm gonna watch you."

"Are you crazy?"

He pushed her gently back down and pulled the sheet away. "You just lay down, close your eyes and think pretty thoughts, and I'm gonna sit and appreciate that beautiful body of yours." He settled comfortably in the chair.

"Achille, this is without a doubt the weirdest thing you've ever done."

"We'll see," he said. "But don't talk."

For the first few minutes she just felt strange, vulnerable, and exposed. Then she opened her eyes and glanced at Achille. In the dim light, he was staring fixedly at her body, absolutely absorbed, an enormous erection jutting from his lap.

He leaned forward briefly, slowly spread her legs wide so that he could see, then settled back again.

It had the strangest effect on her to be appreciated in that way. Her whole body was beginning to feel warm, starting with her breasts. She closed her eyes again as she felt her nipples grow full and hard. She felt a familiar stirring between her legs, and heard herself give a little moan.

She knew he was still watching her with that particularly exciting intensity. It went on for several minutes, maybe a half hour, maybe an hour; she didn't know. It just seemed timeless. She was very aware of the sensations that simply being looked at produced in her.

She kept expecting him to touch her at any second, and her body was anticipating it, producing delicious little tingles, goose bumps that rose of their own accord to meet his hands. The longing was starting to drive her crazy.

She didn't open her eyes, but eventually she felt him sit near her, on the edge of the bed.

By now she had to have him touch her, she couldn't stand it, but he seemed not to be moving. She moved her own hands, one to her breast, the other between her legs.

Achille gently took both her wrists and held them above her head.

"Oh . . . no . . . ," she whispered. But he said nothing.

Other than that, he made no move to touch her, and she felt that her body was on fire. She could feel his breath, just above her nipple, and she arched her back toward him and felt him retreat.

After a few more minutes of this, she was dying, her body twisting toward him, her wrists still held above her head. She had never been so aroused. She was almost crazy with it.

His lips grazed her ear and he whispered, "You're beautiful. I think I should open the shutters and let every man in New Orleans see you like this."

When he said that, Mae felt her whole body explode in a way it never had before. It wasn't an orgasm, but almost; it was different, strange. It was more than she could stand: she had to have him inside her right then, or she'd kill him. Later, she vaguely remembered saying so.

He released her hands and she wrapped her legs around him, forcing herself down over his erection, arching her back, pulling his head down and raising her breasts to his mouth. It was a frantic, violent coupling that blinded both of them to any kind of subtlety, and it seemed to go on forever.

Afterward, they both lay gasping for breath on the floor, across the room from the bed.

Achille raised himself up on his elbows and looked around. "How'd we get down here?" he asked.

"I have no idea," she told him. "Jesus, every muscle in my body hurts."

"Want to do it again?"

"Not in this lifetime."

Mae got unsteadily to her feet and pulled the sheets and pillows off the floor, putting the bed more or less in order. She climbed in and pulled a pillow over her head. "I never knew I was such an exhibitionist," she muttered.

"I knew," Achille said, slipping in bed beside her. "All beautiful women are, a little.

"You know, Mae," he said thoughtfully, "you would have made a good loup-garou."

She pulled the pillow off her face. "Oh yeah? Why is that, because I'm an exhibitionist?"

"No. Because there's something unpredictable in you, uncontrollable. Except in bed, I have a hard time reading you, Mae. I'm never sure what you're thinking, what you're going to do until you do it. I think"—he stopped, as if this had just occurred to him—"I think that's what keeps me fascinated with you."

"I don't know if that's a compliment or not, white boy. I thought you loved me."

He pulled her close and kissed her hair. "I do love you, chérie. But I can't always figure you out, and that's a good thing."

He was quiet a moment. "I'm going to live a long time, Mae."

"I know that, Achille; don't talk about it."

"Much, much longer than you. I don't know if I can take it. Stay with me, Mae."

Mae felt an ache deep in her body. She ran her hand along Achille's chest. Amazing. Twenty years she had been with him and he had hardly aged at all. He looked younger than Mae, although he was two years older. Loups-garous can disguise the fact that they're not aging—to human eyes—by changing outward features. Achille recently had his hair streaked with a little silver in an attempt to *look* forty, but he only managed to look a prematurely gray twenty-three or -four. It wasn't appearances that grieved Mae, it was the reality beneath. She was aging. He, for all practical purposes, wasn't. She was going to die. Achille would, too, but not for five or six hundred years, maybe longer. At times, she would have given anything to live those years with him; at others, she was appalled. Mae tried to see the world as getting better, but in truth, she felt that things were getting worse. She had no wish to live in a poisoned world filled with illiterates breathing toxic air, watching the human race make the same mistakes in every generation.

And the life of a loup-garou wasn't for her. She could appreciate their purpose in their existence, she could even understand it, but she couldn't live it. She was a healer, she tried to bring harmony. How could she bring death?

"I can't live that life, Achille. And I have an obligation to my people. Please don't bring this up again. Aren't we happy the way we are?"

She reached out and traced the furrow between his brows.

"I won't bring it up again," he said with resignation. He turned over on his side, away from her, and fell asleep.

Achille lay on his back, enjoying the late-morning sun warming his chest as it streamed through the bedroom window. He heard water running in the bathroom and the soft swish of Mae's moving into the hall. It was Sunday morning and he felt lazy, indulgent. He felt fine. He stretched, satisfied at the feel of muscles tensing and relaxing. And almost immediately, he had an erection. He looked down, frowned, then laughed.

He thought of calling to Mae and surprising her, but he never knew what mood she was in. He got out of bed and padded down the hall to find her.

She was the most beautiful woman he'd ever seen. He thought so when he'd first met her and nothing that had happened to her in between then and now had changed his mind. Age had brought Mae grace, a measure of control that counterbalanced the occasional lavish displays of emotion.

What a werewolf she would have made! A streak of wildness was born in her, an earthy quality like a pagan goddess. For all her refined, delicately boned beauty, there was something truly intimidating inside Mae, a terrible challenge that was unspoken but very much in evidence. Brave men had tried to seduce Mae and had folded. When she wanted to, she could scare the hell out of them.

She'd never been able to scare Achille. Drive him out of his mind with lust or fury or aggravation or an overwhelming wave of love—she could do that. Easy. But scare him, no. The first time he saw her, a wise sixteen-year-old staring at him with eyes like a tiger cub that hadn't been fed in a while, he wanted her. Absolutely had to have her, no matter how long he had to wait. He knew she felt it—Mae never failed to pick up things like that—but she'd tear out her own tongue before she'd admit it.

He had been patient, out of deference to her youth and her awesome powers. He knew she'd make the first move, and eventually she did. She'd known better than he did when the time was right, and it wasn't right for almost two years.

Now she sat at a small table in the parlor, frowning over a deck of cards. She turned them over, one by one, taking a deep breath before her fingers touched them.

Achille knew enough not to speak or disturb her.

Finally, the cards were all spread. Mae stared intently at them, touching each one lightly, her hand moving forward, then retracing its path over previous cards. At last she closed her eyes and sighed, tilting her head back slightly. After a minute she opened her eyes, looked at the cards, then looked up at Achille.

"You in a lotta trouble, white boy," she said.

He pulled out a chair and sat across from her. "I don't need the cards to tell me that, *'tite cher.*"

She picked up the cards and put them back in the deck. "Neither did I, but it helps to get information from wherever you can. You want to tell me what's bothering you? Or you want me to find out for myself?"

"Nuh, uh! Don't you hoodoo me, woman." He reached over to run a hand up her bare arm. "You know how I am: fuck me and I'll tell you anything."

"So tell me about the body in the cemetery. Nasty business, Achille."

"He *was* nasty business. Now he's just another piece of paperwork. You tell *me* about Papa Lucifer."

"Talk about bad business," she said, shaking her head. "You know, I never thought Antoine would go this far. I think he's lost control of himself. Even the name: Papa Lucifer. That tells you exactly how far he's gone from his roots. A true Voodoo would never use a name like that.

"I wasn't surprised when he broke away to form his own group; I expected that. It happens. It even happened to Marie

Laveau, you know. Followers of hers set themselves up as queens and attracted a little following. But all they wanted was the glory—they didn't have the power, and the people found that out fast.

"But Antoine has the power. I don't know how. He never did before. The kind of power he has isn't the kind Pauline had, it isn't the kind you're born with. And the kind of magic he's practicing isn't true Voodoo, either; in fact, it's a kind of religion not seen around New Orleans since *la Reine Blanche*. You know about her?"

"Only what I've been told, and that's scary enough, yes," Achille said. "But I see Papa Lucifer's thing all the time now. It started with church burglaries: vestments stolen, altar candles and chalices, somebody stealing the consecrated Host. Then we found ritual killings, small animals killed and the blood drained. That's been around for years, crops up every once in a while. But now it's a regular thing. Hell, I've even seen ritual murder before. But I've never heard of the killer sticking around to be found with the body."

Mae leaned forward and put a hand on Achille's arm. "The whole thing in the cemetery is a warning. First of all, look where the body was found. In back of Marie Laveau's tomb. That's a message: it means that even the most powerful of Voodoo queens isn't safe from Antoine. Then you saw the gris-gris around the body. Black and red, black candles, black pins stuck in the corpse, nine coins as an offering to the spirits. You've been to my meetings, Achille, how many times have you seen me burn black candles with black pins stuck in them?"

"I haven't."

"And you won't. Used like this, they're to bring death. No, this killing was a challenge. Why else would Antoine have chosen one of my old followers to do the murder, and to stay there until he was found? It's Antoine's way of telling me that he has control now."

"Does he?"

"No. And he never will. I'd never let his kind of Voodoo get a foothold in New Orleans again. It's the same technique Papa Doc Duvalier used to control Haiti. He perverted the

religion of the people so that he could use it for intimidation. That's how those South American drug dealers keep the
troops in line. They make the people believe that the demons
of vengeance obey them and will destroy anyone who steps
out of line. And Antoine's learned a lot from them, especially
about making sure that his people are loyal. He makes junkies
out of them."

Mae got up from the table and grabbed the back of her chair,
her knuckles turning white.

"It's taken blacks over a hundred years to wipe off the marks
of those slave chains," she hissed, "and Antoine can clap the
irons back on in the time it takes to slip a needle under the
skin. That's what it is, you know: slavery. In place of the ol'
white massa, we've got the cool black drug dealer. Our own
people are our slave traders."

She lifted the chair and slammed it back down.

There really was nothing in town that Mae didn't know. He
hadn't described the body to her, or the circumstances of the
killing. Achille was always a little shocked that she got the
information she did, and got it so fast. It happened often, but he
was surprised every time. In this case, she was right on target.
There was more than a little evidence that Antoine was keeping
his flock faithful through drug dependence. Nothing fancy or
trendy; Antoine's communion wine was good old-fashioned
heroin. Quick, sure, and deadly.

Of course, if the situation warranted it, like persuading
someone to cut out a man's heart and sit by the body, a little
angel dust worked wonders on the recalcitrant sinner.

Achille had seen Mae mad before, but never like this. Her
eyes were narrowed into cat's eyes, her body was rigid, and
she shivered in fury.

"He's taken the only thing that black people had to hold on
to when they were ripped out of Africa and stuffed into stinking, diseased slave ships, the only thing that kept the people
from going insane with grief and gave them comfort: the old
gods and religion of our people. He's bent it and twisted it,
and I'll never let him get away with that. I'll kill him first."

Achille was struck cold by her anger. He reached out to
touch her, but she didn't seem to feel it.

She didn't seem to hear the phone ring, either, but the first peal made Achille jump. He answered it, listened for a few minutes.

"Ya kiddin'," he said into the phone. "Jee*zuz*, Joe Ed, how do these things happen? Yeah, yeah . . . I'll be there in a few minutes."

When he hung up, Mae had recovered, but she was still angry.

"That was Joe Ed," he told her. "They took LeRoy Dufresne from the hospital to the station house. When he got out of the car, he started chanting gibberish at the top of his lungs, then went absolutely rigid. Joe Ed said his whole body was stiff as a frozen mackerel, it felt like rigor mortis. His eyes bulged, his tongue protruded . . . and he stopped breathing. Just collapsed and died right there on the sidewalk."

Mae turned slowly to look at him.

"I've got to go. Joe Ed wants—"

"I'm going with you." She started to gather some things into her basket.

"What for?"

"Call Joe Ed back now. Tell him not to let them take LeRoy to the morgue. If he's already there, don't let them autopsy him, for God's sake. He isn't dead."

Achille, still confused, reached slowly for the phone.

"Move it!" Mae yelled at him. "Come on, white boy. Surely you've heard of zombies before?"

The city morgue had never been so quiet, especially considering how many people were crammed in there.

It wasn't the first time the police had had the cooperation of the Voodoo queen, but this entire operation spooked even the hard-core cops.

The overhead lights were out. The only light in the room was the spill from the hall and the ring of white candles arranged around the metal autopsy table.

LeRoy Dufresne lay on the table. The lower half of his body was covered with a sheet on which Mae had drawn several elaborate symbols in red ink. These were the sacred signs, the vevers: signatures of the *loa*. Mae had drawn the vevers for

Baron Samedi, the Lord of the Dead.

One of the longtime cops, standing in the back, whispered to Joe Ed Landry.

"This is the spookiest thing I've ever seen," he said. "Is this guy dead or ain't he?"

"I guess we gonna find out, Cap," Landry said. "The Voodoo queen don't think so. She says the dubiously deceased there has been slipped some kinda zombie drug that only makes him *look* dead for a while. The witch doctor gives 'em a dose, the family plants 'em, and the witch doctor digs 'em up and revives 'em when he needs somebody to mow the lawn and paint the garage."

"No shit?" the officer said, watching Mae intently. "I should give that stuff to my kid. Eighteen years old and he can't take out the garbage."

"Yeah, well, if this bozo comes back from the dead, he's gonna put ol' Papa Lucifer away for life and then some."

Mae stood at the head of the autopsy table, three of her female followers attending her: Sisters Delphine, Laylah, and Odette. Beside her was a smaller table crowded with jars, small vials, a crystal bowl, and various paraphernalia.

As Mae dropped each ingredient into the crystal bowl, she made magic signs and whispered a few words that the onlookers couldn't catch.

Finally, she took a slender plastic tube with a funnel on one end and inserted it into the corpse's mouth. She poured the liquid from the crystal bowl into the funnel, where it would go down the throat, not into the lungs, then removed the funnel and dropped it into a plastic bag held by Sister Delphine. The sister was careful not to touch it.

Mae and the sisters chanted several prayers. Then Mae closed her eyes and took a deep breath as the women opened the lid on a large wooden box, inlaid with ivory panels carved with magical symbols, pierced with carving all over, like old lace, shedding light and air into the box.

Opening her eyes, Mae ran her hands over where the lid of the box stood open, not touching what was inside, but spreading her hands to catch the power emanating from it. She took another, deeper breath and knelt before the box.

"Come . . . come, Damballah," she breathed softly. "Give me the power of the earth, of the universal heart, of the dark magic at the core of the world, to do what must be done."

"Holy shit!" Joe Ed breathed. Everyone in the room was mesmerized by the gigantic snake undulating up from the box, winding itself sinuously around Mae's outstretched arms. Up and up it wound while Mae knelt motionless, nuzzling its great head against her cheek, drawing back to look into her eyes.

Mae took in a great gasp of air as the power flowed from the gods of the earth, through the snake, to her body. She shuddered and trembled, the spirits shaking her flesh as they entered her. Her eyes rolled back in her head, so far that only the whites showed under her fluttering lids. She began to speak softly, in a language not meant to be heard.

Then Mae relaxed, having taken control of the transfer of power; the snake, his purpose served, coiled his way back into his box, to sleep undisturbed.

Sister Odette shut the lid and Mae stood up. She stretched out her arms, her hands, and flexed her fingers, tingling with the power.

Mae looked just above LeRoy, looking for what only she could see: the fluttering veil of the *ti bon Ange*, still clinging to the body. It wasn't there. So Antoine had not released it or manipulated it. He couldn't have: LeRoy was never really dead, only close to it. What Antoine had done to LeRoy was purely chemical and psychological.

She moved close to the body, her lips brushing its ears. What she whispered to LeRoy and in what ancient language of their people, remembered in the soul if not the mind, no one could hear but the two of them.

She stepped back and slapped LeRoy suddenly on both cheeks, the crack of her hand so loud that the medical examiner and several of the cops jumped.

"LeRoy Dufresne! Get up! Listen to me! It's Madame Mae who calls you back to the living! Get up, LeRoy, open your eyes!"

There wasn't even the sound of breathing in the room.

Mae laid her hand on the body's chest and closed her eyes. She took a deep breath.

"Get up, LeRoy!" she shouted again.

The corpse opened its eyes.

"Look at me, LeRoy!" Mae commanded. "When I call, you have to answer! Get up! Breathe!"

There was a plainly audible whoosh of air as the body's chest rose and its mouth opened.

LeRoy started to quiver.

"I said get up! You're alive, LeRoy!"

He started to sit up stiffly.

Mae looked at the sisters. "Help him," she said in a low voice.

One of the women supported his head and the other two lifted his shoulders as LeRoy got to a sitting position. Mae moved so that he could see her face. "LeRoy, do you hear me? Do you know me?"

He nodded his head.

"Give me your hand, then."

He lifted his arm and put his hand in hers. Mae looked at the medical examiner. "Check his pulse now."

She smiled at LeRoy and patted his arm. "It's all right," she told him softly, "you're free of that man now, LeRoy."

Some of the onlookers applauded softly; most were too flabbergasted to do anything but stare.

Joe Ed Landry looked around just in time to see the cop next to him sink to the floor in a dead faint.

The medical examiner frowned. "His heart's pretty fast," he told Mae. "Let's lay him back down."

Mae's women eased LeRoy back down on the table. Mae felt LeRoy's hand tighten around hers as tears fell across his cheeks and onto the metal table.

"Madame Mae," he whispered, his voice harsh and weak, "forgive . . . me. . . ."

"LeRoy, did Antoine make you kill that man in the cemetery?"

"He got the power, Madame; I have to do what he say. He'd make me touch it and I'd die!" The man's eyes were wild with terror.

"Calm down, LeRoy," Mae said softly. "Touch what? What do you mean?"

"The black heart. The White Queen's black heart . . . you touch it . . . you die. . . ."

"Oh, Jesus," the medical examiner swore, still listening to LeRoy's chest, "we're losing him!"

"LeRoy!" Mae said desperately. "You can't die now! No! Listen to me. . . ."

"Forgive me, Madame . . . ," LeRoy said, his voice merely a remembered breath, "help me die right. Help my soul."

The medical examiner looked up. "Mae, you've gotta get away from him. His heart's fibrillating, we're going to have to shock him." Three paramedics were moving evil-looking equipment into place.

LeRoy's eyes never left her face. He was too weak to talk, but his eyes pleaded for him.

"I forgive you, LeRoy. I'll take care of you," Mae said, and LeRoy smiled and died.

Mae felt as if the floor had given way beneath her. Achille caught her as she sagged from shock and exhaustion. He eased her into a chair and she watched the medical examiner confirm what they already knew.

She was hardly aware of the sounds in the room, the groans of disappointment, the sounds of sympathy, the swearing from the cops who had seen everything but had hoped that, just this once, things would work out the way they should.

The medical examiner came over to Mae and Achille.

"He just couldn't take it, Mae," the M.E. said. "God knows how long he'd been on the junk, and the hot shot of PCP, plus whatever Papa Lucifer gave him to make him look dead. His heart and his respiratory system just couldn't take any more."

"Come on, *chérie,*" Achille said. "Let's get you home. Mae, don't cry."

"Jesus, Mae," Joe Ed said, coming up to them, "nobody woulda believed you could do what you did for that guy. You just made believers out of half the force."

"Did LeRoy say enough to incriminate Antoine?" Mae asked.

From the doubtful faces around her, she knew the answer.

No one else could read it, but the look in her eyes gave Achille that same cold feeling he'd gotten back at the house.

"That son of a bitch," she said, and Achille knew she meant Antoine.

Sister Delphine touched Mae's shoulder. "Madame," she said, apologetically, knowing how the concentration of power had drained Mae, "we got to take care of LeRoy's soul."

Mae rose wearily out of the chair to do what must be done.

Alone in the car with Achille, Mae leaned her head against the window, letting the slick glass cool her face.

"The police won't be able to stop Antoine, will they?" she said.

"We can't seem to get enough evidence to prosecute," he said, "and unless we can link him to this murder or to the drugs, we don't have a crime. The bastard never has drugs around him, and he's got a layer of people catching flak for him. It's not against the law to be a devil worshiper."

They drove in silence for a few minutes.

"You know, *chérie,*" Achille said slowly, "you've never asked me to honor my obligation to you."

She was so tired that the meaning of what he said passed right by her for a minute, then she raised her head and looked at him. "Do you mean to say you'd kill him if I asked you?"

Achille kept his eyes on the road. "You forget. I'd have to. I'd have no choice."

Mae sighed and leaned back against the seat. "I don't know, Achille. Did you hear what LeRoy said about the White Queen's black heart?"

"Yeah. Strange."

"If it's really true, if Antoine really has some link with *la Reine Blanche,* that's just about the worst news we could get. It explains a lot: his sudden power, the drastic change in his personality, the black magic. That kind of power doesn't come cheap, but the returns are tremendous."

"Such as?"

"Such as, in the first place, as long as he's got that stone, and depending on what he did to get it, we might not be able to kill him."

Achille pulled the car over to the side of the road.

"Mae, listen to me. Are you saying that this rock has made Antoine immortal or something?"

"No, I'm saying that he can kill you with it. LeRoy said that if you touch it, you die. That's always been part of *la Reine Blanche*'s legend, that she could kill people by infusing an object with evil, then leaving the object where the victim would touch it. To tell you the truth, I never believed it. But I believe it now. A dying man wouldn't lie."

"And how come Antoine's not dead?"

Mae stared straight ahead. "If Antoine did what I think he did to get that stone, he might as well be dead."

PART
THREE

✝

The Child
of the Moon

10

Andrew sat in his study, working on Sunday's sermon.

It was a beautiful room. Bookshelves covered three walls, reaching around the walls and above the carved mahogany doors almost to the magnificent coffered ceiling. At one end, a comforting fire lit the room. Andrew loved that fireplace; his great-grandfather, a sea captain, had brought it from Europe while the house was being built. It was a great baroque masterpiece, and his great-grandfather had had the room designed around it. The rest of the house was a typically southern and typically New Orleans Greek Revival, filled with light and pastels, and the study was a real beaux-arts surprise.

Despite its size, the room was perfectly proportioned and caught lovely slants of light all day through three Palladian windows. Andrew's desk sat between two of the windows. He loved the desk, too. It had been his father's, an expanse of polished walnut with an inlaid leather top worn and polished to a rich sheen. The whole atmosphere of the room and the furnishings was designed to promote contemplation and ease.

Too bad it was haunted.

In the past, a suicide and an attempted murder had taken place there. No one ever talked about it, and Andrew's children didn't know the room's history, but Andrew had to overcome a slight hesitancy every time he walked in there.

The room's haunted past didn't seem to bother anybody else, though; he was always finding one of his kids in the study when they were little. They'd fall asleep on the Oriental carpets, play board games spread out on the deep window seats, make popcorn in the fireplace. Walt, especially, loved the figures of gods and goddesses carved into the mantel-piece and used to make up stories about them to tell his friends. Recently, Walt had become absorbed in a worn copy of Bulfinch's *Mythology;* he was even more delighted with the real stories than with his invented ones.

One of the double doors slid open.

"Dad?" Sylvie said, sticking her head in. "Everybody's gone out. Can I come in here with you and do some reading? I'm lonely."

"Sure, honey. Where's your mother?"

"Remember? It's parents night at Walt and Geo's school. First, it's the Camellia Grill for cheeseburgers, then school, then Mom will be so upset by what the teachers tell her that she'll have to stop someplace afterward for a double hot fudge sundae."

"Oh yeah. She promised to do the duty this year. I went twice in a row and had to look concerned when Walt's teachers told me that his best subject seemed to be stand-up comedy."

"Walt's crazed," Sylvie agreed, settling her books at a small Queen Anne secretary opposite the fireplace.

Andrew watched her a minute as she switched on the desk lamp and started leafing through books. Every word Achille had said to him came back clearly.

"Don't let her suffer for your past," he'd told Andrew. "The girl is a true daughter of the moon . . . she's one of us."

He watched Sylvie's hands flutter through the pages. She had her mother's hands, delicate and long fingered. The soft lamplight spilled over the fragile skin.

As he watched, Sylvie's fingers lengthened, the bones grow-ing thick and deformed. Dark hair sprouted around the begin-nings of claws that curled and moved of their own volition toward his throat.

He shook his head quickly to clear it of the dream image.

Sylvie had settled at the secretary, making notes.

Talk to her, Achille had told him. How could he talk to her about something he'd spent twenty years trying to understand himself? Something he'd never made any sense of? He knew that what really scared him was that if he talked about it, that would make it real. Once those wheels were set moving, it was impossible to stop them from crushing his life and Sylvie's.

Achille was wrong. He just wanted to believe something was wrong with Sylvie in order to justify his own life. For some sick reason, he wanted to harass Andrew by planting doubts about his daughter. He had probably never forgiven Andrew for turning away from him so long ago.

Sylvie's restlessness was a phase; she'd start college soon and that would take care of everything.

He went back to his writing.

After a half hour or so, he became aware of a tapping sound, light but annoying.

"Sylvie," he said, looking over at her. She was tapping her pencil on the desk, looking toward the window, where the sun had just gone down.

She looked up, startled. "Oh. Sorry."

The room was still again, except for the ticking of the mantel clock.

After a few minutes, the tapping sound came again, louder. With an unconscious sigh of impatience, Sylvie pushed her chair back and started pacing back and forth, still watching out the windows.

Andrew was more irritated this time, but he didn't look up. "Sylvie, do you think you could be still? If you don't want to read, go out to the kitchen and get a snack or watch television or something. Just do it elsewhere, please?"

She went to the window and unlocked it, trying to open it. The window hadn't been opened in a while, and it stuck. She struck at it with a furious, impotent gesture.

At almost the same instant, a warning bell went off in Andrew's head.

"Christ!" Sylvie said in a voice Andrew didn't recognize. "Get me some air! How the fuck do you breathe in here?"

This got Andrew's full attention.

Sylvie looked awful, pale as silver except for her eyes gleaming dark and feverish. Something in her manner, her stalking posture, her hysterical clawing at the window, looked morbidly familiar. As surreptitiously as he could, Andrew got up and shut the study doors.

Sylvie had given up on the window and had started pacing the room, running her nails convulsively over every surface she passed. Her eyes had the look of an animal about to bolt toward a cage door. She passed her hands over a small love seat. Andrew watched, astonished, as the silk damask upholstery ripped in the tracks of her nails, the stuffing swelling out like blood from a wound. She seemed not to notice it.

She pulled at the neck of her sweater. "I can't breathe!" she said, panic starting in her voice. "There's no air!"

He caught and held her. "Sylvie. Calm down. What's wrong with you? Come on, honey, just sit down and talk to me."

But there was no holding her. She pushed him away with twice the strength she usually had.

She threw herself against the doors, screaming in frustration, scarring the fine old wood into deep grooves as she ran her nails down them. Andrew tried to control his own rising panic: he had only shut the doors, not locked them. The problem seemed to be that Sylvie had lost the finer motor functions of her fingers. She couldn't turn the knobs.

She turned back to Andrew. "I have to get out!" she said in that unnervingly unfamiliar voice. "Damn you! Let me out of here, you bastard!"

With a terrifying sound, half-human, half-animal, she charged at Andrew, sweeping heavy Victorian furniture out of her way as if it were paper.

Andrew stood stunned, watching her eyes: they were totally black, all pupil, no whites showing. She was coming closer, and Andrew knew that she had every intent to kill him, but he couldn't move. Her hands flexed, reaching out for him.

And then she stopped. It was as though she'd hit an invisible wall.

Andrew still watched her eyes. They looked confounded, then started to return to normal, the pupils shrinking back into the whites.

In an obvious state of total confusion and fear, like a sleepwalker waking in a strange place, she looked around the room and saw the furniture, the door, the sofa with its gaping rents.

"Oh . . . *Daddy*!" Her voice was tiny, childlike, terrified as she collapsed into his arms.

Andrew always thought that fear left you cold, numb. He had certainly had enough experience with it in the past, but it was never anything like this. The grief and guilt were volatile catalysts that started as an explosive fire in his chest, spreading over his soul, burning him past repair. As he held his daughter, rocking her back and forth in his arms, as much from his own suffering as to calm her, he knew he had to tell her everything. Even if it drove her away from him.

"When I was twenty years old," Andrew told Sylvie, "I thought I had everything. I had a wonderful, loving family— a little eccentric, some of them, but good people. I'd just met your mother and it looked like things were going to happen between us. I was doing the one thing I'd dreamed of all my life: studying for the priesthood. I can't tell you how much I wanted that, Sylvie. I'd asked myself over and over whether it was really a call from God or just the echo of my own ego. I think that if you can ask yourself that question, then it really is a genuine calling; egomaniacs rarely question themselves.

"Then, a few years later, it all just fell apart. This was about the time my father won his Nobel prize."

"And he had his heart attack," Sylvie said.

Andrew shook his head. "It wasn't a heart attack, Sylvie. I didn't want you kids to know, especially you. You've always been so proud of your grandfather, I just couldn't tell you. But he was a suicide. Shot himself through the heart."

"Grandfather killed himself?" Sylvie said, bewildered. "But why? Did he leave a note? Did anybody find out why he did it?"

At that moment, Andrew could see Walter's body as clearly as he did the day he found it in this same room, collapsed behind the desk, the Oriental carpet soggy with blood. A finely crafted antique pistol had fallen a few feet from Walter's hand. Even in his disoriented panic, Andrew had noticed the five silver bullets scattered on the desktop. He had known immediately where the sixth one was. The most disturbing thing of all was the look on Walter's face: profound peace, as if he had recovered something wonderful after years of searching. At the time, Andrew had no idea why his father had chosen this way out, but as time went on, the question became not why he had killed himself, but why he hadn't done it sooner.

"Oh, please, honey," he told her, "don't ask questions. If I don't tell you all of this as quickly as possible, I'll lose my nerve. Anyway, after that, I entered the seminary.

"On the night I was ordained, I was feeling a little dizzy. I'd been sick during the ceremony—nerves, I figured. I went into the cathedral garden for some fresh air and I . . ."

He had intended to tell this story as plainly, as impersonally as possible, in an effort to mitigate some of the horror. But he found that every word called up a thousand images, vivid scenes that provoked an actual physical pain, so that it was impossible to stop his mind from lingering over each one. It was like slowly pulling scabs from a score of just-healing wounds.

He took Sylvie's hands, as if holding on to her could save both of them. "Sylvie, you have to understand . . . the Marley family was cursed."

For the first time that night, her face brightened and she laughed. "A curse? Dad, our family isn't old enough to have a curse. Don't you have to go back to medieval times or something for that? What is it, a hound of Hell? A vengeful ghost? A streak of unnatural insanity?"

"You've heard me talk about my great-grandfather, Stephen Marley. He was a good-looking bounder, and he didn't have much in the way of conscience. In the grandest nineteenth-century tradition, he seduced and abandoned a young girl. What he hadn't counted on was that this particular young girl was no victim. She had been a dabbler in Voodoo, but after the way Stephen treated her, she got involved with it in a big way.

"After a while, everybody in New Orleans started to hear about *la Reine Blanche*, the White Queen, probably the most evil woman New Orleans ever produced. She wanted her revenge on Stephen and she was willing to wait until it could be as bad as she could make it. So when she got the power, she placed a curse on Stephen's family. Not on him, mind you, but on his children and descendants. No, Stephen had to stay alive, to watch what happened to his precious firstborn child. He died after that, but *la Reine Blanche,* they say, was immortal. And as long as she lived, her curse lived.

"Think about it, Sylvie. Your wandering in the night, not knowing why you do it, remembering only bits and pieces, not quite knowing where you go or what you do, only remembering that something pulls you outside and makes you restless. What was this episode tonight, Sylvie? An accident?"

She frowned and tried to pull her hands away. "I don't want to talk about it. Is that what this is all about? Is that what this 'curse' is supposed to be, sleepwalking? You're upset because I wander around at night?"

"Yes. It's more complicated than that, but when you boil it all down, yes. It is about that, about what's happening to you."

She made an impatient sound. "Look, nothing's 'happening' to me. I'm just a night person, I guess. When I go out at night, it's not a frightening thing. It feels good, it feels right. I like the way the air smells differently, the way the wind feels, the moonlight. Okay, so maybe that makes me a little eccentric, but you're acting like I'm insane. And I *don't want to talk about it.*"

He held on to her, his grip stronger than he thought it could be, but it was his daughter's life he was fighting for.

"I'm not accusing you of anything, Sylvie. You're entirely innocent. It's me who's at fault. There are things I should have told you long before now, and I'm afraid that because of my cowardice, you might be in real trouble."

He felt her tense. "What kind of trouble?"

"Now, Sylvie . . . just listen to the story and don't say anything until the end. You can laugh if you want to, or get mad, but for God's sake, don't disbelieve anything I tell you, because no matter how outrageous and insane it sounds, every word is true. I can prove it all, and there are people you trust that you can ask. Your mother, for one.

"On the night I was ordained, I went out into the cathedral garden. The moon pulled me outside, just like it pulled you, though I didn't realize that's what it was at the time.

"I was feeling sick before, but suddenly I was seized by a pain so bad that I thought I was dying. I couldn't even stand up. Just when it was at its worst, I looked up and saw my dead father. He was just staring at me with such sorrow it almost broke my heart. He held out his hand to me, as if he was pleading with me to help him, and I saw that it wasn't human. It was the hand of a monster, half-human, half-animal. My father was a werewolf, a loup-garou, and he had killed himself because he couldn't stand the guilt."

Sylvie gave a choked scream and tried to pull away from him, but he held her there.

"I told you that it would sound insane, but just listen . . . for God's sake, Sylvie! Your life depends on your believing me!"

"Why are you *saying* this?"

"It starts when you find yourself drawn outside under the full moon, and you feel strange, but strong. You once asked me if people changed under the moon, and I lied to you. I told you it was a foolish idea. But I know that some people do, some people become beasts and do things they can't control."

"You can't possibly know that. Just because of a dream you had about your father?"

"It wasn't a dream, it was real. Because the same night that I saw my father, the same night that I was ordained, I inherited his curse. The pain was the pain of transformation; that was the first night I became a werewolf."

Sylvie screamed and put her hands over her ears. She broke away from him and backed toward the wall, looking at him as if he were a dangerous stranger.

"I didn't want to tell you this. God knows I never wanted to revive this nightmare after twenty years of doing penance for it. But I'm afraid for you."

"You're lying! All this is a lie! I don't know why you're saying these things, but I know they're not true!"

"Sylvie, I broke the curse. God help me, it almost cost me my soul, but I ended it. Or, at least, I thought I had. Until this started happening to you. Now I don't know what's going on, but I'm panicked about you."

"Me?" she said incredulously. "You tell me a story like that and you're worried about me? You're the one who's insane! My God! All my life I've trusted you and admired you, and now you can stand there and tell me these lies! My grandfather was a wonderful man, a respected scientist! *He had a heart attack!* He didn't kill himself, and he wasn't any monster! You're telling me this because you're jealous of his memory! What's *wrong* with you?"

He turned away from her, not knowing what to say. He had fought so hard against his curse that he hadn't taken time to learn the finer points that were now so important to Sylvie. He had done this all wrong, he had to try and soothe her and start over. He got up to take her in his arms.

She backed away, looking at him with an expression he'd never seen.

"Get away from me! Don't touch me! Don't *talk* to me anymore!" Her voice was building to that hysterical edge again. She backed toward the doors, blindly groping for the handles. The doors opened and Sylvie fell backward.

Straight into the arms of Achille Broussard.

Sylvie gasped and looked up at the face she'd never seen before.

Achille kept his arms around her. "Hey, *'tite fille,*" he said, smiling. "What's the problem, eh? It's okay, you safe now, yes."

Sylvie couldn't believe it, but she did feel safe. She felt perfectly comfortable in the arms of this huge, beautiful stranger, as safe as she'd felt in the arms of another stranger who carried her home. Her hysteria began to drift away as she realized that her father recognized him.

"Hey, Bishop, where y'at?" he said to Andrew. "What you been telling this child that you got her so scared? Come on, daw'lin," he said to Sylvie, settling down on the sofa and pulling her next to him, "let your Uncle Achille tell you the stuff you need to know."

Andrew looked at Sylvie's bewildered but expectant face. He never would have dreamed he'd be so glad to see Achille again.

Between the two of them, they managed to explain things to Sylvie in terms she could deal with. Andrew had to admit that Achille was better at it, but then Achille had always had the peculiar ability to empathize perfectly with anyone.

"Now, look here, daw'lin," Achille said. "I know you're scared, confused, and you're probably worried about your papa here being a little crazy. He tells you he's a loup-garou. But let me ask you something. When you were little, do you remember hearing stories about the loup-garou?"

"Yes. I guess every kid from around here does," Sylvie said.

"And what did you think? Did those old tales scare you?"

It grew very quiet between them then, as Sylvie held motionless, gradually remembering old stories and feelings. It took a long time for the memories to grow out of the foggy confines of where she'd hidden them, but when they came, they came with the illuminating clarity of revelation. When she spoke, it seemed that she was unaware her father was in the room.

"No," she said slowly, "never. Just the opposite, they fascinated me. I was the only kid I knew that *wasn't* scared. All I could think about was how great it must be to change and run anywhere you wanted in that powerful body, seeing things through a wolf's eyes. To live hundreds of years and witness the future.

"I thought I had forgotten them," she whispered, almost to herself, "those old loup-garou tales, about how they gathered to dance on Bayou Goula, how they changed and made love and ran in the night. And I forgot how the stories made me feel, how I cried sometimes, wanting something I couldn't even understand."

"And you never had the slightest idea why?" Achille asked.

"No. Those old legends excited me, made me feel like something was missing from my own life. I wanted to know what it was like to be a loup-garou, but I knew those feelings were wrong, crazy, and I never told anyone. I kept it a secret so long that I forgot about it."

She turned furiously to her father. "And now you tell me that you were a werewolf, and my grandfather was, and he killed himself because of it. In the first place, how can I believe you? And if I believe you, what happens to my dreams? You say that it was hell on earth. Wouldn't there have been anything good about it at all? Wouldn't the experience have given you something?"

In the face of his daughter's anger, Andrew had nothing to say. He remembered Achille's question: Do you still feel it, the pull of the moon? Does your body burn with longing for what you gave up? And he remembered his answer. It seemed to Andrew that the misery in his soul would kill him.

Achille put his finger to Sylvie's lips. "Sylvie, don't do this to your papa. He only tried to do what's best for you. You think he'd make up a crazy story like that? Now you ask yourself: why would he tell you something like this in the first place?"

"I don't know!" Sylvie said miserably.

"Sure you do, *'tite chère.*"

She took a deep breath. "Because it's true. Because he thinks I'm like him. He thinks . . ." She had to stop for a second. The sound wouldn't come out. "He thinks I'm a loup-garou, too."

Achille took both her hands in his and looked seriously into her eyes. "And does *that* scare you?"

It was on the tip of her tongue to say yes. But she found herself saying no and was shocked that she meant it.

"But, Achille," she moaned, "I don't know what to do!"

He patted her hands reassuringly. "Aw, that's no problem, *'tite fille*! That's why I'm here, to help you."

Then it struck her to ask the obvious. "You're a loup-garou, aren't you?"

His face broke into a huge grin. "Hey! Born and bred, *chérie*! You looking at the biggest, baddest, meanest ol' loup-garou on the bayous—and you don't even look scared no more! I guess you pretty sure by now I'm not gonna eat you up, eh?"

Sylvie laughed. She really did feel good with Achille around.

"The most important thing to remember, Sylvie," Achille said, "is that your papa broke the Marley curse. That means that he gave you a choice. You can choose the loup-garou's life or you can walk away from it."

"How?" Sylvie asked Andrew suddenly. "How did you break the curse?"

Andrew looked up from his misery, startled by the question.

Achille watched him carefully. This was something Andrew had never told. The entire community of loups-garous had pondered that same question, and had never developed a satisfactory answer.

When he finally answered, Andrew's voice was controlled—and cold. "It only matters that it's broken. After all this time, it makes no difference how it was done."

Sylvie stared at Andrew. Something told her not to pursue this question, that the answer would never be forthcoming. It was one more revelation about him: she had thought she knew everything about her family and especially her father. Now that certainty, the touchstone for her whole life, was crumbling. She had never felt so lost. The most important thing in her father's past was something he would never share with her.

Achille jumped into the awkward pause. "Now, let me tell you what," he said to Sylvie. "Me and your papa got a lot of things to say to each other, but if it's okay with him I'm gonna take you to meet a very special lady. She's a very old loup-garou and she knows everything there is to know. You can stay with her for a while and learn more in a month than you could learn in a lifetime on your own. Her special interest is the history of the werewolf, and she can tell you *stories*— Ooo-*wee*! But if you hate the whole idea, you leave. Nobody's gonna hurt you or pressure you or blame you. It's your choice. But in order to choose, you have to have knowledge. You can't just hope that all this will go away."

For the first time, Sylvie looked at Andrew not as a child looks at a parent, but as an equal. It was frightening, heartbreaking. And liberating. "I have to do it. I have to go with him. I want to."

Andrew raised his head, and the pain in his eyes made Achille flinch. Only he knew what this was costing Andrew.

Andrew couldn't speak. He nodded his head in assent, knowing that Achille was right.

"Sylvie," Achille said softly, "you said some pretty mean things to your papa. Someday you gonna understand how much he gave up for you and you gonna remember these things and wish you'd never said them. Why don't I wait for you outside while you talk to him, yes?"

Achille left the room, closing the door quietly as Andrew folded his arms around his daughter.

11

Luna was an opulent shop on Royal Street. It looked both enticing and forbidding, a discreet sign on the door stipulating By Appointment Only, intimating that only a select few were to savor the delights it offered. Most of the shops on the street had that traditional New Orleans look, but Luna sported the *fin de siècle* swirls and tendrils of an elaborate Art Nouveau cast-iron facade, salvaged from a doomed chocolate shop in Paris. Whoever had designed Luna, or perhaps it was the owner, had made it a very personal expression of taste.

It was only about nine P.M., but Luna had been closed for several hours. Achille slipped a key into a shining brass lock.

"Why are we going in here?" Sylvie asked him.

"Remember I told you I was going to introduce you to someone special? This is her shop. She owns the entire building; there's a house over the shop, a courtyard, and a guesthouse in the old slave quarters across the courtyard. Zizi lives here. You gonna like her, *'tite fille.*"

Inside, Achille threw a switch and three exquisite Venetian glass chandeliers dripped discreet light on an array of unusual objects. Luna's walls were lined with pale rose moire silk. Deep wing chairs of a darker rose were scattered around, so one could inspect the merchandise at leisure and chat awhile. The merchandise! Sylvie gasped slightly at the round tables with silk tablecloths. Precious objects sat casually on their surfaces to be touched and considered by Luna's elegant patrons. There were sculptures of jade in all its variations, rock crystal set with precious stones, jewelry so intricate that Sylvie knew it was shaped by the hand of an old master, and some intriguing contemporary pieces. Old books with gilt edges and rare bindings reposed in stacks on the tables and behind glass shelves in mahogany breakfronts. A fragile blown glass moon was suspended over one of the tables, lit softly by a tiny fiber optic cable that conducted violet light into its globe, illuminating the moon's craters. There was a magical scent in the air: roses and sandalwood wafting from huge crystal potpourri bowls.

"This is incredible," Sylvie said.

"Zizi sells antiques, art, and rare books, all relating to either the moon or wolves," Achille said. "Look at this." He picked up a polished walking stick, the wood glowing with a rich, oiled surface. The head was a silver wolf's head.

"Lovely," Sylvie said.

"More than that," Achille said. "This is the cane Lon Chaney, Jr., carried in *The Wolf Man*."

"You're kidding," Sylvie said, peering closer at it.

"It's kind of an in-joke. You'll see."

Sylvie paused in front of a portrait of a woman in eighteenth-century court dress. The picture looked so real that it was eerily compelling, and Sylvie wished she had more time to look at it. She knew she shouldn't do it, but she couldn't resist touching her finger to the face.

"Achille, who is this?"

"Someone from Zizi's past. I told you she was very old."

Sylvie leaned closer and read the little brass plate on the frame. " 'Annette Louise Catherine de Valois, Marquise de Guibert.' She's just fabulous. Was she a loup-garou?"

"Who knows? Zizi won't say much about her, no."

A sound came from the back of the shop beyond a pair of rose-lacquered doors, a burst of laughter from several voices. "Well, you gonna meet Zizi," Achille said. "It sounds like she's entertaining, too. Come on, little one." He took Sylvie's hand and pushed open the doors.

It led to a short corridor, then a comfortable living room decorated in the same rose shades as the shop, but more informally. Several people were gathered around a large-screen TV recessed into the wall. The golden young man pouring drinks behind a bar of glass bricks caught Sylvie's eye immediately.

Jeez, it's Apollo the Sun God, she thought. He's too perfect. I wonder if it was God or surgery?

A tall blond unfolded her rangy frame from a low, rose-cushioned couch. She seemed to glimmer as she walked across the room, her topaz silk dress perfectly catching the color of her eyes. Sylvie thought that she had never seen a more attractive woman; she was exactly what Sylvie wanted to be when she was older: self-assured and expensively cared for. It was hard to guess her age, but Sylvie put her at around thirty-eight or forty. The blond greeted Achille with a kiss that was partly friendly, partly a little more.

"*Ma chère*," she said to him, then turned her jeweled gaze to Sylvie. "Oh, my," she said, "how wonderful that you're here, Sylvie. Achille says that you're going to stay awhile and learn everything there is to know. I'm Zizi. Just Zizi; no one ever calls me anything else. Oh, but this is marvelous!"

She turned to her guests, some of whom were watching the TV and some of whom had risen to greet Achille. "Tear yourselves away from that tube," she commanded. "Achille's here, and look who he has with him! Andrew Marley's daughter!"

The murmur of recognition embarrassed Sylvie and she flushed. Several people came forward to take her hand or kiss her, some to mention her father. Sylvie wondered how they knew him.

"I have very fond memories of Andrew Marley," Zizi told her. "Such a perfectly sweet man. Is he well?"

"Yes," Sylvie said, feeling a little more comfortable, "he's fine."

"Still married to that pretty redhead, I guess," Zizi sighed.

"Twenty years ago, when your father came to Bayou Goula for the first time," Achille explained, "Zizi almost seduced him. They had an immediate attraction."

"He wasn't married then," Zizi added quickly and emphatically. She sighed again, regretfully. "If he hadn't been in love with someone else, well . . ." She gave a typically Gallic shrug. "But . . . *là*, it was not to be. He married your charming mother and here you are. Such a beauty! And one of us! Oh, my dear girl, such a stir you'll make among the boys!"

She looked around, smoothing her hair back. As her long fingers moved, Sylvie noticed the ring she wore, a fantastic creation, a wide silver band set with a tiny gold wolf with canary diamond eyes, howling against a silver full moon. The detail was unbelievable: the hair on the wolf looked real; the moon was sculpted not with craters, but with the serene face of a goddess.

"Christian! Gabriel!" Zizi called, then moved toward a door.

"I thought you told me she was old," Sylvie whispered to Achille.

Zizi's supernatural hearing caught this and she laughed. Coming back to Sylvie, she kissed her impulsively. "Oh, my innocent little one, I *am* old," Zizi said. "The oldest loup-garou in Louisiana. I'm over three hundred years old. One thing about the loup-garou's life, it's a long one, about one year to a human's ten, some of us more and some less. We age very slowly and very well. No face and fanny lifts for us, sweets! And, oh my, those long-term investments and CDs! Now, where are those boys?"

The handsome blond at the bar came over and slipped an arm around Zizi's waist. "This is Christian," Zizi said, "and this . . . ," she said, gesturing toward a rugged-looking dark-haired boy about Sylvie's age, entering from another room, "this is Gabriel. Sweets, Achille told you all about Sylvie Marley, and here she is at last."

Both men gave Sylvie a chaste kiss on the cheek. "Welcome to our little wolves' den," Gabriel said. "I was just making up your room across the courtyard. I think everything's in order, but if you need anything, just howl."

"Gabriel," Zizi said with a pained look, "could you hold off on the insider jokes until the poor girl gets settled?" She looked at Sylvie with a helpless gesture. "We talk like that so often that we forget ourselves."

"I think it's kind of funny, actually," Sylvie said, smiling at Gabriel.

"Well, a sense of humor will definitely stand you in good stead with this bunch," Zizi said. "We want you to be comfortable and happy while you're with us."

"This is very kind of all of you," Sylvie said.

Zizi took her hand, the soft, warm touch of it making Sylvie feel that she knew this woman better than she did. In fact, Sylvie felt that she knew them all, though she had never seen these people before in her life.

There was another burst of laughter from the other side of the room.

"What's everybody watching?" Achille wanted to know.

Zizi rolled her eyes. *"The Wolf Man.* For the eleven hundredth time."

Achille laughed as five or six people, riveted to the screen, chanted along with Evelyn Ankers.

"Even a man who is pure in heart,

And says his prayers at night,

May turn into a wolf when the wolfsbane blooms

And the autumn moon is bright!"

The entire company simply cracked up at this and Sylvie blushed again. "I suppose they don't know . . . well . . . about us," Sylvie whispered to Achille.

He looked at her, amused. " *'Tite fille,*" he said, *"everybody* knows. These are all our people, *your* people. They're all loups-garous."

Sylvie's eyes went wide, and she tried to be polite and not to show her astonishment. "But they look so . . ."

"Normal," Achille said.

"I thought they would be more . . . I don't know . . . dramatic. Exotic, maybe."

"Some of us are," Achille said, "then you got ol' Robert Duplantier over there, ugly as month-old crawfish." He pointed at a perfectly good-looking man whose face bore the aristocratic stamp of the true Creole. Without looking up from the screen, the man made a graceful, but familiar, digital gesture at Achille.

Zizi laughed. "Achille, let her alone. It's a shock for her, all the newness of it. You're plunging her into things too fast. I'm sorry, little one," she said to Sylvie, "if I'd known you were coming tonight, I would have shooed everyone out. But Luna is a gathering place for the loups-garous, an informal place in town where we can relax and be together and talk. People just show up all the time, in and out. It's quite nice, really. We're terribly social and love each other's company. You'll get to like it when things have settled down for you."

"Actually, I like it already," Sylvie said, looking around. For the first time in her life, Sylvie felt like she was exactly where she belonged, among the people to whom she belonged.

Achille and Zizi exchanged a pleased look over Sylvie's head.

"Gabriel, Christian," Zizi said, "introduce Sylvie to everyone, and don't get bogged down in that movie. Get her a drink and something to eat." Zizi waved a gold-braceleted arm, indicating the room in general. "When you've met everyone, little one, I'll show you your room and you can get settled in."

"Thank you," Sylvie said, "this is awfully good of you . . . I mean, this whole thing. Your letting me stay here."

Zizi smiled and put her arm around Sylvie. "Listen to me, Sylvie. We're your brothers and sisters, as close to you as blood relatives, maybe closer. You'll find that we all share a common history, common experiences; we share our lives, even if we choose to live apart from each other. The most solitary werewolf in the most remote corner of the world is as close to us as those we see every day. We're all connected in ways that ordinary people can never understand. Your being here is as good for me, and Gabriel and Christian and all of us, as it is for you. So you needn't feel obligated. It's only right that you come to your own people. Our community is so small, really; when you consider the world, so tiny. Each one of us is terribly important to all of us. You'll see."

While Sylvie met the others, Zizi led Achille upstairs to her sumptuous white lace bedroom, which she usually shared with both Gabriel and Christian. Achille sat in a white silk chair while Zizi sat at her dressing table, brushing her long, gold hair.

"What does Andrew really think?" Zizi said, frowning.

"He says he's willing to send her here, that he realizes she needs what he can't give her."

"But that isn't all," she said, turning to him.

"It's killing him," Achille said.

Zizi's gold eyes shone with slight tears. "I thought as much. He never knew, Achille. He never even realized what he lost."

"I think he did, eventually. But he was convinced he was right and we were wrong. And he might have been right, you know; this life really wasn't for him."

"I think it was," she said sadly.

Achille got up and held her. "*Chérie*, you mustn't think about what could have been. Things worked out for the best. Could you have given up the loup-garou's life for him? You would have had to, you know."

"Maybe I could have convinced him to stay with us."

Achille smoothed her shining hair. "You shouldn't be thinking things like that, no."

"I know. I haven't, not for years and years. Sylvie is so like him, not just the way she looks, but I can see that stubborn streak in her, that extraordinary determination. Do you think she'll be happy with us, Achille?"

"I think that she wants this life as much as her father didn't want it. But we owe it to him to give his daughter every chance to back out, to go back to her father's world and make her peace there."

"But she couldn't do that!" Zizi protested. "She's ours!"

"And it's our job to make her realize that, Zizi. All we can do is teach her everything we can, show her what the loup-garou's world is like, and let what will happen, happen. But we have to be prepared to lose her, if it comes to that. Remember, Andrew was ours, too."

Back in the sitting room, Sylvie was settled in front of the TV with everyone else, a large plate of jambalaya and a cold Barq's root beer in front of her and Christian and Gabriel on either side. The movie had just reached the part where Lon Chaney was attacked by a werewolf.

The werewolf bit Chaney and everybody cheered. "Ya-a-y!" one of the women said. "The *baiser du loup-garou*!"

"Yeah, right," Gabriel said derisively, "hardly."

"It counts," the woman protested, "even if it isn't so subtle."

Chaney started to kill the werewolf with his wolf-headed walking cane, the same one Sylvie had seen in the shop.

A general chorus of boos and rude remarks went up.

"You *dickhead*," three people shouted together. This was obviously a familiar ritual.

"What I want to know," a man said, "is, what the fuck is wolfsbane?"

"Who cares? Are we gonna show *An American Werewolf in London* next?"

"No. Bob's got film of Maria Ouspenskaya naked." A general chorus of cheers for Maria's ninety-year-old tits.

Gabriel put his arm around Sylvie. "I guess this isn't a lot of fun for you. You come to meet the loups-garous and you end up watching old movies with a bunch of lunatics."

"No. I'm enjoying it. It isn't what I expected, but I like it."

"We want you to feel at home."

"I do. I really, really do."

"Come on," he said, getting to his feet and pulling Sylvie after him. "You look exhausted and I know you're staying awake just to be polite. Okay, everybody," he said to the group, "you've bored Sylvie to death and she's leaving."

People gathered around Sylvie and said wonderful, welcoming things to her, wishing her good night, kissing her on the cheek and telling her they'd see her again.

One of the women, a black woman with cat's eyes, as exotic as Sylvie had expected, smiled at her and pressed her hand. "We'll dance at Bayou Goula, Sylvie," she said.

Sylvie smiled politely, but was a little confused at the remark.

Taking her bags, Gabriel led her across a courtyard lit softly by Japanese lanterns and garden lights.

"This is wonderful," Sylvie told him.

"Be sure to compliment Christian," Gabriel said. "The landscaping has been his little pet project all spring. He got so deep into it that he actually wanted to start a compost heap for the flower beds, but Zizi drew the line there."

The flagstones and the central fountain, three cast-iron water nymphs dancing while water flowed from their entwined hands, were very old, probably installed when the house was built. There were lacy iron benches and beautifully planted flower beds, with geraniums in every shade. More electric lanterns were scattered in the tree branches, glowing like enchanted fruit. Across the courtyard were the old slave quarters, now transformed into three guest rooms.

Sylvie's room was a well-thought-out Victorian period piece of rosewood, lace, and satin in shades of ivory and pale gold. There was a marvelous canopied bed and a Queen Anne love seat in ivory damask stripes. A large bookcase secretary held old and new volumes behind gilt-grilled doors.

"Zizi loves to go to auctions," Gabriel said, "but some of these pieces she's had for years. And I mean she bought them when they were new, when Victoria was still queen. If you think this stuff is nice, wait'll you see her collection of Louis Quatorze. It freaks me out to think of all the distinguished buns that sat on our dining chairs."

Sylvie shook her head. "I just can't believe it. That she's so old, that she's seen so much history. Imagine what she knows!"

"And she'll tell you all about it if you ask. What I admire about Zizi is the way she's always able to adapt to whatever century she's in, without losing her sense of the past."

Sylvie couldn't stop herself from asking, "And how old are you, Gabriel?" He looked only about twenty.

He laughed. "Young. No, I mean *really* young, twenty-three. I haven't been a loup-garou long, just four years. But Christian's—um, let's see, I think he's almost a hundred and twenty years old."

"Good Lord! He looks like a college student!"

"Well, he was when he met Zizi. He was a medical student at Tulane. He finished, too, he's a board-certified surgeon. And the funny thing is that he enrolls every twenty or thirty years and graduates all over again just to have a current date on his diploma and keep up with new developments. Tulane's very proud of the fact that father, son, and grandson—all with the same name and with an incredible family resemblance—have gotten their training there."

Sylvie burst out laughing.

"But Christian's sort of an exception to a rule," Gabriel said. "He's had the same profession all his life. Loups-garous usually don't do that. When your life span is six or seven centuries, you tend to get bored, you shrug off an old life or even an old passion and start up with a new one. Some loups-garous even change personalities like you'd try on a new haircut, something radically different."

"How can you change your personality?" Sylvie asked. "Basically, you are who you are."

"Time. Time alters all things. Are you the same person now that you were at fourteen? Or the same person you'll be at forty? Zizi says that sometimes you get more mature and other times you retreat back to simpler things. Here's an example for you. You'd figure Zizi for a levelheaded type, right?"

"She seems like it."

"And she is. During the Crimean War she was taking care of the wounded British soldiers—with Florence Nightingale, no less. After that, she came right back to the South and applied what she'd learned to the women who nursed the Confederate army. And then, around about 1900, she completely ditched being an angel of mercy and became a lady of the evening. She ran one of the glitziest bordellos in Storyville and was the most irresponsible, shallow harlot in the city. She told me she was a complete featherbrain until the district closed in 1917, and that the few years she spent thinking about nothing but screwing and money and dresses and fancy stockings did her a world of good.

"Me, I'm a bum," Gabriel said, shaking his head. "I simply work in the shop and basically hang out with Zizi and the other loups-garous. I dabble in goldsmithing, some of my stuff is for sale at Luna. I'm not a master at it yet, but the good thing is that I have *lots* of time to perfect it. In fifty years I'll be as good as Carl Fabergé. And I'll only be twenty-eight."

Sylvie looked a little wistful. "I want to be a doctor, too. A psychiatrist. At least, I thought I did. Now I don't know where my life's taking me."

Gabriel patted her hand. "You can be anything you want. You'll have the time. That's one of the most wonderful gifts we have."

"Gabriel," Sylvie asked as he was leaving, "what was that the others were talking about? The . . . um, something-or-other *du loup-garou*?"

He laughed briefly. "The *baiser du loup-garou*. Well, it's a little complicated. But don't worry, you'll learn about that and everything else while you're here. I'll knock on your door tomorrow for breakfast in the courtyard, and I'm sure Zizi will start telling you more than you ever thought you wanted to know." He kissed her on the forehead. "Welcome to the family, little sister."

The next morning at breakfast, Sylvie commented on the ring Zizi wore. She had noticed that Gabriel and Christian wore the same design as neck pendants.

Zizi stretched out her hand to look at it. "It's Gabriel's work. Isn't it marvelous? He's much too modest about how good he is. It's the symbol of the Krewe of Apollonius, the loup-garou's Mardi Gras association," she told Sylvie.

"A krewe!" Sylvie laughed, delighted. "Do you mean you have a parade, and throw doubloons, and hold a ball?"

"Hardly," Zizi said, "but I think we have a better time than Rex or Comus or even Zulu. On Mardi Gras eve the loups-garous prance in the Carnival streets, in all stages of transformation. We laugh, we dance, we make love with humans, and no one knows we're real. For the humans, it's a delightful little thrill; they sense our power, and being close to a loup-garou, even if they're unaware of it, is a sensuous experience."

"Wait a minute! I've heard of that krewe! The one that's supposed to be so impressive with makeup effects."

Zizi laughed. "Never wore a stroke of it. It's all real."

"And sometimes," Gabriel said with a sly look at Christian, "we seduce a willing human with the *baiser du loup-garou*." Christian blushed a little and Zizi laughed.

"I met Christian at Mardi Gras," Zizi said tenderly, giving Christian's cheek a light pinch.

The French term clarified itself for Sylvie: *baiser du loup-garou*, the werewolf's kiss. This mystifying phrase was starting to creep into several conversations and Sylvie wanted to ask about it.

But Zizi was off on another subject.

"If you want to understand the loup-garou, you must go back to the old stories. We named the krewe after Apollonius of

Tyana, the philosopher and magician. 'Apollonius the Deliverer,' he used to be called in the sixteenth century, though that's overly dramatic. But it *is* accurate; if not for him, we would be simple monsters, brute killers, animals. The story of Apollonius symbolizes the struggle that each loup-garou must face sooner or later."

Sylvie noticed that, even though they must have heard this story, and perhaps heard it more than once, Gabriel and Christian ignored their steaming coffee, beignets, and omelets to listen, enraptured and respectfully, to the story of Apollonius of Tyana.

12

Rome, A.D. 61

"Even you will die," said the Greek casually to the Emperor Domitian, "though this can't be of any surprise to you."

A slight scowl marred Domitian's pretty face. "This isn't the kind of prophecy I expected from you. Why, it isn't a prophecy at all! It's merely a fact. Have I bothered myself with your case only to hear facts I could hear as easily from cheap fortune-tellers?"

Domitian's anger passed. He reached across a small table for a pear, bit into it, and sat back, regarding the tall man still standing in the middle of the room. His face became sly. "However, you may be wrong even in that," he said. "Jesus the heretic said that *his* followers will never die. What if I decided to follow this rebel's teachings? I wouldn't die and your prophecy would fail."

The man shrugged. "Shall I tell you of your death?"

A shudder passed over Domitian, and the pear suddenly tasted of poison.

"No, thank you just the same," Domitian said.

"You see? We always think we want to know the future, but to be certain of it is frightening. We cling to the hope of better things." The glow from the flickering lamps illuminated the painted walls of Domitian's palace. The Greek stood so straight and with such authority that he seemed a part of the mural scenes of gods and warriors.

Domitian leaned forward. "Then let us discuss the past, and the present. You're a Greek. . . ."

"I was born in Tyana, educated at Tarsus and at the temple of Aesculapius."

Domitian considered. "Hmm. A hotbed of radical thought, Tarsus. Full of heretics." Domitian saw a heretic in every shadow. "And you learned magic . . . where?"

The man frowned. "I am not a magician. I am a philosopher, a follower of the Pythagoreans." He started to elaborate, but Domitian's lavish yawn stopped him.

"Did you know this rebel heretic?" Domitian asked. "The Nazarene?"

"Jesus? I have heard of him. I didn't particularly agree with him; however, even dead, he will have great success at proving his point. His ignominious end will be the undoing of Rome."

"Aha! You see!" Domitian said gleefully, pointing a gilded finger at the man. "You do have the gift of prophecy! But you believe in his miracles?"

"I do not."

"And yet," Domitian reflected, "like him, you raised the dead. A young girl of good family, a daughter of the consul. And this was done right here in Rome, where Roman citizens could see it, not in some heathen town with only superstitious louts for witnesses." Domitian leaned forward. "The heretic's followers hate you for that, you know. They resent the fact that you can do the same tricks he did. How did you do it? The girl?"

"Perhaps the lady wasn't really dead. I don't know. I can't explain everything I do. If I knew, I would tell you."

Domitian seemed to accept this, though a little huffily. "The oracles say the same thing. They can't explain how the gods speak through them. How very tiresome. It was a shame about the girl, though, what happened later."

Domitian watched for a reaction.

"Went completely mad," Domitian said, "killed all four of her children, all sons. Did you hear that story?"

"Yes." Apollonius's face was still as ice.

Domitian sighed. "Ironic, isn't it? You snatch her back from death and she proceeds to murder her children. One simply never knows about the workings of destiny. If you hadn't saved her . . ." Domitian took a sip of his wine and frowned slightly at the taste. "But tell me about Ephesus, your miracle there."

The Greek made a dismissive noise. "Hardly a miracle. It was mere investigative work."

"Yet you predicted the plague that almost destroyed it. And you ended it. How?"

Domitian was pleased to see the break in the cool demeanor of the Greek. He looked very troubled, he shuddered slightly, as if with a passing ague.

At last, he spoke. "By a method that was my undoing. The shame of it has haunted me, and I don't speak of it."

There was a loud bang as Domitian, his temper piqued, slammed his gold goblet down on the table, crushing the vessel's delicate stem. "You *will* speak of it! Remember that you're here because you're charged with a serious crime. Take care not to irritate me, Apollonius, or your punishment will exceed the usual imprisonment. Now speak!"

Apollonius's face reflected a great melancholy, but as he spun his tale, the weight seemed to gradually lift from him, as if the telling of it relieved him.

"I was passing through Ephesus," he told Domitian, "and warned the people of the plague that was coming. They laughed, they ridiculed me, they kept on with their giddy way of life until the plague was actually upon them. Then, with much wailing and many apologies and bribery, they sent for me.

"Wandering the streets was a poor, maimed beggar, hardly able to walk, dragging himself about from place to place. And at each place he stopped, the plague visited." Apollonius broke off his story, his face changing with horror as he remembered, even now, the nightmare of what he had learned in Ephesus.

"I recognized the beggar as the enemy of the gods, one who had so offended them that they afflicted him with the ability to bring the plague. I pointed the man out to the people and insisted that they stone him, as the gods require. They were reluctant, the Ephesians being rather simplemindedly softhearted, but their fear of the plague was stronger than their sympathy for one useless beggar. They pelted him with stones until he lay buried beneath them, completely out of sight. The plague ended immediately."

Domitian stared in speechless awe for a few minutes before remembering the matter at hand. "The gods truly work through

you, Apollonius. That is no small benefit in your favor. Yet
here you are before me, charged with a most outlandish crime:
lycanthropy. Are you a lycanthrope, Apollonius? Can you
change yourself into an ass and move through the towns with
impunity, as they say?"

"I am afraid not," Apollonius said, a trace of a smile beginning on his face. "Though if it were true, I should take up the
trade of a farmer and grow rich working my own land and
pulling my own plows. And think of the political advantage:
I'd disguise myself as a pet monkey and eavesdrop on my
enemies, who would grow mad trying to discover which of
them had betrayed the others."

"A useful talent, to be sure," Domitian said, laughing. Life
had grown stale and boring lately, dull with predictability, and
Apollonius was at least something new and different. He had
quite grown to like this self-assured, amusing philosopher.

"Well, I'm inclined to believe you," Domitian said. "In any
case, I should pardon you merely out of gratitude for the
entertainment you've provided me." He picked up a paper
sitting before him and wrote for a few minutes. He set his seal
impressively across the bottom. "The charges are dismissed,"
he said, handing the paper to Apollonius, "and I hope to hear
more stories about your exploits. But not, I suggest, in Rome.
Not for, say, a few months?"

"Your generous nature shames me," Apollonius said, taking
the paper and bowing to Domitian. "As for the other matter, I
feel that the gods have directed me to travel in the East, where
there is knowledge much different from ours."

Safely out in the street, Apollonius breathed deeply. He had
told Domitian the basic truth of the story of the Ephesian
plague, but had left out most of the important details, details
that made him shiver even under the warm sun of a Roman
summer.

It wasn't a regular plague visited on the Ephesians. The
people called it that, but only for lack of a better name. The
Ephesians were being murdered, with such swiftness and in
such numbers that the only word they had to describe it was
plague. And the frightening part was that no one saw these
murders, though they were horrible. Some victims disappeared,

some were found days later, some found immediately, all with the same wounds on the bodies: the throat and heart torn out.

And the beggar who caused it wasn't maimed or crippled. He was a bright, shining man, as powerful as Domitian himself. In nightmares and in prophecy Apollonius had seen him disguising himself as a crippled beggar during the day, so that no one would take undue notice of him, then changing shape in the dusk and stalking the Ephesians by night, a great monster half-wolf, half-man, a lycanthrope who reveled in the killings.

Calling on all his magic and all the gods to protect him, Apollonius had confronted the man, challenging him to stop his slaughter. The man had looked at him with hypnotic eyes and an audacious smile.

"Call me by my name," the lycanthrope said, "Lycaon, King of Arcadia, beloved of Jupiter, who gave me this gift and abandoned me." Lycaon's voice had grown bitter. "Would you have me deny my deity?"

"You must stop this!" Apollonius demanded.

Lycaon looked at him, puzzled. "Why?"

"Because it's wrong," Apollonius said, astonished at the man's amorality. "You can*not* take human life so casually."

Lycaon grew reflective. "I suppose I've forgotten what human life is, how terribly important it seems to those who have only a few years of it. Yet, to me it seems so trivial. Human beings are only fodder to me; what do I care how soon they die or by what method? Yet this seems of consuming interest to you. Why is that? Do you eat meat, Apollonius, or the shining fish that light the depths of the sea?"

"Fish and fowl do not think. They don't create beauty. They don't better the human condition or challenge the mind."

"Oh. Then simply to have life isn't enough. So it isn't life that's precious to you, it's the possibilities of it for enriching your world. Well"—Lycaon stretched and enjoyed the feeling of his own body—"I'm just as selfish as you are. Killing human beings enriches *my* world. I enjoy doing it. Moreover, I must feed, and human beings are my food. So sometimes I kill solely to eat. Do you believe in killing, Apollonius?"

"No!"

"Ah. Then murderers and criminals should go amongst the general populace and continue their vicious ways?"

"Punishment for crimes is not the same as killing for sport. This is a sophistic argument."

"Please. It isn't an argument at all. I'm merely giving you something to think about. Isn't that what philosophers do? How wonderful it must be to be a completely moral man, convinced that you know for *sure* what is right and wrong," Lycaon said. "For instance . . ." He leaned forward and smiled maliciously at Apollonius. "Is it right to wake the dead?"

Apollonius froze.

"I mean," Lycaon said airily, "what are the moral consequences of resurrecting the dead, only to have them kill? It could be a simple question of mathematics, of course," he said with mock reflection. "You snatch one from death and she dispatches four more to Hades. Hmm. I suppose that means that the god of the underworld is four souls to the good, five if you count the mother's suicide. How very fascinating."

Apollonius stood stonily through this discourse.

"Was that moral, Apollonius," Lycaon said, his voice low and serious, "to change the course of events simply because you *could,* disregarding the will of the gods, unmindful of the consequences? Is your wisdom so complete?"

For a moment, Apollonius forgot Lycaon. For years, in his most troubled dreams, he had seen the consul's daughter, standing over the bodies of her children. And in those dreams, her hollow eyes had turned accusingly to him.

He had never raised the dead again. When it was requested of him, her pitiful specter laid her hand on his shoulder.

"What do you believe in, Apollonius?"

"I believe in justice," Apollonius said.

"Oh! Justice!" Lycaon's eyes went wide with amusement. "Excuse me, I had no idea we were speaking of such a noble ideal."

Apollonius was losing patience. "Without justice we are savages, animals. It is the highest of human ideals, and without it there is no order, no peace. The just may not be rewarded, but the unjust must be punished. You are an unjust man, Lycaon, a murderer without remorse and a heart without pity. I know you, and I know your story. In your audacity you plotted to kill Jupiter, and he punished you with the curse of lycanthropy so that you might contemplate the difference between man and animals. But your curse has taught you nothing; it has only given you a weapon with which to exacerbate your compulsion to kill. You are an abomination, and your retribution will come, never doubt it!"

"Is that what you think?"

"Obviously."

"Then you *don't* know me. You don't understand the stillness that comes when a man accepts himself and his world for exactly what they are, no more, no less. You strive to change it; you rail against injustice and pander for beauty. You devise complicated systems of right and wrong. You try to mold the world into your idea of what it should be, even to the extent of cheating death. Are you a happy man, Apollonius?"

"As happy as one can reasonably expect to be."

"Ah, but how blissful to live in a just world, free of rapacious characters—like me, for instance. That would be worth any small personal sacrifice, wouldn't it?"

"It's strange to hear you speak of sacrifice. I'm sure you're familiar with it solely in the abstract."

But Lycaon only smiled and looked up to the sky. Apollonius followed his gaze and saw the sun retreating, the stars winking into light, the moon rising full and virginal, like Artemis herself.

Lycaon, his teeth now lengthened and his fingers grown into claws, embraced Apollonius, his breath filling him like a powerful drug. Apollonius felt the front of his garment tear, the sharp pain over his breast, and then a magnificent burst of energy charging his entire body and brain.

He clung to Lycaon, his fingers digging into the lycanthrope's shoulders, as the energy crested, blinding his eyes and shutting out the sound from his ears.

Then the power subsided, leaving him limp and confused. Lycaon let him drop to the ground.

Lycaon stood over him, still changing. When the transformation was complete, he laughed and leaned over to whisper to Apollonius.

"Now my curse is your curse, Apollonius. You'll live longer than you ever dreamed possible. What you do with the time is up to you, but what you do at the full moon is entirely at the gods' discretion. We're brothers now, bound in blood; I kill the innocent, and you will kill the guilty. Think, philosopher! I've just given you the means to bring justice to an unjust world."

And he ran off, with the wolf's speed, to disappear in the groves toward Ephesus.

The next day, Apollonius led the citizens of Ephesus to the beggar, lying in a bed of filthy rags, and denounced him as the cause of the plague. The beggar looked up at Apollonius as if he knew that what would follow was inevitable.

The citizens seemed reluctant, but when they hung back, it was Apollonius who cast the first stone.

As it struck the beggar, he stood up, the blood streaming from his cut and bruised head. The entire crowd was silent and motionless as he regarded the transfixed Apollonius.

The beggar whispered one word: "Judas."

And then the crowd was on him, hurling stones that broke his body slowly, each crack of the stone a shattered bone. Only Apollonius stood mute and stunned.

When the stones were removed the next day, the Ephesians found a great black wolf lying where the beggar had fallen. Again, the Ephesians sought the counsel of Apollonius, but in the bleakness of his pain and his doubts he had no answer for them. And when they returned to see the body of the wolf, it was gone.

Apollonius left Ephesus, losing himself in vast lands where he could pass unnoticed, waiting in terror and resignation for the full moon to claim him. He returned just once to Rome, where whispers of lycanthropy reached the ears of Domitian, and he was charged with the crime. Where the story about his transformation into an ass began, Apollonius wasn't certain, but the ironic misinformation afforded him the only amusement he had enjoyed in the years since Ephesus.

Apollonius wandered the world after that, gathering ancient wisdom and earning a place in history as a great moral philosopher, guided by revelations from the gods, who were said to have rewarded him for his strict asceticism with the gift of

eternal life. In some stories he was also known as a powerful necromancer and magician, but this Apollonius strictly
denied.

Of the life and works and miracles of Apollonius of Tyana
there were many stories, written and oral, but of his death there
was only a phantom whisper drifting back from wild lands,
perhaps simply the imaginings of unreliable wanderers.

13

"A very strange story," Sylvie said to Zizi.

"But illuminating for several reasons. First, Apollonius and Lycaon represent the dual nature of the loup-garou. Killing is the nature of the animal, and it's a heady experience. We can't stop doing it. But we can make a choice. Like Apollonius, we can kill the guilty, those people who have escaped the fallible justice of human courts. Some of us feel that executions are the reason for our existence, but I don't think so. Like so many of the conventions that govern civilized life, it's something we agreed on. Apollonius felt that justice was the highest of human ideals; we feel that it's also the highest ideal of the lycanthrope."

"You mean that killing scum mitigates some of the guilt of killing in the first place?" Sylvie asked.

"We never feel guilt about killing, Sylvie," Zizi said firmly, "it's completely beyond our control. But we can select our kills, and many of us do. Learning to do it is a struggle, but one that can be mastered with varying degrees of success."

"So there are werewolves who only kill people who deserve it," Sylvie concluded.

Zizi smiled. "So far, no one has that much control. Nobody, human or loup-garou, achieves perfection. But it's the striving for it that makes us strong. I think, of all history's werewolves, only Apollonius kills solely for justice."

"Apollonius!" Sylvie exclaimed. "He's a real person? I thought he was just a legend!"

"Absolutely real. Apollonius and Lycaon are immortal, not because of their lycanthropy—immortality isn't one of our curses—but because of other factors. Lycaon because he was

125

cursed by the gods, and Apollonius because of his magic."

"But what about his raising the dead? Can all werewolves do that?"

"*No* werewolf can do that, except Apollonius. And that's not because he was a werewolf. He was a powerful magician, and had the gift of resurrection long before his lycanthropy."

"But where are they? Have you seen them?"

Zizi hesitated a moment, then shook her head. "Lycaon supposedly comes to werewolves who are cursed, probably because misery loves company. Lycaon never wanted to be a werewolf, remember, so he never developed a sense of purpose to mitigate his lycanthropy. Apollonius did and achieved peace. Lycaon only grew bitter. Meeting him would definitely not be a pleasant experience.

"So far," Zizi said, "every instance we have of werewolves meeting Lycaon has ended in tragedy. Peter Steubbe was one of history's most infamous werewolves, a cold-blooded killer of children. Steubbe saw Lycaon in 1589 and later told the authorities that the man he saw was the Devil. Jean Grenier saw him in 1603 and went mad. Grenier called him 'The Dark Man of the Forest' and said that it was this man who made him a werewolf.

"Apollonius, on the other hand, seems to bring a special wisdom to those who meet him. He's a wanderer, always learning, always sharing what he's learned. I suppose the New World was irresistible to him as a source of information. The Native Americans knew him; they called him 'the Man of Light.' I think they called him that from a combination of things. His light skin, his wisdom, a certain aura of authority he had."

"If you'd lived as long as he has, and seen all that he's seen," Christian said, "you'd have an aura of authority, too."

Zizi shook her head. "Imagine," she said admiringly, "after all those centuries, still taking an interest in the world, still finding new things to learn."

Gabriel, who had been silently listening to all this, spoke up hesitantly. "We don't know for sure," he said, glancing at Zizi, "but there is one of us who is supposed to have met Apollonius."

Zizi looked at him sharply. "Gabriel. Respect the man's privacy. That's only a rumor." She sighed and looked back to Sylvie. "He never speaks of this, and he won't respond when asked, but the only Louisiana loup-garou in hundreds of years to see Apollonius is Achille."

Sylvie was confused. "But why wouldn't he say so? I'd think he'd be honored."

"Exactly why I don't think it's true. And all our psychic attempts to read Achille on this point are useless. But if it were true, it would explain several things. Achille's insistence on striving for the ideal, while acknowledging that werewolves, like men, are frail creatures when it comes to self-control. His extraordinary command of his own powers, which are considerable even by our standards. And his leadership of the loup-garou community. Achille is a very young loup-garou, but his instincts and his knowledge far outstrip his age. Achille, in human reckoning, is just about your father's age, Sylvie, only forty-two years old, that's around four for a loup-garou. Yet he has the unquestioned air of a leader; no one elected him or chose him, and he didn't campaign for the job—we don't do that. It just happens that one of us is the leader, and that leader is Achille."

"Another thing about Achille," Christian said, "is that he's a true loup-garou, born with a sure knowledge of what he was. Some werewolves come to the decision later in life, but Achille was a child of the moon from out of his mother's womb. This is sort of a mark of honor among us. Some of us don't even recognize what we are and then one day—wham!—something happens that enlightens us."

"Is it always always so complicated to learn?" Sylvie asked, a little intimidated.

"Oh no," Zizi said. "One may become a loup-garou in a minute, with no preparation, and pick up the knowledge along the way. It's done all the time, usually with the were-wolf's kiss, like my luscious Austrian pastry here." She poked Christian with a long gold-painted nail and he laughed. "But you're special, Sylvie, partly because of your father. You must understand that he did what no loup-garou has ever done. He gave it all up. That indicates strong feelings, to say the least.

Achille wants you to know what you may be getting into. It's better this way, and we prefer to bring a young loup-garou into it slowly, when we have the time. Oh! But look at this! We've let your breakfast get cold and you haven't had a bite of it."

Zizi looked resigned. "Well, the hell with it," she said with a sigh. "Everyone get dressed. We'll join the tourists at Brennan's."

But Sylvie had one more question. "What about you, Zizi? Were you born a werewolf, too? How did you know what you were?"

Zizi laughed. "I'm too old to even remember my story. And if I could, it would probably be boring."

Back in her room, Sylvie started to dress but gave it up. She sat on the edge of her bed and let her mind wander. She had so many questions, so many feelings to sort out, but two questions that kept coming back to the forefront of her imagination were: What in God's name is the werewolf's kiss? And why was Zizi so evasive about discussing her past?

PART FOUR

†

The Mother of
Werewolves

14

France, 1722

The courtroom, large as it was, seemed to have no air at all. Perhaps it was the summer, perhaps it was the crush of people. Marie-Thérèse waved a square of lace in front of her face and tried not to faint.

"Duchesse de Marais," the man said, somewhat impatiently, as if he had had to repeat it several times.

Marie-Thérèse looked up. She sometimes had trouble thinking of herself as the Duchesse de Marais, even after two years.

The man, the king's magistrate, looked at her sternly.

Marie-Thérèse turned her head away from the magistrate and looked miserably at Alexandre, half sitting on the edge of his seat, as if he would leap up at any moment and sweep her out of here. In his eyes was the desperate madness of someone who has realized that all his money, his influence, and the power of his name and title could not keep his wife from this ordeal. He had even appealed to his friend, the Duc d'Orléans, the young king's regent. Orléans seemed as anxious as Alexandre that Marie-Thérèse not go to trial and further complicate an already notorious scandal, but it was precisely that scandal that made a public trial necessary.

"Her name must be cleared, Alexandre," Orléans had said. "Good God, no one believes such an outrageous charge against her, but for her sake—and yours—she must be found innocent. And I'm sure she will be."

But Marie-Thérèse wasn't so sure. And now she sat in this place waiting for a verdict.

"Marie-Thérèse Madeleine de la Rochette, Duchesse de Marais, you have been charged with the crime of lycanthropy and have been found guilty."

The entire courtroom erupted with outraged noise. This woman was, after all, the wife of one of the richest men in France. If she hadn't been of the aristocracy herself, she was at least married to the cream of it. And the charge—an outdated statute that hadn't been invoked in a hundred years, and then only in ignorant provinces—was absurd. The spectators, all Alexandre's peers, were incredulous that things had come to this. In the eye of the storm, the Duc de Marais stood frozen in horror.

The Chevalier d'Arcy clapped his hand on Alexandre's shoulder. "No one even considers such a travesty to be true, Marais," he said defiantly. "This verdict is politics, not justice. It's not the king's judgment."

Another man took his hand. "This isn't the end of this farce, Alexandre."

But the magistrate was speaking again. "Marie-Thérèse de la Rochette, taking into consideration your tender age, your rank and title, and the noble services your husband has rendered France, we are inclined to be lenient. It is our judgment, therefore, that you be exiled from France to the colony of Louisiana. You are to be held in La Salpêtrière until such time as the first prisoner ship leaves."

There was a stunned silence, then another indignant roar. "So that's the plan," d'Arcy said to Alexandre. "Your enemies are sure you won't let her go alone, that you'll follow her. And so you're out of France and out of the way with no overt political maneuvering. You must not go, Alexandre! The time has never been worse for you to leave Paris."

"How can I not?" the Duc asked in anguish. "Look at her, d'Arcy. She's only twenty and so innocent. How will she survive in that hellhole colony? Who will protect her?"

Marie-Thérèse, her sorrowful eyes never leaving her husband's face, was led out of the courtroom.

"We'll write to Bienville, tell him this entire preposterous story. He's the governor of the colony and a kind man; he'll watch out for her."

Marie-Thérèse still couldn't believe this had happened to her. It wasn't supposed to be this way: things like this simply did not touch the pristine slippers of the French aristocracy, and especially not when they were as highly placed as the de Marais family. That was one of the reasons she had married Alexandre in the first place. Oh, she was very fond of her husband, and as happy as she could have been with anyone, but the protection that his position and money *should* have afforded her was undoubtedly an attraction.

She thought about her husband. Poor Alexandre. He was an old man who had conceived a passion for a young woman and it had been his Achilles' heel. He had been kind to her, and if perhaps she hadn't loved him with the ardor he deserved, at least she was devoted to him and tried to make him a good wife. She had watched over his health and his diet, making him avoid rich foods and seeing that he got enough exercise. She had run the household and staff like a particularly well trained army, so that Alexandre never had to be distracted by a dusty bookshelf or an indolent housemaid. She was an excellent hostess and had made her own friends at court, tactfully navigating the treacherous political waters of France with neither selfish intent nor ambition. Alexandre's sons had accepted her with no objections, since their mother had been dead almost fifteen years and Marie-Thérèse brought with her no sons of her own who might make sticky work of the inheritance, and she showed no signs of producing any. In fact, until this shocking unpleasantness, coming out of the blue as it did, life had been uneventful and Marie-Thérèse had been contented.

Her married life with Alexandre had been like pouring oil on wild waters after the years she spent with Paul-Joseph and Cathérine, the Marquis and Marquise de Guibert.

Marie-Thérèse, then sixteen, was the Marquise de Guibert's hairdresser. She had been trained for this since she was a child, and showed great talent. One of her greatest pleasures was to brush the Marquise's hair in the evenings; the thick black strands, glinting with burgundy lights, felt like a satin cloak under Marie-Thérèse's hands. A faint trace of antique roses always shimmered in the air around Cathérine.

"You have such a lovely touch," Cathérine said to her, "such adept hands, Marie-Thérèse. It will be a very lucky man someday who receives caresses from those hands." Cathérine often paid her these pretty little compliments. A few times, Marie-Thérèse had caught the Marquise looking at her in the mirror, her eyes bright and speculating, and at those times, Marie-Thérèse would blush and feel slightly disoriented.

Marie-Thérèse had a little secret: she had a painful crush on the Marquise de Guibert. She wasn't sure if she loved Cathérine or merely wanted to *become* Cathérine, who was everything Marie-Thérèse wanted to be. The way she entered a room, a certain movement of her hands, the exact octave of her laugh, her ability to enchant without effort or obvious design. There were a thousand tiny parts that made up the whole of Cathérine's charm. It wasn't something acquired, it was inborn. It drove Marie-Thérèse wild to think that she could watch Cathérine for a hundred years and learn to mimic her style, but that she would never be Cathérine's equal, even if she had been born to her station. I love her for everything I'm not, Marie-Thérèse often thought. But it was love all the same, and of the most frustrating character.

Sometimes, in her bed, she would think about the graceful Cathérine and twist in the sheets until dawn. Cathérine's perfume clung to Marie-Thérèse and haunted her on those nights.

It was precisely one of those nights that changed Marie-Thérèse's life.

As usual, she could not sleep. It seemed that the moon through the window was particularly bright, shining into her face and inciting lustful thoughts. She was too awake to stay in bed, so she moved to the window.

The Marquis and Marquise were out on the lawns, in the rose garden. They were wearing only their nightclothes. The Marquis, Paul-Joseph, held his wife in the sort of embrace Marie-Thérèse had only dreamed of. She couldn't see very much from the high attic window, but her flaring jealousy and the natural curiosity of a sixteen-year-old virgin drove her to do something reckless: she slipped downstairs to watch them.

It was a chilly night, but her very audacity heated her blood. Dressed only in her flimsy shift, she crept out toward the garden until she found a suitable hiding place.

She watched, entranced, as Cathérine and Paul-Joseph undressed each other, slowly. He dropped to his knees to ease her nightgown down over her hips, and she bent to kiss him. The moon shone on their bodies and caught the gleam in Cathérine's hair as it fell over her husband's upturned face. Then they were facing each other, both on their knees in the velvety grass, talking briefly, holding hands, occasionally stroking each other's skin. There seemed to be an excitement between them, beyond what was happening at that moment, as if they were waiting for something else. Both of them lifted their faces to the full moon, drinking the light like wine. Paul-Joseph leaned over and ran his outstretched hands over Cathérine, his fingers skimming her throat, the tips of her breasts, and disappearing between her legs, his movements so authoritative and possessive that Marie-Thérèse grew dizzy with longing. Cathérine threw her head back, arching her back so that the moonlight reflected on her white skin, and her long hair swung free. Marie-Thérèse felt her head pound, her body burn, her own voice harsh in her throat as she inadvertently cried out.

Both of them turned their heads toward the place where Marie-Thérèse crouched, the shock of humiliation and fear choking her. Paul-Joseph, with a puzzled smile, dragged Marie-Thérèse out of the hedges, not too roughly, but his hold on her would obviously brook no opposition.

"And what is this?" he asked, raising an eyebrow. "Are we performers now, Cathérine?"

"It would seem so," Cathérine answered, laughing.

Marie-Thérèse wanted to die.

"You liked what you saw, child?" he said, not unkindly. "Have you ever seen anyone make love before?"

"No, sir," Marie-Thérèse gasped.

"And you certainly haven't done it yourself?"

"Oh, no!" Marie-Thérèse said, mortified.

"And yet you seem so sensual, so ripe," he said slowly. "Your eyes are not the eyes of a virgin. And your reactions"— he touched his lips tenderly, but maddeningly to the sensitive skin of her throat, and noted the instant gooseflesh he raised— "are not the reactions of a virgin. You seem very aware of sex, my dear, and I think you're fascinated by it. What do you think, Cathérine? Is she a daughter of the moon?"

Then the Marquise pulled Marie-Thérèse close. Once again, her perfume seduced and confused Marie-Thérèse, stirring the same feelings she had when she dug her nails into the stifling sheets of her bed. The Marquise gathered Marie-Thérèse's shift in her hands and quickly pulled it away. When Marie-Thérèse tried to cover herself, the Marquise stopped her, holding both of her hands at her sides. Marie-Thérèse was humiliated, and undeniably excited.

"Such perfect beauty," Cathérine said. "Such fine features and delicate skin, such golden hair. What sacrilege for them to waste away, for time to be allowed to desecrate this body. It must not happen, Paul."

Then the Marquise laid Marie-Thérèse down on the grass and touched her in exactly the way she had dreamed. The black hair brushed Marie-Thérèse's body, soothing and exciting her with every touch. Cathérine's fingers floated over her skin, the tips of her nails leaving delightful little scratches. She moaned as Cathérine's hand probed between her legs, teasing her until she felt a warm rush of moisture and sensation. It was almost more than she could bear. Cathérine and Paul-Joseph each took one of her breasts, sucking and running their tongues over the sensitive flesh, teasing the nipples to an inflamed hardness. The very sight alone almost drove her insane. Then Cathérine withdrew slightly, and there was Paul's lips on her throat, her face; she was aware of his hands gently opening her legs. As Paul's body covered Marie-Thérèse's, she felt Cathérine's deep kisses. Paul's slow thrusts, the slight, shuddering pain—all of this delighted Marie-Thérèse beyond her imagining. She felt her body explode in a long, slow quiver that started in her genitals and seemed to spread through her overheated blood. Her back arched and she tightened her legs around Paul-Joseph's back, pulling him deeper inside her, as he moaned at exactly the same time she screamed. She had imagined what sex would be, but she never expected anything so wonderful.

Then Paul-Joseph was retreating, and Marie-Thérèse caught the shadow scent of roses in Cathérine's hair. "Just a little

more pain, beautiful one," Cathérine said. "Only the slightest and sweetest, and then the rebirth. Then years will pass,
decades will pass, centuries will pass, and still your beauty
will remain."

Cathérine's lips brushed Marie-Thérèse's breast, and she
felt a sharp pain over her heart and felt the warm blood
flow from the shivering wound under Cathérine's mouth. This
second orgasm was more all-encompassing than the first. All
her nerves seemed inflamed and alive, revitalized, as if a
galaxy of glittering stars were sizzling through her veins.
The light of a brilliant sun burst before her eyes, blinding
her, then lighting the night to clear brightness. Her brain
felt rejuvenated, as if every cell was being brought to a new
awareness. She moaned and embraced Cathérine, and was surprised to feel rough fur where there had been soft skin. When
Cathérine drew back, Marie-Thérèse could see the growth of
sharp fangs.

Cathérine rose and moved to join her husband, both rapidly
changing. As Marie-Thérèse watched, the metamorphosis continued, human being into wolf-creature, the teeth sharpening to
full sets of fangs, the limbs stretching, the nails darkening into
great claws, the muscles rearranging themselves into powerful,
living machines.

The thought came to Marie-Thérèse that she should be
afraid, but she found that she was merely excited. There was
a fever in her blood, her eyes seemed to see for miles in the
dark, her ears drowned in a hundred sounds of the night that
she had never known before. They seemed to come at her
from everywhere: the sound of crickets, the shiver of birds'
wings as they moved in the trees, the breathing of the sleeping
household servants, and the hot, urgent sounds of someone
in the house making furtive love. Marie-Thérèse clapped her
hands over her ears, trying to shut out the sounds.

"It will subside," Paul said to her. "Just a few minutes and
you'll adjust to it, you'll learn to shut out the sounds you don't
want and pick out the ones you do."

She looked down at herself and saw her own body under-
going the same changes. She laughed out loud with pleasure,
and she didn't know why.

"I told you, Paul!" Cathérine cried delightedly in her changed voice. "I knew the child was one of us! Look how easily the change comes on her! Come, Marie-Thérèse," she said, holding out a paw of ebony silk, "run with us, rejoice in the night and the kill and your own new life."

And Marie-Thérèse, having just escaped the bonds of time and convention, eagerly joined them.

They ran with a speed that amazed Marie-Thérèse, covering a great distance in a short time. The countryside flew by, but she could catch every little detail with her new senses. The flicker of a candle flame in a maid's room, the scent of a late supper being consumed indifferently by a pair of lovers who would shortly ignore the food, the dank smell of death crawling from a peasant's hut, the dust of many roads in a mare's coat as she slept in an inn's stall. The lusty, slurred voice of a soldier singing his regimental song as he left his whore.

Paul, his dark copper coat leading the way, slowed to veer off toward the soldier, but Cathérine nudged him away. A drunk was too easy prey. She had caught a more exciting scent.

In a clearing there lay a small band of sleeping soldiers, clustered around the dimming embers of a supper fire. Paul and Cathérine circled the group slowly, silently, choosing the strongest, the one whose dreams were untroubled by doubt. This was to be Paul's kill; he chose and nodded at Cathérine, then disappeared into the trees with Marie-Thérèse.

Cathérine closed her eyes and transformed quickly to her human form. She knelt and lightly touched a single fingertip to the soldier's cheek, gently, softly as a night moth flutters. He opened his eyes and saw a dream: a beautiful naked woman, motioning him to be silent. She nuzzled his ear and whispered for him to come with her. She held out her hand and he followed her, sleepwalking and dazzled, into the forest, deep into the grove where no sound could emerge. She held out her arms.

Paul sprang from the darkness and knocked the soldier to the ground with one blow. The man staggered, but recovered. When he looked up to see what had hit him, he was too stunned to make a sound. His mind refused to give credibility to the beast he saw, but his military training took over his body. He backed off, stalling for time, planning his moves. He knew sudden flight was useless; his best chance lay in battle. He was trained to kill with his bare hands if necessary.

The werewolf also waited. Paul's nostrils dilated, anticipating the scent of fear. It was there, but it was only a sudden flash as the soldier's disciplined mind overrode his body's instinct to flee.

The soldier made his move, charging suddenly at the werewolf's midsection to knock out his wind.

But the werewolf, with a deft move, sidestepped.

The two circled. The werewolf, for sport, swiped at the soldier with his claws. He was rewarded by a quick burst of terror. He suddenly charged the man and easily lifted him up over his head, and the man gasped and made a short, terrified sound.

Marie-Thérèse, driven out of hiding by the irresistible scent of fear, emerged from the trees, her eyes burning with hunger and excitement. When the man caught sight of her, the scent grew stronger, almost overwhelming, as his terror took him.

Still, he fought, raining blows on the werewolf, kicking, clawing, biting, fighting from a deep instinct now, all the rules of training giving way to the will to survive. When the werewolf made a mighty slash, almost severing the man's arm, it only slowed him for a moment, then he jumped back at the monster with renewed, desperate strength. He threw himself on the werewolf, but the werewolf's height and superb balance made him impossible to tumble. It was then that the man knew he was finished, and when that happened, an inappropriate calm settled him. The scent of fear subsided.

Man and werewolf were motionless for a moment. Then the man dropped to his knees, crossed himself, and began to pray, determined, for how many seconds he had left, to make peace with his sins.

Marie-Thérèse was driven by a voracious hunger. She made a slight move, but Paul-Joseph waved her back.

The man finally lifted his head and merely waited. The werewolf lifted him again and, with one mighty shake, quickly broke his neck and it was over.

Paul-Joseph bent over the body, turning and motioning for Marie-Thérèse to come closer. "Your lesson begins," he said in his raspy whisper.

His claws opened the soldier's chest like a master chef slicing a delicate roast woodcock. He snapped the ribs and extracted the warm heart, filled with sweet, salty blood. Closing his eyes in rapture, he swallowed the heart like a rare oyster, savoring the taste and texture as it filled his senses and renewed his strength until another full moon.

Marie-Thérèse watched carefully.

Paul-Joseph took a deep breath and opened his eyes. "You see how it's done?"

Marie-Thérèse nodded. Her hunger, which had only abated a little at her fascination with Paul-Joseph's feast, now returned ten times stronger, gnawing at her in a way that human hunger never did. It was ripping her apart from the inside.

"Now, one for you," he said. Taking Cathérine on his back, he led Marie-Thérèse back to the encampment, where they lured another soldier to the forest with the very same techniques. Marie-Thérèse learned the wicked pleasures of toying with a kill to extract the addictive scent of fear that so delighted the senses of a werewolf. But when it came time to actually kill her man, she was clumsy in her new body; she inadvertently crushed his right rib cage, piercing a lung. The man was in agony until Paul reached out and snapped his spine, cutting off his nervous system. He felt no pain, but he still lived.

"You must do the kill yourself if you're to eat," Paul told Marie-Thérèse. But she was afraid to try to shake the man again. She laid him on the ground and with a fast motion, crushed his head. It was crude, but quick. Marie-Thérèse learned something: that the actual moment of death brought no pleasure to the werewolf. That was simply something to be done as quickly and painlessly as possible. It was the chase, the scent of fear, and the consumption of the heart that was at the center of the werewolf's life.

Marie-Thérèse had another awkward moment extracting the heart, but she was rapidly mastering the use of her claws and made a very good first attempt. She swallowed the heart while Paul and Cathérine looked on like a young couple watching their child's first steps.

"But what about the bodies?" Marie-Thérèse worried.

"Their regiment will assume they've deserted. The animals of the forest will finish them," Paul said. "That's always the case when you kill in the wild. Never leave evidence of a kill, child," he said positively. "Bury the body or sink it in a swamp or toss it in the ocean, where the rocks on the coast or the fish will take it. And when that isn't possible, you must eat it—all of it, except the bones. Bones are easy to get rid of."

Marie-Thérèse's eyes went wide again, and Paul laughed. "It isn't difficult," he said, "and you'll find the taste is lovely. Some of us are quite fond of it and do it every time. But consuming an entire body takes time. And tonight, time is something we don't have enough of. Come, child; Cathérine has a special friend expecting us. I don't know if you'll like him, but the experience will definitely teach you something new."

Paul took Cathérine on his back again, her white skin lucent against his coppery pelt, and the three of them ran back into the night.

They stopped at the door to an elegant house, as beautiful as the de Guiberts' own. It seemed unnaturally quiet, almost deserted, but Marie-Thérèse's senses could detect motion inside, someone coming closer.

Marie-Thérèse was instantly attracted to the man who greeted them. He was tall and elegant, with a heavy, powerful body that nonetheless moved easily and confidently. He wore deep burgundy red, a color most complementary to his pale skin. But, Marie-Thérèse thought on further consideration, there was something about him that was repellent, something strange beneath the skin, a stain of sin and dissipation that colored the atmosphere around him.

He was not at all frightened or even surprised by the loups-garous. He only expressed a slight curiosity as to the third party.

"Beautiful Cathérine," he said, embracing her, "we can't let you become chilled!" He settled his own burgundy dressing gown around her shoulders. "But who is this?" he said, looking at Marie-Thérèse.

Cathérine laughed. "Our new daughter. I'll explain later. But how marvelous to see you, François! Have you a wonderful treat for me?"

"Most wonderful, I think you'll agree, and worth the wait since the last time I saw you. Come with me."

They wound their way through splendid chambers of gilded walls and old tapestry, of heavy silk couches and marvelously wrought furniture and glowing carpets under candlelight reflected in crystal facets. The house was very large, but through the whole place they saw not one other soul. Marie-Thérèse knew by the scents that there were other people present, but they were either asleep or had been instructed to keep silent and out of the way.

François opened a hidden door, and the four of them descended a long set of stone steps. Marie-Thérèse heard the echo of her claws scratching as her hand trailed along the stone walls. She expected cold, but the passage was unusually warm, with currents of heated air rising from below. She could see a light coming from another door at the bottom of the stairs.

When they reached the bottom, François stepped aside to let them enter first. Marie-Thérèse heard an iron door bang shut behind them, and stopped in terror. She found herself in prison.

At least, it looked at first glance like a prison. There were several unoccupied iron cages, three feet square and seven feet high, lined against one wall. Iron rings and manacles attached to chains were set into the stone walls. An array of instruments, the purposes of which Marie-Thérèse tried not to contemplate, were laid out on a long oak table. An X-shaped cross, as tall as a standing man, also set with manacles at the top and bottom, was attached to the wall.

The source of warmth was a huge fireplace, blazing away. Large enough to roast a man, Marie-Thérèse thought with distaste. Why, she wondered, had that particular image popped up? The atmosphere was getting under her skin.

Facing all this, along the opposite wall and scattered throughout the room, were couches and cushions as luxurious and richly upholstered as anything in the rooms upstairs. Little gilded tables held crystal glasses and decanters of wine. It was an unusually decadent and unspeakably strange theater.

Paul-Joseph caught Marie-Thérèse's confounded look and gave a very brief and unconvincing laugh. "Don't look so apprehensive," he whispered to her. "It's only that Cathérine shares with François an unusual little amorous preference. Quite the renegade, our Cathérine." But despite his laughter, Marie-Thérèse could see that Paul was distracted. He never took his eyes off Cathérine.

Amorous? Marie-Thérèse thought. What could a place like this possibly have to do with love?

A square frame of hewn timber posts was mounted in the center of the room. Identical iron manacles studded it at the top, sides, and bottom, so that a prisoner could be fastened with his arms above him and his legs together, or his arms and legs stretched out to the sides, or any combination. The entire arrangement looked ominous to Marie-Thérèse.

She was obviously the only one who felt uneasy. Paul and Cathérine were chatting quietly with François, and there was a strange current of subdued excitement among them. François settled all of them on the cushioned couches, and poured wine.

"What do you have for me, François?" Cathérine said. Her body leaned eagerly forward, restless and excited.

François smiled as a young man of about twenty, his dark looks amazingly like François's, brought a tray of sweetmeats and set it on one of the little tables.

"You haven't seen this young man since he was very small, I think. My son, Donatien Alphonse François. Donatien, you remember the Marquis and Marquise de Guibert? And this is their ward, Marie-Thérèse."

The young man bowed and exchanged a few words with his father.

"Oh, yes," François said, "bring him out now. And don't let him give you any trouble. If he does, you know how to curb him."

Marie-Thérèse watched Cathérine, who was finding it difficult to contain herself; her face was tense, her breath came a
little heavier.

Donatien, carrying a long bamboo switch, returned leading
a man in chains. The man was about the same age as Donatien,
but with a stocky, muscular peasant's body and a rough-hewn
face, set in defiance. Every time the man pulled back, Donatien
turned and struck him with the switch. The stroke was light, but
the bamboo cane made an evil, eerie swish as it cut the air. A
red welt swelled under every stroke. The man's buttocks were
covered with such marks, some still oozing blood.

Donatien manacled the man to the timber frame as he
squirmed, spread-eagled, against his captivity. Every motion
of his body as it tensed and relaxed produced in Marie-Thérèse
a slight frisson of excitement. She despised herself for it: this
was a perverse preference of the rich, not to the taste of the
lower classes like her, to whom misery was anything but a
diversion.

She felt a tiny pang of sympathy for the chained man.

At second glance, Marie-Thérèse realized that her sympathy
was wasted: the man had a rock-hard erection.

"Look at him!" Cathérine exclaimed, standing mockingly
before the man. "Even chained and helpless, his body insults
me. What an insolent creature!"

"Unfortunately for him," François sighed, "he's intractably
stubborn. Examine his buttocks, madame; you're familiar with
how precise Donatien is with the cane? Well, this brute took
thirty-five strokes from him this afternoon and he absolutely
refused to make a sound. He knows that it's his shrieks I
want to hear and he is determined not to oblige, the rude
monster."

Cathérine's eyes glowed with a strange pleasure. "Let's see
if we can produce screams for you, François." She stroked the
man's body and he flinched away. She frowned slightly. "What
is this? He doesn't like women? Oh, François, you *haven't*
brought me a sodomite?"

"On the contrary, dear, his affection for women is why he's
here. The wretch violated two—*two,* mind you!—of my kitch-
en maids, spotless virgins that I was saving as the centerpieces

for my entertainments. Because of this oversexed addlebrain, I had the embarrassing inconvenience of informing my guests that there were no longer any virgins to be had that evening."

Cathérine expressed sympathy for this unforgivable social gaffe forced on the elegant François.

"His capacity for pain seems enticingly high," Cathérine mused.

"It's your pleasure to find out," François said, easing himself down beside the werewolves on the cushioned couches.

Silently, Donatien offered Cathérine a whip, an elegant thing with a silver handle enclosing several braided leather lashes, each with a knot on the end. At the sight of it, the man tensed. Cathérine ran the whip over his body, letting the braided lashes brush and tickle his skin, and every place the whip touched seemed to set the man on fire. He closed his eyes as Cathérine teased his flesh.

She stepped back and weighed the whip in her hand, becoming familiar with its feel. She eyed the man's body like a sculptor studies a block of marble before making the first chisel stroke. Then she drew back her arm, and with a subtle flick of her wrist, snapped the whip across the man's thighs.

The sound was sharp, but light. The man winced, but didn't seem to be in unusual pain.

Cathérine took the next stroke, then turned her back on him, walking away, her fingers tensing against the whip's handle. Suddenly she turned back and, with an uninterrupted series of backhand and forehand motions, laid six lashes across the man's back, each stroke a little harder than the one before it. By the last one, the man's eyes flew open and he half gasped, half screamed.

Cathérine circled the whip above her head, building up momentum, and, with a loud crack, landed three crosswise strokes over his back, each stoke drawing blood.

The man's tears tracked his face. His erection was, if possible, even more pronounced than before.

Marie-Thérèse had never seen Cathérine so intense, her face so flushed with pleasure and concentration. She felt herself squirm among the silk pillows.

Cathérine shrugged off the burgundy cloak in one supremely seductive motion. She draped the whip around her neck, its silver handle and leather thongs brushing her breasts as it hung over her shoulders. She dropped slowly to her knees and drew the man's erection into her mouth, inch by inch, with an excruciating slowness. She would withdraw, then advance, each movement bringing a groan from the chained man. Her hands moved gently around his welted buttocks, holding him, the fingers of one hand probing deep inside his anus.

This went on for a few minutes. The young man's eyes rolled back in his head with pleasure as he hung suspended and helpless there.

But Marie-Thérèse could see what the young man couldn't— the first faint sproutings of fur down Cathérine's back.

Cathérine never broke her rhythm; back and forth her head moved, her fingers probing deeper. Marie-Thérèse was riveted with horror: she could see the tapering fingers of Cathérine's free hand beginning to grow claws, which must mean that the teeth were also changing.

The man's eyes opened in shock and he gave a faint, surprised shout as the first shimmers of pain ran through his body.

Cathérine either didn't hear or didn't care. Her head continued to move back and forth, her hands to massage deeper and faster. The black fur was growing fast now, covering her whole body as she changed.

A single thread of blood ran in a red track down the man's thighs, only the thinnest and finest trickle, so faint that it seemed a crimson illusion. Then, as his shock wore off and his screams began, the trickle became a running river, a torrent of blood splashing the floor, staining Cathérine's fur.

Still, she did not stop. And he continued to scream.

Marie-Thérèse turned to look at Paul. He watched with a slight edge of distaste. The scene apparently wasn't to his liking, although he was willing to indulge Cathérine. For the first time, Marie-Thérèse realized that Paul-Joseph was as much a slave of his wife as this tormented creature was of François's.

François was a different story. He reclined on the cushions, his head turned to watch, his eyes glittering. His fly was unbuttoned and his considerable erection rampant under his stroking hands. As appalled as she was, Marie-Thérèse was appreciative of the fact that he had to use both hands.

Never breaking the motion of her head, which now seemed in synchronization with the man's screams, Cathérine, fully changed, reached up and rested both hands on his shoulders. With a long, slow motion, she raked her claws from his shoulders to his hips, opening great rents of flesh that hung in dripping strips.

The man's eyes bulged from his sockets, his face turned the shade of old parchment, his tongue protruded from his mouth, muffling the shrieks. But only for a moment.

As the man's agonized wailing began afresh, François moaned and his hands moved faster.

At last Cathérine withdrew. Still on her knees, she smiled and considered the man's agony. He moaned and sobbed, in unbearable pain but obviously relieved that the worst was over and that, perhaps, he might live.

Cathérine lunged forward. The great snap of her teeth echoed on the stone walls like an explosion as her jaws closed. The man's final bellow and François's climactic outburst broke simultaneously. Paul jumped, and Marie-Thérèse gave a faint scream.

Cathérine spit something into her hand.

The man slumped in a faint, held upright only by his manacles. François collapsed against the silk cushions, his eyes closed in exhaustion. He never noticed as Cathérine extracted the man's still-beating heart.

In a few minutes she stood over François, the sweat and blood making glistening highlights in her black fur. For one moment—and it was gone in just that instant—Marie-Thérèse caught Cathérine's slight sneer of contempt.

"Oh, my God, Cathérine!" François panted in a ragged voice. "Your inventiveness always overwhelms me. I have to take to my bed for days after you're here, trying to recuperate from the effort."

Cathérine wiped the blood from her face and mouth with one arm. She tossed something vile next to François's outflung hand. He turned to look, then burst out laughing.

"*Memento amore*, my love," Cathérine said lightly. "We have to go. Thank you for the diversion."

"My pleasure," François said, waving a limp, exhausted hand.

"But exactly," Cathérine said, sweeping Paul and Marie-Thérèse along before her.

After that night, Marie-Thérèse was no longer in love with Cathérine. Under her spell, yes; it was possible to be repulsed by certain things Cathérine did but still to be charmed by the force of her personality and swayed by her beauty. Cathérine had made Marie-Thérèse a werewolf not out of noble motives, but in the same spirit that a spoiled child demands another child's attention—and with as much regard for her feelings. Paul, with his small acts of compassion, was a better person than Cathérine, but his unquestioning love for her and the helplessness it produced was Paul's tragedy. Cathérine's brutality was Paul-Joseph's blind spot; he was willing to overlook it, obviously hoping that experience and age would soften her.

Women have a strange cynicism toward each other's faults, and are never so forgiving as men in love. Marie-Thérèse knew that Cathérine would never change.

Still, Marie-Thérèse gained something from her first outing as a werewolf. The differences in Paul's and Cathérine's ways ran to either end of the moral spectrum. The most valuable lesson she learned that night was that she had a choice, that she could live her werewolf's life in her own way and kill as her conscience or her preferences dictated. Taking the heart of her victim, one of the few absolutes of a werewolf's existence, was a soberingly intimate act: the victim was the werewolf and the werewolf was the victim. Paul's toying with his prey was not completely frivolous, as she had first thought, even though it was calculated to produce the scent of fear. Paul gave his victim a chance to fight with valor, even if the outcome of the battle was heavily weighted in the werewolf's favor. However, there was the slim chance that, by accident or an act of God or a miscalculation on the werewolf's part, the prey would go free. Paul gave his opponents the dignity of taking that chance. It was an honorable death.

Marie-Thérèse thought of all the variations that life held for her and the many years she would have to explore them, and though she might not savor the same delights that Cathérine did, she was excited by the endless possibilities. Only one thing puzzled her: why the choice? Why not simply kill, if one had to in order to live? Why had the loup-garou, unlike other animals, been given the power to make a moral distinction?

After that night, Marie-Thérèse's position in the household changed. Cathérine and Paul-Joseph made her their legal ward. She was taken from out of the attic servants' rooms and ensconced in large, airy apartments on the second floor. If the other servants were shocked by this change, they would at least say nothing in her hearing. What they said in private, Marie-Thérèse knew, was a different story. She was certain that they thought she was the Marquis's mistress. Her bedroom was a froth of pale blue watered silk, set against the intricately plastered and gilded walls. A pair of curved glass doors opened to a terrace. She was denied nothing: Cathérine sent her personal dressmaker to fit Marie-Thérèse with everything from the skin out, and she had her own maids and hairdresser. Cathérine gave her a black pearl ring and a diamond comb for her hair. Paul-Joseph gave her a curious pendant: a silver charm in the shape of a full moon, surrounded with moonstones. "You're a child of the moon now," he told her, "and this will remind you of the obligation you owe her, always."

As if Marie-Thérèse could forget.

Her position was legally clear, but ethically nebulous to Marie-Thérèse until one afternoon while she was being fitted for a ball gown. The dressmaker and several assistants were chirping noisily about, draping fabrics and lace, sticking pins into large pincushions and occasionally into Marie-Thérèse's rapidly wilting form. Servants hovered about with lemon verbena tea and tiny cakes. In the midst of all this, Cathérine swept in, carrying one of her many small dogs. She took one look at Marie-Thérèse and frowned. The dressmaker and her assistants froze.

"No. It won't do at all. Not at *all*!" Cathérine said. "Good Lord, are you color blind? The girl is a blond, and you're going to put her in that shade of green? Never. What have you got in pink or rose, or a hyacinth blue? And not white lace with it . . . cream. I think the pale rose damask silk, trimmed with darker satin roses, don't you, Marie-Thérèse?" She surveyed the fabrics draped over chairs, running her hand over the little dog in her lap.

As Marie-Thérèse nodded agreement, it suddenly came to her what her position really was: she was Cathérine's pet.

Still, it was certainly preferable to the life she'd led so far, and if the days were marvelous, the nights were intensely sensual. Paul-Joseph liked to change only at the full moon, but Cathérine and Marie-Thérèse changed every chance they got, sometimes three or four nights a week. Marie-Thérèse was still slightly appalled at Cathérine's violent kills: they were neither quick nor painless. She insisted on visiting the Marquis's dungeon torture chamber several times, and though Marie-Thérèse always hung back, she inevitably went along.

"One of these days," Cathérine gleefully told Marie-Thérèse, "I might give old François a taste of his own torture. The temptation is almost too much to resist."

"But his equipment is so impressive, Cathérine," Marie-Thérèse said, laughing. "A shame to lose it!"

"Yes. That's the only thing that saves him," Cathérine agreed. "I'm afraid I'd choke to death!"

Over the next year, Marie-Thérèse absorbed a strange education. During the days, she learned how to seat a dinner party, to carry a fan gracefully, to appreciate opera, to speak flirtingly, yet circumspectly in polite company. She had a dancing master to drill her in the intricate steps of the quadrilles, and a music master to teach her the flute and harpsichord. She learned to sing, to do delicate, useless embroidery, to tell superior lace from the merely acceptable. She learned to read and write, and thereafter was a devourer of books, racing through Paul-Joseph's library.

With equal dexterity, she mastered the deft touch with which to break a man's neck quickly and quietly, and how to extract a living heart with a single series of smooth, efficient motions. She wanted her own kills to be like Paul-Joseph's. She preferred running with him, but he never liked to change as often as she did. When they did go out together, sometimes without Cathérine, he invariably made love to her just before the transformation, which made the whole process more exciting. The pain of transformation never quite abated, but the pain was turned into sexual excitement beyond anything Marie-Thérèse had known. It was like an extended orgasm that exalted not only the genitals, but the entire body, and it lasted for so long!

On the nights they were not changed, there were parties, balls, entertainments. The de Guiberts were expected to keep up a rather lavish social schedule. Naturally, at first, everyone wondered about Marie-Thérèse: where she had come from, who she was, why she was the de Guiberts' ward. Cathérine explained that she was a distant cousin, very good blood but no money, and that her delicate parents had died. The first time she overheard this, Marie-Thérèse wryly thought of her family: stocky, healthy peasants, a sturdy French mother and an Italian father, still living in a little town near Rouen.

Because of her ties to the de Guiberts and the inheritance she was expected to have, not to mention the hefty dowry that Paul-Joseph would settle on her, Marie-Thérèse was a very sought-after dancing and dinner-table partner. The young men, encouraged by their mothers and by their own hormones, paid her extravagant attention.

All this amused Marie-Thérèse. She could have married any of them, but she preferred to wait.

"What are you waiting *for*?" Cathérine demanded to know. "You can have the husband of your choice, as rich or as handsome as you like. And all you have to do is pick a title, and he's yours."

"I'm not looking for either of those," Marie-Thérèse said.

Cathérine shook her head in mystification. "You don't know what you want," she declared.

But Marie-Thérèse did know. She wanted another loup-garou. She could not imagine having to keep her life a secret. She knew she could make anyone a loup-garou, but she wanted someone born to it, like she was, someone who would revel in it with her and understand what she felt.

She began to revise what she wanted when she met the Comte d'Apollonaire.

It was Paul-Joseph's birthday, and Cathérine had arranged a magnificent night: an afternoon musicale, followed by a sumptuous dinner, followed by a ball and a midnight supper.

At dinner, Marie-Thérèse noticed a man she'd never seen before. He was deep in conversation with the Comtesse de Montaigne on his right and the English Duchess of Kent on his left. He looked slightly foreign to Marie-Thérèse: dark hair streaked with gray, and large, dark eyes. He was wearing a wine red silk coat and vest with cream lace at his throat. The color was wonderful for him; it made his eyes smoky, more mysterious. For a few seconds, she couldn't tear herself away from the sight of those eyes. She was vaguely aware of the conversation of her dinner partner, and she was well trained enough to be sure she was making the correct responses, but she didn't hear a word.

It was his hands, too, that caught her fancy. They moved like graceful birds, lightly and fluidly; when he unconsciously caressed his wineglass, his fingers playing up and down the stem and over the bowl, Marie-Thérèse watched, fascinated, imagining those fingers on her own skin.

She looked up to find that he had caught her watching him, and she was positive that he knew what she had been thinking.

She was mortified, but he only smiled at her and, after a moment, resumed his conversation with the Duchess.

Marie-Thérèse's dinner partner said something to her, and she struggled to look interested.

"Jean-Louis," she said casually to her dinner partner, "do you know that man? The one across the table and down three chairs? Wearing dark red and sitting with the English-woman?"

Jean-Louis took a surreptitious look, squinting against his nearsightedness. "I don't know him well. We've only been introduced once. The Comte d'Apollonaire. *Very* old family, ancient, older than the Valois, I understand. You never met him?"

"No. But then, Cathérine and Paul-Joseph know so *many* people . . . it's hard to keep track!" She laughed to indicate how little the whole matter meant, then distracted Jean-Louis with polite inquiries about his sister, who was about to be married.

She resolved to catch Cathérine for a moment and ask her about this strange man. Better yet, she had to contrive to dance with him later. She was sure Cathérine would introduce them. If she forgot, Marie-Thérèse would hound her until she did. Men tended to talk when they danced, and what they generally talked about was themselves. Usually this bored her, but tonight she was burning with curiosity.

But after dinner, Cathérine seemed to have disappeared.

This was so strange, Cathérine disappearing from her own party, that Marie-Thérèse went searching for her, afraid she had been taken ill.

She was not anywhere downstairs; all the public rooms were full of people, and Cathérine was not among them. She was not upstairs in any of the bedrooms. In a last-ditch effort, Marie-Thérèse thought of the Temple of Music. This was a little pavilion at the far end of the garden, built in the manner of a Roman temple. Cathérine used it for musical afternoons with other ladies who were trained to sing and play, more charmingly than well.

As she climbed the steps, she noticed that the door was slightly ajar and the candles inside were lighted. She started to push open the door and call to Cathérine when she heard voices.

A man and a woman were speaking, quite agitatedly, but in soft tones. She recognized Cathérine's voice.

"I tell you, it makes no difference," Cathérine said positively.

"Why, Cathérine? Why this way?" the man said. He had a lovely, lush voice, with a trace of a foreign accent that Marie-Thérèse didn't know. "I taught you," he said with a little sadness. "I thought you understood me; you certainly seemed to live the way I taught you, at one time. And now, look what you've come to: vice and degradation. Thoughtless destruction. You're no better than a common murderer. You could have been glorious, and you've thrown it away."

Marie-Thérèse crept a little closer. She could only see Cathérine, not the man she was talking to, but she had never seen Cathérine so agitated. She paced nervously, unconsciously wringing her lace handkerchief between her hands, her perfect equilibrium thrown off. Nevertheless, her voice sounded brave. "I live my own way. I take pleasure in it. I'm not going to apologize for that!"

The man sounded disgusted. "Pleasure? Good God, Cathérine! And what kind of pleasure is that? I cannot imagine. . . ." His voice broke off.

The door was suddenly pulled open, and the Comte d'Apollonaire was staring at Marie-Thérèse. They stood that way for what seemed like a long time. With a quick, purposeful motion, he grabbed her by the shoulders and propelled her into the room before she could even explain that she hadn't been eavesdropping.

He thrust her in front of Cathérine, who looked at Marie-Thérèse in slight confusion, as though she had never seen her before.

"And what of her, Cathérine?" he demanded. "What becomes of her? Do you take her down that path with you?"

Cathérine made a visible effort at control. "Oh, leave her out of this, Apollonius. It has nothing to do with her. She's fine."

"It has *everything* to do with her, Cathérine. She has choices to make, and it's your duty to tell her what they are!"

Choices? This intrigued Marie-Thérèse, this very question that had been bothering her, the question of ethical behavior. What choices did he mean? She wanted to ask, but the situation didn't seem conducive to a discussion of that sort.

Apollonius looked gently at Marie-Thérèse, and ran a finger softly over her lips. When he did this, it seemed to Marie-Thérèse that she could feel it all over her body. She felt an instant bond with him; not love, but more than that. Stronger. She felt that he understood her, that he could teach her everything that Cathérine couldn't or wouldn't.

"What do you believe in, child?" he asked her.

"Why . . . ," Marie-Thérèse said, thrown off guard herself, "I believe in the Commandments, sir. I believe in being the best person that I can manage, although we all fall short of perfection. I believe in man's dignity."

"And justice? Do you believe in that?"

"Yes, I do."

He looked at Cathérine with a mix of triumph and annoyance. Then turned back to Marie-Thérèse.

"If you ever need me—and there'll come the time when you will," he told her, "then come to me. Even if it's a long, long time from now. I won't forget you, and I'll always welcome you."

Marie-Thérèse was mystified, but oddly comforted.

"Go back now, Marie-Thérèse," Cathérine said to her. "I'll join you shortly. The Comte and I are just having another installment of a continuing and unresolvable discussion."

For many days, the Comte's words stayed with Marie-Thérèse. She played them over and over in her head, as though by repeating them, she could divine some hidden meaning there, as if the words were code. Why would she need him? she wondered. For what? She had everything she wanted, more than she had ever had in her life. Come to him? At first that was cryptic: she didn't even know where he lived. But it was an easy matter to find out; it seemed that everyone knew his family's ancient house not far from the de Guiberts'.

After the first few days, Marie-Thérèse no longer tried to decode what he had said. She merely accepted it at face value. She was sure, though, that there was still a meaning there that would come clear when the time was right.

She never talked about that evening or about the Comte to Cathérine, and she certainly never mentioned it to Paul-Joseph. For Cathérine's part, she was obviously content to pretend it never happened.

A week later, Cathérine and Marie-Thérèse were running together. Marie-Thérèse had made her kill: a robust man driving an ox cart on a dark road. But all through the process, Cathérine seemed preoccupied, jittery with nervous energy.

They ran to a prosperous-looking farmhouse sitting silently among the fields. The occupants were asleep. Marie-Thérèse could separate the family by their scents: there were six, including the old grandmother and the baby. Cathérine motioned

Marie-Thérèse to be quiet, and the two of them slipped in through the front door.

This struck Marie-Thérèse as very strange, and unnecessarily risky. She knew it was possible to kill one of them silently, but why do it here, in the house, where the slightest miscalculation could rouse the entire family? The survivors would spread the alarm throughout the village and it would start a full-scale hunt for werewolves. That had happened in France several times.

Marie-Thérèse's uneasiness grew. Cathérine, on the other hand, seemed excited, jumpy; she kept picking up common household objects and examining them as if she'd never seen anything so wondrous: pots, crockery, a chair cushion, a carved wooden rosary, which she dangled from one claw in amazed fascination. Marie-Thérèse just wanted to get out and go: there was something terribly wrong here, and the feeling was getting stronger by the second.

Suddenly, Cathérine let out an ear-shattering howl, a roar that would shake the dead. Even Marie-Thérèse jumped in startled surprise.

The scent of fear came rolling down the stairs like a cloud of heavy smoke, striking both Marie-Thérèse and Cathérine at the same time. Marie-Thérèse had never felt it so strongly, perhaps because it came from six terrified people all at the same time. The father was the first one down the stairs, naturally. When he saw the pair of werewolves, he froze for a moment, and that was all Cathérine needed to drag him the rest of the way down. He clawed at the stairs, his nails grating on the wood, but it was useless. The scent, if possible, intensified. Marie-Thérèse almost fainted from the power of it.

When Cathérine got the man downstairs, she pinned him to the floor with one powerful hand. She slammed her other fist down first on one leg, then the other: Marie-Thérèse heard the familiar crunch of bones breaking. But Cathérine made no move to kill him. This was strange; why break his legs and leave him in agony? None of this made any sense at all.

Cathérine bounded up the stairs just as the wife was coming down, armed stupidly with a large cane. The wife saw her husband, moaning in pain on the floor, and stopped, stunned.

"Get back!" her husband cried to her. "Protect the children!"

She turned to run, but Cathérine caught her first. She picked her up and slowly crushed the life out of her, squeezing her rib cage, crushing her heart beneath the collapsing ribs, while her husband watched, paralyzed with fear and impotent grief. The woman's suffocating screams seemed to go on forever, dying out into agonized moans. She coughed once, an explosion of blood that splashed onto the white walls.

Marie-Thérèse was paralyzed with shock and disbelief.

When Cathérine started up the stairs, the man screamed. "Not my children! Please, don't hurt my children!"

This was too much for Marie-Thérèse. She ran after Cathérine and caught up with her just as she opened the bedroom door.

Two children and the old grandmother were huddled together in the bed, crying and praying. The children were both under ten. They started to scream when they saw Cathérine and Marie-Thérèse. The grandmother was babbling hysterically, and the children huddled against her.

"Cathérine," Marie-Thérèse pleaded, "you can't do this! How could you do it? Just take the heart of the mother and let's leave here!"

Marie-Thérèse knew that to leave the children fatherless would be the same as killing them.

But Cathérine didn't even answer. She was beyond all reason, staring at the children with eyes that were mad with blood. Marie-Thérèse had never seen her like this; she had become a complete, mindless animal. Cathérine swept aside the grandmother, cracking her skull with one sweep of her arm, and advanced on the screaming children.

"Cathérine! No!" Marie-Thérèse lowered her head to crash into Cathérine's midsection, hoping that the shock would bring her to her senses. She charged at Cathérine, who now held the little girl by the arm. But Cathérine sidestepped and smashed a terrible blow to the side of Marie-Thérèse's head. It was so strong and so sudden that Marie-Thérèse was temporarily blinded by it. She fell to the floor, stunned and barely conscious.

She was unable to get up, but she could hear the children shrieking as Cathérine killed them, each in turn. She could smell the blood, could hear the sounds as Cathérine extracted their small hearts, could hear the father downstairs, crying in anguish. She put her hands over her ears and howled to drown it all out.

And then she heard a tiny cry. The baby.

Oh, no . . . she wouldn't kill it, not a baby, not that little, helpless thing! Marie-Thérèse struggled to get to her feet, but was still too dizzy from Cathérine's blow. She managed to reach out and grab Cathérine by the leg, trying to pull her feet out from under her. She got a good grip and tugged, but Cathérine shook her off and slapped her hand away with a stinging blow. Marie-Thérèse got to her knees, groggy but ready to fight.

She was a heartbeat too late.

In the house, there was now only the silence of the dead, and the wrenching pain of the sole survivor.

Marie-Thérèse crawled to the stairs, and was able to stand up and maneuver her way down, holding tight to the railing. Cathérine was still upstairs, occupied with the bodies of the children.

When the man saw Marie-Thérèse, their eyes locked for a moment. She wanted to tell him . . . what? That she was sorry? That there was nothing she could have done?

It was a lie. She could have killed Cathérine, or she should have tried to.

As he looked at her, she saw the look that so many victims had: resignation. He was already mad, he had that vacant blindness in his eyes. She had no idea what Cathérine had planned for him, but she wanted to thwart her, whatever it was. Marie-Thérèse leaned over him as he whispered his prayers by rote, clinging to the only thing that had any meaning for him now. She put her hands on his neck.

"I'm sorry," she whispered. "Pray also for me when you stand before God." She twisted his head powerfully and swiftly to one side. He was dead instantly.

Cathérine was coming downstairs. Her face darkened when she saw Marie-Thérèse standing over the dead man, and Marie-Thérèse's look of unashamed triumph. For a brief moment, they stood like that, and Marie-Thérèse realized that she hated

Cathérine. She couldn't stand to look at her, to be with her, to see her covered in the blood of children. What she had done was beyond redemption, beyond anything permitted a werewolf. And she had done it for no reason, only because the brutality excited her.

Marie-Thérèse ran into the cool, cleansing night air. She was surprised to feel the cold stream of her tears—she never knew that werewolves were capable of it. The farther and faster she ran, the more her tears came, wetting her fur and streaming down her face. She had no idea where she was going, but the run was cathartic for her; the farther she got from Cathérine and that farmhouse, the safer she felt. It wasn't her physical safety she was worried about; she knew that Cathérine would have forgiven her for trying to stop her, but it was her own soul she wanted to save. She never, never wanted to kill like that. Better to die in a rain of sharp silver knives than to kill like Cathérine had killed tonight.

She ran until she found herself at an unfamiliar house. She stopped just at the door, panting in great, sobbing gasps. She dropped to her knees and began the transformation, the pain this time almost like a penance.

As it ended, she crouched on the ground on her hands and knees, drenched in sweat despite the night's coolness. She heard the front door open and knew that a man had stepped outside. The Comte d'Apollonaire.

She knew what he was.

Sobbing all over again, trying to catch her breath, she turned her head to look at him. "Why?" she demanded. "Why am I not like her? Why does her kind of killing repulse me?"

He said nothing, but wrapped her in his jacket and helped her to her feet. She leaned unsteadily against him as he guided her into the house.

"You'll never have to go back to her," he said positively. "You'll stay here, where all your questions will be answered. You'll learn another way of life, Marie-Thérèse, one with more purpose and with principle."

She buried her face in his shoulder and cried harder.

Apollonius had a bath drawn for her, and a warm robe and thick towels brought in. The patchouli-scented steam from the water soothed Marie-Thérèse as she settled into the tub. It was a lovely room she was in, very like her room at the de Guiberts'. The large copper tub sat in front of a marble fireplace, in which a fire danced hypnotically. Marie-Thérèse sat back and sighed. The flames seemed to be burning away all the horror of the night.

Apollonius rose to go, but she caught his hand. "Stay," she told him, "I'm not embarrassed for you to see me. And I don't want to be alone."

He looked doubtfully at her, but turned back. He sat beside her, settling himself on the floor beside the tub.

"You have so much you want to ask me," he said.

That was true, but Marie-Thérèse said nothing. She was aware of his watching her, and aware of the heat rising in her own body. She slid the creamy soap over her skin, sliding it slowly down from her throat as she tilted her head. She arched her back as she soaped her breasts, very slowly, never taking her eyes off Apollonius. She saw him close his eyes briefly, and saw his fists clench. She reached over the edge of the tub and took his hand, covering it with her own as she glided it over her body, over her breasts, and down between her legs. Without her encouragement, he moved his fingers briefly to tease her clitoris. It swelled and excited under his touch.

She knew exactly what she was doing. She wanted him from the first second she saw him across the de Guiberts' table, and he knew that. What better time than tonight, when she needed so badly to blot out the bewilderment that overwhelmed her. The familiar ritual of sex was the only thing she knew to do, the only comfort she could find. She could concentrate on her body and still the turbulent waters of her mind.

The look in Apollonius's eyes was everything she wanted. He moved his hand away from her pubis, and caressed her cheek gently.

But she had misread him.

"Your feelings are too confused now," he told her, "and to make love to you would be to confuse them further."

Marie-Thérèse didn't know what to say. She stared at him for a moment, then buried her humiliation in her hands. He lifted her face and kissed her.

"You think I don't want you, but you're very wrong," he told her.

"I don't understand!" she said desperately.

"It's more important now that I be your teacher, not your lover. I have so much to tell you, Marie-Thérèse."

She looked at him strangely. "Were you Cathérine's teacher?"

"Yes."

"And her lover?"

"No. I was never her lover."

"But she wanted you to be." This was a sudden insight.

"I don't know. Yes. I think so."

"Was it you who made her a werewolf?"

At this, a pained look came over him, as if the question were too complicated or too hurtful to answer. "No. It was someone else, someone I know well. But I found her shortly afterward. I thought I could save her, I thought I *had*. I know what happened tonight, Marie-Thérèse. I always know when things like this happen. You yourself are beginning to understand the werewolf's bond, that psychic connection that we all have. With me, it's stronger than in others. It's a curse sometimes, like tonight." He stopped and ran his hand over his forehead, as if it hurt him. "I knew she was playing dangerous games, I knew she was willful. But I never thought she could do this."

"But if you knew . . . couldn't you have stopped her?"

"No. I never interfere. To interfere would be to challenge destiny. I had no way of knowing that Cathérine's killing that family wasn't meant to happen. Or what the consequences would be if they lived."

But Marie-Thérèse couldn't see how something so monstrous was ordained by fate. She thought that if he could have stopped her, he *should* have. This argument about interfering with destiny was philosophical; what Cathérine had done had nothing to do with philosophy, and not stopping her—especially if you had the power to do it—was wrong.

"Who are you?" Marie-Thérèse asked. "I mean, who were you before this? I may be inexperienced, but I know how long a werewolf lives."

"My name really is Apollonius. It always has been, for all the centuries I've been alive, since the Roman Empire, when I was called Apollonius of Tyana."

This stopped Marie-Thérèse short. "Good Lord! The Pythagorean philosopher! I was reading about you—just last month!—in one of Paul-Joseph's books. But . . . how have you lived this long?"

"I can't die. Lycaon, the werewolf who gave me the kiss, was immortal, a demigod. I was a necromancer and magician and knew the darkest secrets of death. We are the only two werewolves who suffer the pain of living forever."

Apollonius sat very still, his eyes far away.

"He wanted, I think, an opponent, an adversary to keep him interested and make him strong. If you know about the Pythagoreans, you know about the Seven Hermetic Laws. According to the Hermetic Law of polarity, everything must have its opposite. For evil to flourish, there must be good; the opposite is equally true. So I am immortal, to provide the balance and to keep Lycaon from growing too powerful. He and I have fought this battle of ethics for centuries, and I'm afraid that the werewolves are our soldiers. Cathérine was one of his. You, by your act of conscience, are one of mine."

"I don't understand. How did I become one of yours? What does it mean?"

"All werewolves stem from the two of us, from me and from Lycaon. There's a genealogy that can be traced there. The werewolves he made begat others; so did the ones I made. And mine are predisposed to justice and principle. Lycaon's . . . well, you've seen what they can do."

"So we really don't have a choice? Heredity is destiny?"

"No. I said 'predisposed,' not 'preordained.' You wondered why Cathérine's irresponsible killing bothered you. It's because you were meant for better things, Marie-Thérèse. You were meant to kill in the name of justice. What is a werewolf, if not a force of nature and magic? And isn't it our duty to use our powers well? We must kill; it's our nature, as it is the nature of the bear or the lion or the shark. But we have human intelligence, human complexity. With it comes responsibility. And that responsibility is to choose our kills carefully. There are people who are evil. There are people who have no conscience, no love for mankind, no respect for life. They have made, or will make, life miserable for others. They will never nourish the earth, they will never benefit mankind, they will only hurt.

"And those people are the werewolf's kills. Killing one of these is a noble act, Marie-Thérèse; it exalts a werewolf, it confirms our purpose. On the other hand, killing the innocent is a disgraceful act, abhorrent to nature.

"There are those of us who regard lycanthropy as a wonderful gift and we would never do anything to degrade it. So we do what we must do, and we do it in a manner that does us honor. You instinctively understand the underlying principle of this. That's why you always preferred Paul-Joseph to Cathérine. Paul-Joseph is one of my werewolves."

Marie-Thérèse thought about that, and she knew he was right. Apollonius had recognized the kind of werewolf she was from the first time he saw her. He had known that there would come a time when she would not be able to stand Cathérine's way of life.

"Cathérine wasn't always this way, was she?"

"Yes. Unfortunately, she was. I taught her what I'm going to teach you, and tried to change her, and for a while I was successful. But Cathérine's nature was always wild and willful, and in the end, it overcame her. The veneer cracked. She was my greatest challenge and my bitterest defeat. Cathérine is one of Lycaon's werewolves."

"I still don't understand. Cathérine made me a werewolf. Doesn't that make me a child of Lycaon?"

"A werewolf always has a choice, Marie-Thérèse. That's what Cathérine failed to tell you. And you, out of instinct, chose a more responsible path. It was your nature. You were always a compassionate woman; it stands to reason that you would be a responsible werewolf."

Marie-Thérèse bit her lip in confusion. There was so much hidden here, so much she couldn't see. It was like one of those clever drawings that changes form when you look at it long enough; she couldn't tell which had the real meaning.

Apollonius put her hand gently to his lips. "Don't be confounded, Marie-Thérèse. Everything will become perfectly

clear to you. You'll live here, with me, and learn everything
I have to teach you. You'll run with me under the moon
and find a purpose and a new glory in the kill. You'll
understand why you're the kind of werewolf you are, and
you'll rejoice in it."

Marie-Thérèse looked at him in wonder. Apollonius: the
Pythagorean philosopher, the magician, the ageless wanderer
and the keeper of aeons of secrets. It was just beginning to
awe her when she considered who he was and how many things
he'd seen.

He stood up and held out an enormous sheet for her. When
she stepped out of the water, he folded it around her, wrapping
her in the linen and in the comfort of his arms.

"Just be patient, Marie-Thérèse," he told her, "your life
hasn't even begun to blossom yet."

In the months to follow, Apollonius's prophecy proved true,
like everything else he had told her.

He taught her about the Lunar Goddess, whom the Romans
called Diana Trivia, Diana of the Three Ways, and about Her
three aspects: Diana the Huntress, the Goddess of Creation;
Selene, who brings about solutions to all problems; and Her
darker aspect, Hecate.

Hecate, Apollonius said, was the Goddess of things hidden
and secrets held, the dispenser of justice, the Queen of the Dark
of the Moon. She was, and is, revered by the werewolves.

"We must kill, or we would die," Apollonius told Marie-
Thérèse. "It isn't because we like it. You know that the
moment of death is no pleasure to a werewolf like you.
But to change, to run under the moon in freedom and
euphoric joy, to feel our heightened senses and sexuality—
all that has its price. And its price is the kill. That's our own
darker aspect."

Marie-Thérèse came to understand that killing, a necessity,
could be offered in the service of Hecate, to mitigate the fact
of killing at all.

"That's why we have a heightened psychic ability," Apollonius said. "So we can judge without question who is guilty
and who is not. It isn't enough to take someone's word that

another man is guilty or innocent—we must know for certain. And so Hecate gave us this gift."

Werewolves like Cathérine, Marie-Thérèse discovered, were an abomination. They killed only for selfish, sadistic pleasure, disregarding the guilt or innocence of the victims. What was abhorrent about it was that the werewolf always had that choice, and Lycaon's werewolves chose murder.

"It may seem incongruous to say so," Apollonius told her, "but the werewolf respects life. We respect mankind. And in our way, we try to do mankind a service."

He also explained to Marie-Thérèse why werewolves are vulnerable to silver. "Silver is sacred to Hecate," he told her, "and only the Goddess can kill one of Her own. Silver never succeeds unless the Goddess chooses to make it so . . . however, I've rarely seen it fail."

At the next full moon, Apollonius took Marie-Thérèse with him into the night. Marie-Thérèse, used to Paul-Joseph's love-making before the transformation, had hoped that Apollonius would do the same, but it wasn't to be. As the change began, he took her hand and closed his eyes. Marie-Thérèse was amazed at the stillness in his tranformation: he passed through it quickly and serenely, not moving a muscle, as if there were no pain, no traumatic mental upheaval. And when her own change began, she felt anchored to his hand, a calm, warm energy flowing from his body to hers. It made the change— while not as meditative as his—much easier and smoother. For the first time, Marie-Thérèse was able to observe and appreciate the changes taking place in her own body, and it was a marvel to her.

Apollonius made a handsome werewolf. His dark pelt, shot through with silver strands, reflected the moonlight and reminded Marie-Thérèse of what he had told her about the Lunar Goddess.

Apollonius chose the victims that night, a pair of robbers and murderers who had committed several crimes and not been caught. Apollonius led Marie-Thérèse to a crude, one-room cottage, where the dim lights of cheap lamps flickered and smoked, filling the air with the foul odor of rancid oil.

"Use your power of smell," Apollonius whispered to Marie-Thérèse. "How many are inside? And tell me something about them."

She sniffed the air. A thousand scents of the night washed over her. Knowing what Apollonius meant, she made herself blot out the other scents and focus on the cottage. She closed her eyes and inhaled deeply, concentrating. Suddenly, two special odors stood out.

"Two," Marie-Thérèse said, then, as other smells enhanced the basic two, "and they've eaten . . . ah . . . mutton, and drunk too much wine."

Apollonius looked pleased and surprised. "Very good. You have unusual concentration for your age. Now, we need to know if these are indeed the two we want. I know they are because I have their scent from the scenes of their crimes. But how are you to know? Use your mind, Marie-Thérèse."

She closed her eyes again, but nothing came except the scents. He knew it immediately. "Blot out the scents, like you eliminated the others. Shut off your hearing, keep your eyes closed. The five senses are shut down. That leaves you with only one. Concentrate and use it. Use what comes into your mind and trust your vision."

She methodically closed off her other senses. Making her mind go blank was much more difficult; unrelated pictures and words kept intruding. But suddenly, a scene came to her with such force and clarity that she knew without doubt that it was true. She saw two men robbing an old gentleman, then sadistically beating him until he died. She could see the glee on the older one's face as he kicked the old man in the head, opening a bloody wound. She could see the casual evil of the other murderer as he used his knife on the man, cutting off his fingers to steal the man's rings. The picture was so clear that Marie-Thérèse knew she would never forget these faces. She also knew that what she was seeing were the murderers' memories. She opened her eyes so as not to see any more.

She turned to Apollonius in wonder and dismay. "I saw . . ."

"Oh, I know what you saw," Apollonius said grimly. "I told you, Marie-Thérèse . . . it's a gift, but it's also a curse. Let's not wait any longer."

Apollonius burst into the cottage, almost tearing the door off the hinges. Both murderers were sitting at a crude table, among the ruins of a mutton supper. Before they could scream, Apollonius picked the two of them up by the throat. He tossed the younger one to Marie-Thérèse, who caught him around the shoulders.

"You're going to die," he told the murderers. "If you know how to pray, confess to your God and ask absolution of your sins, for which you are about to be executed."

The man only struggled to tear himself loose from Apollonius's grasp. But in the extremity of his terror, his arrogance asserted itself. He produced a knife out of his pocket and plunged it into Apollonius's chest.

Marie-Thérèse, horrified, let out an agonized howl. She immediately snapped the young murderer's neck and tossed his body aside to run to Apollonius.

"Take him," Apollonius said. Marie-Thérèse held the man tightly, pinning his arms to his side. Apollonius looked down at the knife protruding from his body. Taking hold of the handle, he pulled slowly until the knife was out. He stared balefully at the murderer.

The murderer began at once to babble. His face was chalky pale, his eyes huge with fear.

"Move your arm, Marie-Thérèse," Apollonius said. She moved her arm away from the man's chest. In a movement almost too fast to see, Apollonius stabbed him through the heart. He slumped against Marie-Thérèse, who let him drop to the floor.

"Apollonius . . . your chest . . . we have to do something!"

He took her hand in his and pressed it over the wound. She could feel that it had already closed.

"The knife wasn't silver," he told her. "If it had been, I'd be dead by now. As it is, there'll be no trace of this wound by morning. Remember, no matter how terrible it looks, unless it's caused by silver, a wound never really harms a werewolf."

"Did it hurt?"

He was amused by the childishness of the question, and smiled. "No. It didn't hurt, it was only uncomfortable. But we must finish off these bodies. We'll take the hearts and go, leaving the bodies as warnings to murderers."

"But Paul-Joseph taught me never to leave evidence of a kill"

"And he was correct. But these were notorious criminals and were killed in accordance with justice. These bodies are meant to be found."

Marie-Thérèse needed no instruction on how to take and consume a heart. But a few minutes later, running into the night, she asked Apollonius to stop for a moment. "I feel so very strange," she said.

"And how is that?" he said, smiling at her.

"Wonderful! I usually feel good after the kill, but . . . this is different. More exciting! As if my blood were on fire!" She couldn't stop herself from laughing. "I feel . . ." She thought a moment. "Satisfaction."

"That's what it is, Marie-Thérèse, to have killed in the name of justice. You've fulfilled an important purpose. You've just done what a werewolf was born to do. You should feel satisfied with yourself: you did very well tonight."

"I want to change back. Now."

He looked at her strangely, but took her hand through the transformation. When it was over, she pressed close to him, her lips against his skin. The pure delight of his nakedness warmed her, the sight and scent of him inflamed her.

"I love you," she told him. "From the first time I saw you, I knew it was supposed to be that way. I felt a bond between the two of us, something mystical that I didn't understand but I knew was right. All these months with you have only convinced me that I was right." She sighed and nestled closer to his chest. "Don't make me wait any longer, Apollonius."

He stroked her hair. He knew what she meant, and he couldn't lie to her. He, of all people, knew about the werewolves' bond. It was a tie forged in inevitability and sustained through complete fidelity, something stronger than love. It was what every werewolf waited for, that mating between two bodies and two souls that lasted for life. It was a joy and a completion of the werewolf's life.

And of all the world's werewolves, only Apollonius couldn't accept it.

He had lived too long. Through all those centuries, he watched mankind make the same mistakes, over and over. He had been a philosopher, a lover of man and nature, with optimism for the future of the human race. He had hoped, within his endless life span, to be able to watch the blossoming of humankind, as each generation learned from the mistakes of the previous one. Instead, they repeated them. Nothing changed. And Apollonius at last learned the real meaning of immortality: despair.

At first, after three or four hundred years, he thought he'd go mad. Then he learned to protect himself by closing off his emotions, one by one. It took an enormous effort of will and a hundred years of training, but he did it. He could watch dispassionately as the tragedies that led the Roman Empire into ruin were repeated in Europe. He watched the worldwide hysteria and horror of nine million people tortured and killed for witchcraft and he steeled himself into a cold blankness. Three hundred years of sadism and mercenary motives disguised as Christianity finally laid to rest the lingering ghosts of his optimism.

He looked around him now, at the vast discrepancy between rich and poor in France, and could predict what was going to happen—could almost predict exactly when. He doubted that the monarchy would last into the next century, and he was certain that the end, when it came, would be cloaked in the kind of righteous indignation that made atrocity acceptable. The indifference of the rich toward the poor was about to bear bitter fruit, ripened in blood and in anger. He could read the future because he'd lived the past so many times.

All he could do was look away. Compassion would destroy him, and his passivity was his salvation.

It was his burden that, along with his other emotions, he had also destroyed his capacity to love.

But Apollonius wanted to feel. He wanted to regain the fire of emotion that he once had, and that is so perfectly catalyzed by love. But it was much too late. Even he, who had the gift of resurrection, could not resurrect his own soul.

He wanted to explain all this to Marie-Thérèse, but what would he have expected of her? What did he want her to say? He didn't want to lose her, but he could never give her what she had every right to expect of him. It was indeed the werewolves' bond between them, and it would last for the rest of their lives, but it was Marie-Thérèse's great misfortune that it was Apollonius she loved. His misfortune was greater.

He tightened his arms around her and felt her slight movement against him.

"Marie-Thérèse," he told her, "if I could love, if I were capable of it, it would be you. But I'm not capable, I don't love. I've forgotten how."

She drew back and looked at him, and the look in her eyes caused him more pain than he thought he could feel. "Everyone can love, Apollonius. In this, I can be *your* teacher."

"To someone as young as you, everything is possible. But optimism loses its illusion after as many years as I've lived. Just take what I have to teach, Marie-Thérèse. It's all I can give you."

She shook her head. "I won't take your word for that." She reached up to touch his face. He turned his head and pressed his lips to her palm. She moved closer to him and felt his beginning erection under her hand.

"You aren't as dead as you thought," she said lightly.

"I never said I couldn't fuck," he said with a casual brutality. "A werewolf can always do that, no matter what. It doesn't mean love. If that's all you wanted, I could have done that from the first night I saw you. *Is* that what you want?"

She stepped back, hurt, and he hated himself for doing what was necessary.

"If that's all you have to give, then it's what I'll take," she said quietly.

Confused and angry, and not at her, he turned away, toward the house. He broke into a fast, cleansing run and never looked to see if Marie-Thérèse was behind him.

The next morning she was gone. In the days to come, he discovered that Marie-Thérèse had proven herself more perceptive than he was: his carefully crushed emotions were not all dead.

*   *   *

She went to live in Venice in the Palazzo Giuliana, a guest of the prince and princess, friends of the de Guiberts. Marie-Thérèse quickly became one of Venice's most charming women, renowned for her changeless beauty. There was a sadness to her, lying just under the laughter, that gave her beauty a mysterious depth. She was courted by several Venetians of good family, but she didn't want a foreigner, she wanted a Frenchman. A year later she met Pierre Louis Alexandre de la Rochette, the Duc de Marais. She married him out of loneliness and melancholy, and because he loved her. She realized that her own capacity for love was becoming as dead as Apollonius's, and if she didn't do something about it now, she'd never experience it again.

Alexandre came along at a good time. Marie-Thérèse admired Venice and was happy there, but was a Frenchwoman to her core. She wanted to go home. She missed Apollonius desperately, but was afraid to admit it to herself. Being in France would at least make her feel closer to him, even though seeing him was out of the question.

Back in France, Marie-Thérèse and Alexandre preferred their country house to court life, but living near the king was a political and social necessity. She kept her lycanthropy a secret. Marie-Thérèse prudently limited her transformations to the full moon, when she could travel to the country place, but it was getting harder and harder. The few kills she permitted herself had the effect that one drink has on an alcoholic; the taste drove her wild with the hunger for more. That and her boredom with the gossip and shallowness of the court was driving her mad, and one night she couldn't stop.

Disregarding everything she had been taught, she plunged into an orgy of killing, culminating in a careless kill too close to a village. One of the villagers shot her through the shoulder. She knew she wouldn't die, but Marie-Thérèse had never been injured before, and the sight of the gaping wound and the cataract of blood terrified her. When she transformed back into human form, it looked even worse. She made it as far as her own doorstep, then fainted.

She was found by the servants, cleaned, bandaged, and put to bed. Both the doctor and Alexandre were summoned.

The irony of this, Marie-Thérèse thought with unease, was that for the first time, the kill hadn't satisfied her. Neither had the transformation, something she usually loved. To kill like that, mindlessly and without thought of justice or honor, left her feeling degraded and unnatural. She thought of what Apollonius would have said, and was deeply ashamed. She had made four kills that night in a frantic orgy of despair, and on the fifth attempt she was shot.

But already the damaging stories were circulating; how the villager had shot at an abnormally large marauding wolf and wounded it in the shoulder. Servants who lived in the village carried the tale of the duchesse's wound and her odd appearance on the doorstep at dawn. The whispers of "loup-garou" were everywhere.

Alexandre was furious when he heard these stories. Most incriminating was the fact that by sundown the next night, the duchesse's shoulder was healed, with only a slight redness marking what had been a frightening wound.

Marie-Thérèse found that Alexandre was as blind to his wife's imperfections as Paul-Joseph had been to Cathérine's. He attributed her recovery to her youth. Despite his efforts to quiet the stories, they reached the ears of his political enemies; hence the charges and the trial.

And now she languished in prison. Because of Alexandre's money and influence, she was comfortable there: she had privacy, a carpet and a feather bed, rich food brought in from her own cook—which she shared with the other prisoners—and books to pass the hours. But she was unable to read or to think coherently. She couldn't concentrate. A crowd of thoughts, tumbling into her mind one on top of the other, kept her frantic and distracted. She couldn't even turn them off at night, and so was weakened by lack of sleep. Alexandre visited her every morning and stayed as long as he could, either consumed by grief or furiously making wild promises that he would join her in Louisiana or get her back to France as soon as he had ruined the bastards who had put her in this position.

She thought constantly about Apollonius, about what he'd taught her, about the feel of his hair, the warmth of his body, about what she'd tell him now if she could. She berated herself for leaving him: she now felt that she should have stayed and tried to make him love her. She should have had the patience to wait him out until he overcame his fear of love. She should have accepted him as he was. She wondered if he knew what was happening to her.

Most of all, she simply missed him.

Marie-Thérèse couldn't forget about the werewolves' bond, and how it never fails, so she wasn't surprised when the jailer announced a visitor.

"The Comte d'Apollonaire," the jailer whispered to her through the bars.

She was so relieved to see him that all she could do was burst into tears.

"Marie-Thérèse," he said, "why is it that every time we meet, you're in tears?"

"Apollonius, I'm so afraid!"

"Of what? What could hurt you?"

She stared at him as if he were insane. "What could hurt me! Good God, I'm in prison, I'm being shipped to a wild country that I know nothing about, I'm leaving all the security I've ever had . . . my entire life is falling apart."

He took both her hands. "Listen to me. You must stop thinking like a woman, Marie-Thérèse, and start thinking like a werewolf. Security? You need nothing. You're a creature of earth and wind; all you need is to run free in the night. You know how to kill to live. You've let this civilized life drain the power out of you, but it will all come back when you need it."

"How can I be sure of that?"

"It's enough that I'm sure of it, and that you can trust me."

But Marie-Thérèse was very doubtful. "I've always had someone to take care of me. Cathérine, you, Alexandre."

"Yes. And you never had to take care of yourself. But I know you, Marie-Thérèse. I know you have an independent soul, and that being on your own will make that spirit rise.

Don't be afraid of Louisiana, or of any new place. For years, centuries, I've wandered the world, never staying anywhere very long. But every new place had something to teach me, every incarnation made me richer in my soul. It's not a bad life, the wanderer's life."

She shook her head. "It's not for me. I like to be settled. And I don't know that wandering has made you a better man, Apollonius. I think it's left you isolated and cold; you have no close friends, you have no lovers, you cut your ties before they're forged. I believe that you suffer, but you don't even recognize the pain."

He drew back a little and turned his face away from her, going to stand at the tiny slit in the wall that let in a glimmer of light. His hands looked very pale as they rested against the gray stone.

"I won't argue that with you," he said quietly.

She got up and stood behind him, putting her arms around him. "You have your life ordered in the way that it's best for you," she said, "and I have no business trying to change it. But I want you to do something for me, Apollonius, since I know that you'll never see me again."

"Don't say that, Marie-Thérèse. Our paths will cross again."

"No. I don't *want* them to cross. I've learned something from you about self-protection, Apollonius, and being far away from you is *my* self-protection. But for all I know, my life may be ending in Louisiana. Or I could be discovered and killed on the voyage there. Whatever happens, I want you to make love to me before you leave me. I once told you that if that was all you had to give, then I would take it. And I still want it."

He turned around to hold her.

"The werewolf's bond only comes once, Apollonius. Only once in our very long lifetimes. I want to know what it feels like, so that I can remember it through all those years I may have left to live. And if I don't have them, I don't want to die without knowing."

As he kissed her, he picked her up and she settled her legs around his waist, wrapping him in her body. Their undressing was a slow, delicious discovery; she was delighted to find him so strong, his skin so youthful, but she remembered that he had been only in his forties when he was made a werewolf. That and his immortality had preserved the perfect tension of his body. Then Marie-Thérèse was overcome with a fierce emotion, and the heat of their lovemaking was cooled with the sorrow of loss.

A week later, Marie-Thérèse found herself on a ship to Louisiana. Again, the Duc's influence had accomplished a few conveniences: Marie-Thérèse was allowed to travel as a paying passenger with a cabin of her own instead of being consigned to the prisoners' belowdecks hold. She had been allowed quite a few trunks and, although they had been searched, she had a small fortune in jewels sewn into the hems of her clothes.

The journey to Louisiana was a nightmare. The full moon brought her none of the usual joy, only the terror of being discovered. She locked herself in her cabin at the transformation, muffling the sound through a supernatural effort of will fueled by fear. When the other passengers were asleep, she crept along in the darkness and caught a young sailor unawares, the kill coming quickly and painlessly. She dragged him to a secluded area where she hurriedly ripped out his heart and consumed it, then heaved him overboard as lightly as a lady might toss a withered rose. The kill was only a necessity, a means to live, and was unsatisfying and humiliating. Thoughts of Apollonius and her promise to kill for justice only deepened her despair.

She stayed mostly in her bed for the rest of the trip, miserable with frustration, with shame for Alexandre's pain, and from a sense of loss that would not abate. She thought about what Apollonius had told her about her independent spirit and wondered when it would assert itself. She didn't feel independent; she felt abandoned.

Along with these feelings was another, and one that Marie-Thérèse couldn't identify or explain. An expanding restlessness, a feeling of something waiting to start or waiting to end, a harbinger of change. It wasn't just the voyage to Louisiana, it was the feeling that something was waiting for her there, something she had to do that would either complete or destroy her life; she couldn't tell which. Sometimes there was a muffled excitement connected with these thoughts, sometimes terror. The fact that it was so elusive maddened her: she liked things clear cut and decisive, to know what she had to do and then do it. This sense of her life being suspended between the past and the future was driving her insane.

Marie-Thérèse hadn't thought much about what Louisiana would look like, but when the ship docked and she had her first look at the colony, she was shocked. She hadn't expected Paris, but New Orleans was even cruder than the poorest French village, a collection of rough houses made of mud packed between hewn cypress posts. There were no streets; only bare logs laid in the gluey mud in the most haphazard pattern, so that a traveler might have at least some hope of keeping his feet dry some of the time.

What fascinated her was the wilderness surrounding the outpost, the miles of dense forest and swampland in which she might run as long and as far as she wished. She began to feel a little excitement.

The governor of the colony greeted the ship, along with most of the male population who were waiting for the female convicts to disembark. These men had been anxious for wives, and even though the women were not frail flowers of good families, they were still of sturdy French stock and convicts were certainly preferable to celibacy. The men had been here long enough to know that hothouse ladies wouldn't last five minutes in this rough country, but the convict women were tough minded enough to take it, and wouldn't mind work.

When Marie-Thérèse started down the gangplank, Governor Bienville himself offered her his arm. "I have had many letters on your behalf, madame," he said, "and be assured that the deplorable injustice you suffered in France will not be held against you here."

Marie-Thérèse could see that putting on her court airs wouldn't help her tremendously here in the colony, and especially not with this man. She had been told that Bienville genuinely loved this wild place and wished desperately to see it prosper. That meant hard work for everyone, and there was neither the time nor the resources to cater to the rarefied whims of the aristocracy. It was almost a relief. Marie-Thérèse had been a peasant in aristocrat's clothes for too long; perhaps that was at the root of this nameless dissatisfaction. Perhaps that's what Apollonius meant about her true nature asserting itself.

"Why, thank you, Governor," she said, "your gallantry disarms me." She gave him her most beautiful smile. "I have to admit that if one must leave the luxuries of France, one might as well devote one's energies to carving a civilized place out of difficult country. I'm sure I'll find it most exciting as time passes."

Bienville seemed delighted to hear it. "I've taken the liberty of arranging a house for you," he said. "I'm afraid it's nothing like you would expect, but it's one of our best. The duc assures me that he'll be sending furnishings and appointments for you on the next ship."

"Actually," Marie-Thérèse said, considering, "all that space in the hold might be better spent on tools and necessities for the colony. I know the king's financial support isn't nearly enough. Just tell me what you need and I'll be glad to write to my husband."

There, she thought as she accepted Bienville's gratitude, that ought to silence any loose talk about me that might drift over from France.

The house was small, but quite comfortable, fitted out with a few essential pieces of serviceable furniture. The one luxury, Marie-Thérèse was surprised to see, was an elegant four-poster bed. Its hangings were only of homespun fabric, all that was available here, but the mattress was made of soft feathers and covered with smooth cotton ticking.

Marie-Thérèse thanked the governor profusely. When she pleaded exhaustion and Bienville left, Marie-Thérèse took stock of her house. She had lived in better, of course, but she had also lived in worse, and no house in New Orleans was any more elegant than this one. She was actually beginning to feel good. In this new world she could be free of the conventions that had governed her life for the past few years, the need for caution and circumspect behavior. It was almost like shrugging off a heavy cloak.

She wondered what she would do here, where she would fit in. Everyone had some kind of work to do, but all she knew how to do was dress hair. She doubted that would be much help.

Two months later she found that her duty had been decided for her. She was pregnant. The news both elated and worried her. Of course the child was Apollonius's, but would the colonists believe it was Alexandre's? And what about Alexandre? Word would surely get to him that she was pregnant, and he would undoubtedly know it wasn't his. Or, if his memory for time and events was a little lapsed, the idea that he was having another child would send him here as soon as he could book passage. It was this last that worried her the most. She had come to realize that Apollonius's prediction was true: she liked being on her own; she didn't want to be a sheltered, pampered child anymore.

At the full moon three weeks later she made her decision. Just before moonrise, she walked into the swamp and kept walking, so that when her transformation finally came, she could howl her joy and relief without reservation. She began to run, pushing herself farther and faster, feeling the moon on her back goading her on. She would live as a werewolf, not transforming back, until her child was born. By then, she would have learned enough to fend for herself, and she and her child wouldn't have to go back to the colony.

A light in the darkness distracted her, a campfire glowing on the bayou. She crept closer, her curiosity outweighing her hunger. Gathered around the fire were eight or ten men of a sort that she had never seen. They were tall and dark, and braided into their long black hair were feathers and stones and beaded amulets. They wore almost no clothes, and sat around the fire meditatively.

Instead of attacking, Marie-Thérèse stared in wonder at these men. One stood slowly and his eyes went straight to the spot where Marie-Thérèse was crouched. The others followed his gaze. It seemed to Marie-Thérèse that they called to her. Almost without will of her own, she moved into the circle, the fire throwing glints of light onto her glossy fur.

The standing man indicated that she should sit with them.

Marie-Thérèse was confused. The men acted like loups-garous but they weren't, not precisely. They knew they were perfectly safe with her, and that she knew they were to be protected like her lycanthrope brothers and sisters. But who and what were they? She crouched in the circle and waited.

She couldn't understand their language, but she saw the clear pictures the standing man projected into her mind. They were the Indians she had heard about in New Orleans, the Bayougoula tribe. They had been friendly and cooperative with Bienville, and visited the colony often, but Marie-Thérèse had never seen them. The standing man was the religious leader, the healer, the teacher and magician, and these particular men were also holy men.

As Marie-Thérèse watched, the men transformed one by one, not into creatures like Marie-Thérèse, but into wolves, bears, alligators, owls, serpents. Later, she would learn that their forms were determined by their souls. They were brilliant, beautiful, a magical light around them shining in the darkness. Their shapes were perfect and strong, magnificent animals in the purity of spirit. Only the leader, the shaman, did not change, staying with Marie-Thérèse as the others scattered in the night, some to kill to feed the tribe, others to commune with the spirits that governed their shapes.

The shaman spoke to Marie-Thérèse in the crude, but free-flowing French that the Bayougoula had learned in their contact with the colonists.

The ground they were on was sacred, the shaman explained, protected by the spirits of past shape-shifters and great shamans who were buried here. Here, they were free to change without fear of interference, for the spirits watched over them and drove away intruders.

"You also have a guardian spirit," the shaman told Marie-Thérèse, "but you haven't made the attempt to learn from it. Without the guidance of the spirit you have power but no wisdom. You fight your battles alone and then wonder why the struggle is so hard and why your life of freedom leaves you so unsatisfied. You have a mission, a purpose, but you haven't found it."

The knowledge that he was right, and that he had pinpointed exactly what was wrong with her, struck Marie-Thérèse with the force of the truth.

"You have a strong will," the shaman told her, "and we can learn much from you. But there is much you can learn from us. You need to listen to the spirit, you need a home among those who understand you, your child needs protection and love. We offer you a home."

Marie-Thérèse was not even surprised that he knew these things.

"I would like very much to stay with your people," she told him.

"It's the child of the Man of Light that you carry," the shaman said.

Marie-Thérèse didn't understand what he meant.

"The Man of Light," the shaman said, "a wanderer who came to us generations ago, long before the time when the tribes scattered and became many tribes. This Man of Light had no name, but was a great shaman and shape-shifter. He passed through this country as he had passed through many others, gathering wisdom and sharing what he learned. He taught the Bayougoula, but he also learned from us."

From this, Marie-Thérèse knew that Apollonius's lifetime of wandering had taken him here at one time. How long he had traveled, and how far, she thought, and how much wisdom he had gathered. And still, he had never learned to love, the simplest and most universal emotion.

The Man of Light had also given the long-ago shamans a terrible prophecy to be passed down, a portent of great sorrows to come. The Europeans would come, he had told them, seeking not wisdom but gold and power, and to that end they would offer the tribes lies disguised as friendship. The resulting battles to protect the tribes' homelands would be bloody and useless, the bravery of the warriors would be looked upon as mere savagery. The learning and traditions of the tribes would be ridiculed. The Bayougoula and all the tribes of the continent would be dispersed, driven from their birthright, left to die until the shamefully few who remained would serve as a reminder of the arrogance and greed of the intruders. The Europeans would grow rich and have good lives, and with the tribes whom they had dispossessed they would share nothing but disease and death.

The Bayougoula had extended friendship to the European invaders, but they could see the seeds of the prophecy in the condescending way they were being treated, as amiable but backward children.

Marie-Thérèse grieved for the already-foreseeable fate of these wise and gentle people. She could see that they were becoming fixed in history as memories of a lost way of life.

She stayed with the Bayougoula from that night. The colony assumed she had strayed into the swamp and become lost. When search parties were unsuccessful, Bienville wrote to the Duc de Marais that his wife was dead. Marie-Thérèse felt a deep sadness for Alexandre, but it was only right that he be free of his ties to her.

As much as she had learned of the material world and the joys of the flesh with Cathérine and Paul-Joseph, she learned of the spiritual pathways of the Indians. She did indeed learn control and discipline. Even more important, she learned self-reliance. Marie-Thérèse, who had all her life been under the protection or guidance of others, now learned the heady power of being able to take care of herself.

Of all the things that would carry her through the vast stretches of time she had to live, the most important was the concept of justice. She had never forgotten Apollonius's training, and it seemed that he had also made a deep impression on the Bayougoula. They knew all about the loup-garou, although there were no loups-garous in Louisiana except, now, Marie-Thérèse. But the loup-garou was one of the tribe's cherished totems, half-animal, half-human, combining the spirits of both. This made the loup-garou a powerful entity. They believed that the loup-garou, with its supernatural gifts and psychic abilities, was able to tell the difference between the innocent and the guilty, and would avenge the tribe when wrong was done to it. The loup-garou, the shaman told her, has a duty to see that justice is done.

It wasn't hard to see where the Bayougoula had picked up *that* bit of philosophy, Marie-Thérèse thought.

Marie-Thérèse finally found her work in Louisiana. She became the tribe's loup-garou, their arm of justice, and as the old colonists left or died, as the government of the colony changed, as new and more opportunistic Europeans came to Louisiana and encroached closer on the Bayougoula, smothering them and crowding them out, taking advantage of their open natures and most often treating them as idiots or inferiors who didn't deserve courtesy or thought, Marie-Thérèse meted out justice.

The elation she felt from that first kill for justice, when she ran with Apollonius, was repeated every time. It never faded, never wore thin, never became dull with familiarity. Each time was as exciting as the first time, and Marie-Thérèse gloried in it. She vowed to herself that when her child was born, she would dedicate it to Hecate, Queen of the Dark Moon, and that the minute it was old enough, she would make it a werewolf. She knew that her child was meant for it, she could feel the pull of the moon on her growing belly in a way she never felt before she was pregnant. It wasn't for her, it was for the child, and it gave her a deep satisfaction.

The child's birth was a great event for the tribe, attended with much ceremony and preceeded by many oracles and divination. The child of the Man of Light and the tribe's loup-garou was going to be welcomed into the world with love and care. Marie-Thérèse had three midwives hovering over her, while outside the hut there was drumming and chanting for the protection of mother and child. The hut had been sanctified with smoke and prayers so that the birth could take place in sacred space.

Marie-Thérèse had an amazingly easy time of it for a first birth, so the midwives told her, and her son was born without incident. Immediately after tying the cord, the midwives swept the child outside and displayed him to the tribe, and to the spirits of the earth and sky. Marie-Thérèse didn't even see him until this important step was taken for his protection.

She and her son lived among the Bayougoula for another five years. But she had learned all that they had to teach her, and she had given them all that she could. She loved them, and had loved living among people whose bond with the earth and the spirits made them better people, more ethical and moral, than any she had known. But she had begun to miss her own people, and she realized that her stay with the Bayougoula had been, in part, an unwillingness to face living as a woman alone in a world where that was suspect. From the Indians, and from her own inner resources, she had learned to vanquish fear and to take a strong hold on her destiny. She doubted that the world had changed, but she took great pleasure in the fact that she had.

When Marie-Thérèse and her son returned to New Orleans she was a different woman. But then, New Orleans was a different town. A few of the settlers she had known were still there, but many had left, died from the periodic yellow fever scourges or just plain worked themselves to death. Other new-comers, just as eager to build new lives and new fortunes, were pouring into the city. This New Orleans was well on its way to building its glittering reputation. The Marquis de Vaudreuil was governor now, and he had imported the good life from France: the elegant houses, decoration, manners and styles; the parties and entertainments; the corrupt city government. The city was earning its own way, building more elaborate houses. Real streets had been planned and laid out, with the center of the city being the Place d'Armes and the cathedral. The Mississippi was becoming a major asset in the New World, and New Orleans was right in the heart of it.

No one remembered Marie-Thérèse. She was assumed to be one of the recent arrivals, a young widow with her little boy. She could invent her own history and reinvent herself, as she had done so long ago in Venice. This time, however, luring a rich husband was the last thing on her mind.

She still had the jewels she had brought from France, and with the new longing for luxury in New Orleans, there was a seller's market. She built a house on Royal Street and began to settle in to the life of the city.

She decided to shed all the heavy baggage of the past, and so she took a new name, a frivolous name, Zizi, a name that signified nothing and carried no expectations. She never told her son who his father was, since his knowing that would mean nothing. She assumed that Apollonius would be just as unable to love his son as he was unable to love her, and she wanted the boy to be *her* son, hers alone. From the time he was old enough to understand, she had explained about the werewolves, and had let him watch as she transformed. She took satisfaction that the boy was never afraid and understood the role of the loup-garou from the very beginning, and when she found him drawn outside under the full moon and staring up at it in rapture, she was jubilant. She made him a werewolf when he was only eight, and he was more than ready for it.

The only thing missing in her world was the companionship of her own people. She knew how to remedy that. In Louisiana, a new world and a new realm of possibilities, she would create a community of loups-garous, werewolves who would understand and live by Apollonius's principles of justice. It was also her tribute to the Bayougoula, who had taught her so much, and her gesture of keeping the tribe alive in spirit as they were slowly exterminated. And at the most sacred time, at the full moon, when a loup-garou acknowledges his obligation to the Moon Goddess, the loups-garous would gather in comradeship and reverence at that place sacred to the shamans and shape-shifters, now known as Bayou Goula.

PART
FIVE

†

The Loup-garou's Ball

15

In the middle of the nineteenth century, Gallatin Street was the nastiest hellhole in the state of Louisiana, if not the entire Gulf Coast. It was a filthy stretch of street only two blocks long, from the French Market to the Mint, but in those two pitch black blocks there was a universe of perversion, depravity, and murder. The river men and sailors who patronized the smoky saloons and barrelhouses of Gallatin Street were a brutish lot, but the whores were even tougher. The clap was the least of a man's problems on Gallatin Street; here, sex was best performed standing up and with a razor in one hand. This was the place where the six-foot redheaded harlot Bricktop robbed and roughed up more men than she fucked, and she could fuck fifteen of them in thirty minutes. This was the place where a man could start walking down at one end of the street and come out the other without his money, his clothes, or all the bodily parts he was born with. This was the place where a man could take a drink as a respectable lawyer and wake up as a shanghaied sailor on his way to the West Indies.

And this is the place, now, where everybody gathers for the weekend flea markets, a sunny street with the touristy shops of the French Market at one end, and the beautifully restored Mint at the other. Only one thing stayed the same: you could still start at one end and come out the other without any money. Outdoor tables and stalls crowded the street, and you could find anything from antique lace hankies and old silver to fluffy purebred Chow puppies, looking like scowling teddy bears with wise eyes.

Sylvie was looking at some lavish old hats when she looked up and saw a figment of her imagination looking back at her from across the street. She had seen those green eyes and that blond hair before, in a dream, the night she had disappeared from the crawfish boil at the lake and he had carried her home.

That half-forgotten feeling of being warm and safe flooded over her again, but this time, seeing him in broad daylight when she had thought she had dreamed him, stopped her cold. She felt a fast rush of sexual longing that she had never felt for poor Quentin—or for anybody else—and then wondered at the imprudence of it. If there was one thing she didn't need right now, it was to get involved with somebody. She didn't even have her life screwed on straight.

Well, that's rushing it, she thought. I don't even know this person and I'm daydreaming already. This is some hunk I saw on the street one day, and when I had that weird hallucination, it was his face that filled in the blank.

She had to find out why this man figured in her memories. Against her better judgment, she started across the street, with no idea what she'd say to him.

He looked indifferent as he watched her thread her way across the jam of vendors and booths, but when she was almost there, he shook his head, frowned, and almost turned over a display table getting away.

Sylvie took this as an omen.

Consumed with frustrated curiosity, she continued shopping but her heart wasn't in it. She bought some old lace for Zizi, an elaborate antique gold watch fob for Gabriel, and several bottles of homemade herb vinegars for Christian, who loved to fool around in the kitchen.

She waited in line at La Marquise to pick up some pastry, still upset and still trying not to think about that strange man.

Someone cleared his throat behind her and she turned her head slightly to look.

It was her anonymous friend.

"You've annoyed me beyond all belief," she said in a quiet, fierce voice, mindful of the other people in line. "Who the hell *are* you?"

Her unexpected reaction had obviously driven whatever opening line he'd had right out of his mind, and he was too stunned to think of another one. All he could get out was, "Lucien Drago." He looked as though he might say more, but he gave her another intense look and bolted again.

Just then, the clerk called her number. Sylvie looked over the counter, confused. "Oh. What?" she asked the lady.

"That's what I was gonna ask you, daw'lin," the clerk said. "What you gonna have?"

But she knew that name, and now she knew that face. Lucien Drago. He was a composer, mainly of opera. She had watched him conduct his work twice, once at a premiere in Houston and again in New Orleans. There was no doubt that he recognized her, but not from the performances: she hadn't gone backstage. So what did he have to do with her?

"You okay, miss?" the clerk said. "You look like you just seen a ghost."

"Maybe I did," Sylvie said, considering it.

Callou had waited for two hours to see him, two hours' work that she had to miss and two hours' pay, but she knew it would be worth it. When Papa Lucifer heard what Callou had to tell him, he'd reward her well.

Callou was a cleaning woman for several people in the city, but the one that Papa Lucifer told her to watch was Zizi. See who went in, who came out, whether anybody new came around. And now here was this young girl, supposed to be the daughter of a preacher, staying at Zizi's with those two boys around. Callou knew what went on between Zizi and the young men, and she didn't consider it a wholesome thing, the three of them acting like lovers—and sleeping in the same bed, more often than not. She didn't think it was right, bringing a young girl into that house of corruption. Callou squirmed on the little chair in the foyer of Papa Lucifer's house and shredded a couple of tissues.

She remembered when this had been the Reverend Mother Pauline's house, before the Reverend Mother died. Most of Mother Pauline's people followed Madame Mae now, and congregated at Mae's house on Dauphine Street, but some, like Callou, had decided to follow Papa Lucifer. After all, he was Mother Pauline's grandson, no matter what Mother

Pauline had said on her deathbed. Besides, Papa Lucifer had told them that Pauline hadn't meant it, that Madame Mae had put a powerful gris-gris on Mother Pauline when she was sick and confused. It had never crossed Callou's mind as to why Papa Lucifer couldn't remove the bad gris-gris, if he had the power he claimed to have.

Callou had always loved Papa Lucifer, way back when he was simply the Voodoos' bamboula dancer. At the meetings, Callou was mesmerized when Antoine had leaped into the circle of worshipers, his smooth body gleaming in the firelight, his powerful muscles shimmering under a slick gloss of oil and sweat. As the frenzy of the dancing mounted, Callou's favorite moment was when he spun past and touched her. No man that handsome had ever touched Callou before, or even paid the slightest attention to her. So after Mother Pauline died, when Antoine, now Papa Lucifer, came to Callou and put his hands on her cheeks and told her in that silky voice that she was one of his Chosen, there was nothing she wouldn't do for him. He even knew about her little secret vice, the fondness she had for that certain powder that made her feel so fine.

When Callou had imparted her information to Papa Lucifer, he had smiled slowly and had told her she had done the right thing and to keep on doing it. He kissed her forehead and told her that she could have a wish come true. Brother Leon had escorted her politely outside and handed her a small bag of powder and a powerful gris-gris for pretty dreams.

Antoine leaned back in his chair and considered what he'd just heard. When he'd heard the girl's last name, he was slightly stunned. Andrew Marley's daughter. He was slipping; he should have thought about the Marleys the very first thing.

A long time ago, when Antoine was just a kid, Andrew Marley had come to Mother Pauline for help, trying to break the curse that *la Reine Blanche* had placed on his family.

There could be only one reason the girl was at Zizi's: she's a loup-garou like her father. But has she had her first transformation? If not, she's still ignorant about what she is, and that makes her vulnerable. His grandmother had told Antoine how the loup-garou who cannot change suffers, how they sometimes appeal to the Voodoo queens to help them by giving them the magic ointment and performing the old rituals that will set them free, that will bring about the transformation they must have.

Antoine knew that he needed this girl. He needed the power she could give him, the status she would confer, and the innocent soul she could provide. She must be made to believe that Antoine was her only salvation, and when the time was right, she'd give him everything he wanted.

16

"Let me tell you how I became a loup-garou," Achille said to Sylvie. "Maybe it will help you to understand how things work."

They were sitting in Zizi's courtyard, surrounded by palms and bright flowers, listening to the calming splash of water in the fountain. They sunned themselves lazily and sipped icy lemonade laced with grenadine from tall, frosted glasses. Every once in a while, Christian or Gabriel would bring a pitcher of refills out and silently pour, slipping back into the house. If something caught their attention, they'd stay and listen for a few quiet minutes.

"When I was a child," Achille said, "practically still a *bébé,* I was fascinated by the moon. Every once in a while my mama would tuck me into my bed at night, only to find me in the morning asleep on the big screened front porch. I'd gone out there to watch the sky until my eyes got too heavy to stay awake. I used to feel that the moon was alive, that she knew my secrets, that she saw a part of me that no one else could see. And I was right, *chérie;* you know the feeling because you feel the same, yes.

"But there was something else, too: a savageness to my nature, not just the usual rowdiness that boys have, no; this was something primitive and raw that chewed at me from the inside. I saw things no other child noticed, I was aware of scents, of tracks across soft grass, of sounds far away. And I knew about sex without anyone ever having to tell me. I wanted it before the other kids knew what it was. That's why you see a lot of young loups-garous with human lovers much older than themselves: we start earlier. It's our animal nature, yes."

He caught sight of Sylvie's sudden flush and laughed gently. "Don't you be embarrassed, *'tite fille*. I got to tell you the truth. And if we're going to talk about the nature of the loup-garou, sex is an important part of it."

"I'm not embarrassed about that," Sylvie said. "I'm just amazed that we're so much alike. I thought I was the only person in the world who felt like this. A freak. I used to think I was insane, that it was only a matter of time before I exploded."

He could well imagine what she had gone through. A girl like Sylvie, born with her advantages, living in a glass house of parties, social events, charity work. Smiling and trying to fit the mold, fighting down her feelings at every turn. And inside she was terrified because she knew—ah, God! How clear the signs must have been!—that she was not like the others in her circle and never would be. Damn her father! Andrew had to have noticed the signs, but he never said the words that could have helped her. He was so busy denying his own past that he didn't notice his daughter's present hell. Rather, he *noticed;* he just hoped it would go away.

Achille lifted Sylvie's chin slightly and looked into her eyes. "Ah, Sylvie. Please don't cry. Everything gonna be all right for you soon. Now you want to hear the rest of my story?"

"More than anything."

"Well, I'm gonna tell you. So . . . the feelings got stronger. And other things started to happen as I got older.

"One time I was with a bunch of other boys. I was about twelve or thirteen then. There was this old house out on the bayou, everybody said it was haunted. Nobody'd lived in it for a while and it looked pretty bad. I tell you how bad it was, *chérie;* you know how ramshackle a bayou house can get; you can't keep paint on them things and the rain always comes creeping between the boards and into the chinks. And that's the high-rent district, yes. Well, this one had a 'condemned' sign on it, so that gotta mean it gonna fall down on you if you blow on it. But me and my friends don't care. Going into that house meant you were a man, and whoever stayed in there the longest was the most macho of us all. I tell you, *'tite fille,* I didn't want to go in there. All my life I'd heard how old man

Bréaux went crazy and killed his whole family in there. And at night you can hear 'em crying and moaning and looking for someone to take back to Hell with 'em. Ooo-*wee*! I was about to wet my pants, me!

"So we all troop in and settle down, smoking cigarettes and talking tough. Soon night falls and everybody gets a little nervous. But me, all of a sudden I wasn't scared anymore. In fact, I started to feel good.

"But there was something strange going on. 'Hey, John,' I says to my friend, 'what's that funny smell?' He says, 'Don't worry 'bout that; 'Polite's mama made him red beans for lunch.' Everybody laughs and the smell fades.

"Then dark falls for real and it's getting black as the swamp night in there, and the smell comes again, stronger than before. Nobody else seems to notice it. But I feel powerful and excited, like a million little stars are starting to glitter in my blood.

"The wind picks up and the branches scratch against the roof. One of the boys jumps up, terrified, and the smell by this time is overwhelming. And then I notice something. As the smell gets stronger, *I get stronger*, more excited. I look down and I got an erection like no twelve-year-old ever had. But more than that, I find out I can see in the dark. It's like somebody was turning up the light with a dimmer switch, brighter and brighter. But I can tell that my friends can't see or smell the same things.

"Well, I can't sit still. I want to run, to holler, to howl! I can see myself running across the bayous, chasing my friends and laughing like hell as they get more scared. It was almost uncontrollable.

"You know what it was, Sylvie? The smell was the smell of my friends' fear. Every loup-garou knows it. It's what prods you on, makes you chase, makes you kill. Young loups-garous are savage killers: one or two a night won't satisfy them. As long as the smell of fear floods over them, they can't control themselves. They could wipe out ten men in a single night. And they wouldn't be quick kills; they'd be as slow as possible, to prolong the fear and the scent. The death itself is fairly fast, but a loup-garou knows that the chase is everything, toying with the prey, doing battle in a doomed war. That's why a werewolf's preferred kill is a strong man, one who can fight. As long as they're alive, the scent rolls over us like a wave of pure ecstasy. It's the most powerful drug in the world, Sylvie, and the most addictive."

"I don't understand, Achille," Sylvie said. "If it's only the scent you want, why kill them?"

He hesitated only a moment. "A werewolf has to feed. At least once a month, at the full moon. It makes us strong—and it keeps us alive. Sylvie, you must understand this: *we're not human*. We look the same as everyone else, and when we aren't changed we have what we call for lack of a better term, 'human lives.' But we're not really part of the human world anymore. And the physical reaction to fear, the hunt, the kill . . . that's part of our particular reality. We kill because we have to, and we also do it because we want to. That's a hard fact, Sylvie, but one you have to face."

Sylvie's eyes were enormous and bright, her face flushed with a strange, embarrassed excitement.

"You've felt this, eh? This strength that comes from fear. And you had no idea where it came from or what it was. This is something every loup-garou has to learn to control, sooner or later, and it's the hardest thing we deal with. The degree of control is what makes all loups-garous different: some of us have worked long and hard to learn it. But you *have* to learn it, you have to discipline yourself. Otherwise, you're a mindless killing machine, and that's not what we're about."

"What are we about?" she said.

"Justice, Sylvie. The kind of justice you don't find in the world, you find among the werewolves. We're very fundamental creatures, very simple. We know the difference between right and wrong, and we know who's guilty and who isn't. The Voodoos know this. That's why we've been part of their legends forever, and why they come to us when ordinary justice fails. And I believe in justice. I believe in the turning of the great wheel. That's why I became a cop."

"Yes, but how did you become a werewolf?" Sylvie asked.

The memory made Achille laugh. "Ooo-*wee*! You gonna love this story, little one, but you gotta keep an open mind! It's pretty raunchy, but I'm gonna tell you everything, yes!

"Like I told you, I knew I was a loup-garou very young in life. When you grow up on the bayous, all your life you hear stories about the loup-garou: how he changes under the moon, how the loups-garous gather on sacred ground at Bayou Goula, how they run in the night. Most kids were scared by that kind of talk, but me, I loved it. I thought how wonderful it must be to be a loup-garou, to be free like that, to have the power.

"So after that night in the haunted house, I kept thinking about how I was different from my friends. I thought about it for three or four years. I read everything about werewolves, most of it, I know now, useless. One thing was clear, though: if I wanted to become a loup-garou in truth as well as in mind, I had to have the kind of help you don't get from books.

"Now, there are three ways to become a loup-garou. The most natural and the most exciting is the *baiser du loup-garou,* the werewolf's kiss. That's how most loups-garous are made. Ah, it's a beautiful thing, little one," Achille said wistfully, his eyes misting with pleasure and longing. "It's the most precious gift we can give, and we give it very carefully. Werewolves are very attuned to one another and we never fail at spotting our own kind. Even if, like you, they don't know what they are. But *we* know, and we can feel their pain, like we felt yours."

"You knew about me?" Sylvie said.

"Oh, yes," Achille told her. "The werewolves' psychic bond is like radar: we always know when another one of us is in trouble, or if there's something wrong. In fact, one of us, a young man with incredible powers, has been—this is hard to explain—I guess you'd say he's been kind of 'tuned in' to you for a long time. Sometimes he's almost crazy with it. He went out looking for you several times, even though we tried to discourage him. He didn't know specifically who you were, of course, but he knew there was a loup-garou out there who needed help."

"You should have let him find me," she said bitterly.

"No, *'tite fille,* I couldn't do that, for both your sakes. He's too impetuous and you're too ignorant."

She bristled and Achille laughed.

"Don't you look at me like that, no! What I mean is, you need to learn our ways first. That young man would have jumped on you and given you the werewolf's kiss quick like hell! He's an impulsive boy, and he loves the loup-garou's life. But you got to make your own choice. That's one thing I promised your papa. Now, what was I telling you?"

"The werewolf's kiss," she said, somewhat mollified.

"Yeah. Well, our genetic material is carried in our saliva and our blood. And when we bite you and give you a little of our blood, you become a werewolf. There are no accidental werewolves, like in the movies. When we bite, it's either to kill or it's the kiss. And the kiss is a very deliberate action. If, for some ungodly reason, a werewolf is interrupted during a kill and the victim lives and changes—and that almost never happens—we search him out and offer him the chance to learn our ways and truly become one of us. If he refuses, we kill him. We have no choice, although we never willingly kill one of our own. That's an act that is totally repugnant to the loup-garou. Remember, we're pack creatures: our survival depends on our protecting each other. But we can't leave a rampant killer loose out there: it's too dangerous for us all. He would never learn to control his hunger, he might not take care to hide the evidence of a kill, and he'll talk, sooner or later."

"Why won't loups-garous kill each other? I mean, what if some psychopath became a loup-garou by accident?"

"I didn't say we didn't do it, I said we don't *willingly* do it. We're very social animals. By that, I mean that the pack is very important to us, the family. The whole community of werewolves is bound by trust. No loup-garou got a private life, no! Oh, our human lives are our own, but as loups-garous, each of knows what the other is up to. It's not only a safety measure, it's our way, our nature, to revel in each other's company, to share our joy in our strength and freedom. A solitary loup-garou is a tragic thing, little one. We try to limit our numbers and keep close."

Gabriel came out of the house with another pitcher of lemonade.

Achille shaded his eyes against the sun and looked up at the pretty boy as he set the lemonade down. "Gabriel, where y'at? Sit down here and tell Sylvie how you met the beautiful Zizi."

Gabriel looked a little uncomfortable.

"He don't like this story, no," Achille confided, "because he still can't believe he did it and it gives him chills."

Gabriel gave Achille a very sour look. "This was while I was still a human," Gabriel said. "I was going to school at LSU in Baton Rouge. Well, one weekend, I was hunting out near Bayou Pigeon, trying to take down a couple of birds. I had been out there all day and the sun had gone down, so I was on my way back to my car. I heard the shots from another hunter, only it sounded like a much more powerful gun. I figured somebody was shooting at gators. All of a sudden, I saw this beautiful golden wolf run right past me, or at least, I *thought* it was a wolf, but it was bigger and ran upright. Now, that would have scared anyone, but I got the distinct impression that the wolf wouldn't hurt me. And I also had the funny feeling that this wolf meant a lot to me.

"A minute later, this big ugly Cajun—no offense, Achille— comes roaring out of the trees with a huge rifle. He stops, he lets out a long string of swear words, and starts to reload. That's when I notice that he's loading silver bullets.

"The first thing that flashes through my mind is loup- garou! The hunter raises his gun, sights down the barrel, and is about to get off another round. And that's when I shot him. I had no idea why until it was over, but I took his gun and his silver bullets and threw them into the water.

"I ran back into the trees after the wolf, and there was this righteous babe: a stark-naked blond, with tits out to *here*." Gabriel threw back his head and laughed. "I tell you, she was every hormone-ridden college boy's dream! But when I looked closer, I saw she had a nasty gunshot wound in one leg and I was furious. I was so glad I'd shot that bastard.

"I took her home, drove her all the way back to New Orleans, and just never left her. She knew I was a loup- garou, deep inside; that's why I had helped her, why I had felt so close to her. And after a while, she gave me the kiss. It was the most wonderful thing that ever happened to me."

He got up. "And that's it." Gabriel leaned over and refilled Sylvie's glass, then disappeared back into the house.

"We protect and love our own, it's the foundation of the loup-garou's life," Achille said. "That's why the werewolf's kiss is given very cautiously. I'm told that, to the person who receives it, it's an unbelievable experience, that even sex pales alongside it, but I can't imagine that, no."

"You never had it? Then how . . . ?"

"I never did, and it's one of the great regrets of my life. No, when the time came, I went to the Voodoo woman. That's the next way to make a werewolf. The greatest Voodoo woman in Louisiana at that time was the Reverend Mother Pauline. Pauline was a good woman with a kind heart and more magic than you can imagine. She spots me for a loup-garou the minute I walk in the door of her house.

" 'You want the ointment, eh, Achille?' she tells me, and I don't even know what she means.

"She looks real hard at me. 'You want to learn the ritual that will make you a loup-garou.'

"Me, I'm amazed that she knows exactly what's in my heart.

" 'I'm not gonna help you,' she says, and I feel sick. Then she rings a little bell and in walks the most beautiful girl I'd ever seen. She's a little younger than me, sixteen or seventeen, and looks like she's about half-wild. She's got skin the color of café au lait, and long black hair like a Gypsy.

" 'Mae,' Pauline says to her, smiling a little, 'what do you think this young man wants?'

"The girl walks over to me like a cat walking around china plates on the table. She looks right into my eyes and into my soul. 'Loup-garou,' she says, not looking away. It makes me nervous like hell and, if you want to know, hot all over. She's a *very* beautiful girl. She knows how I feel and she laughs.

"Mother Pauline says, 'I'm too old to give you what you want, but Mae can, if you ask her nicely and give her what *she* wants.'

"Well, I'm confused. 'What does she want?' I say, but I tell you, I'm ready to give her anything. She looks in my eyes again, just like before.

" 'What if I said I wanted your soul?' she asks. I don't even hesitate before I say it's hers if she wants it.

" 'You meet me tonight at Bayou Goula,' she tells me, 'and we'll both be satisfied.' I must look scared because she bursts out laughing. 'Don't worry,' she says, 'I don't want your soul. I need something else from you. You be there tonight if you have the courage.'

"She doesn't say what time to meet her, but I'm out there as soon as the sun goes down. The longer I wait, the more like a fool I feel, and I wait a long time. Finally, about eleven o'clock, here comes Mae, carrying a big straw bag and sashaying along like she's going to watch the boat races on the river. By this time, I'm shaking all over, I'm so scared. I wanted this all my life, and it's not that I'm having second thoughts, it's just that I know that my life will never be the same again, and I'm not sure what's going to happen to me. This girl is standing there so cool and confident, and I'm a nervous wreck. She knows it, too.

" 'Calm down, Achille,' she says with this smug little smile, 'I'm not gonna hurt you. So what are you scared of?'

"She drops the bag on the ground, then bends over to rummage around in it. When she does this, she makes sure to lean way over, facing me so I can see down the front of her dress practically to her toes. So now I'm scared, nervous, excited—and horny. She looks up at me. 'Take off your clothes,' she says.

"For some reason this makes sense to me, so I do it. And she stops very still and just watches me. All of a sudden, I'm not scared, nervous, or excited anymore, but I'm sure as hell still horny, yes, and getting worse by the second. When I'm done, she reaches in the bag and pulls out a big jar of what looks like honey.

"Her voice gets very solemn. 'Now you're ready, and we'll begin. Achille, you're sure you want this? You know what it means to be a loup-garou? Because all I do is get you started. After this, you'll be a loup-garou all your life, no going back, and it's gonna be a long one.'

" 'I was born a loup-garou,' I tell her.

" 'If I do this for you, you know you have an obligation to me. Just one thing you must do for me whenever the time comes. And what I'll ask you to do will be to kill someone.

It won't be for revenge, and it won't be out of anger, but it will still be a kill of my own choice, for my own reasons. I may never ask you, but if I do, you won't be able to refuse. Can you live with that?'

"For some reason, I trust her. I'd never met her before in my life except that afternoon at Mother Pauline's but I know I can trust her, that she'd never ask me to do anything I couldn't agree to.

" 'I can live with it,' I say.

" 'Then close your eyes and hold very still,' she says, coming over to me with the jar in her hand. In a minute I feel her touch, light as a cotton dress, sliding something all over my chest. 'This is the magic,' she whispers. Her voice is low now, serious and smoky, intoning some chant I can't make out. Just the sound of it calms me, or maybe it's something in the ointment. I found out later that I only had to touch the ointment lightly to my wrists, ankles, head, and heart, but Mae's doing this for her own amusement. She slips the stuff all over me, slowly. Just the feel and the heat of her hands arouse me, and for one minute, I actually forget why I'm there. There's no spot her hands don't miss, and I mean *no* spot. Her hands close around me and move slowly up and down, sliding, then squeezing, her fingers firm, then fluttering.

"I moan and start to move, following her hands. I can't help it. 'Don't move,' she says softly and firmly. It isn't easy but I stay still, even though the pleasure of what she's doing is driving me insane. I found out later that she had done me a great favor; the pain of the transformation is much easier when you're aroused, I don't know why.

"Then her hands trail away. 'Open your eyes, Achille,' she says. She caps the jar and puts it back in the bag. 'I'm going to leave you now, and the rest of it you have to do on your own. Not even the Voodoo who creates one can control a loup-garou, and if I stay, you might kill me. The change is going to come strong on you, and you won't be able to control yourself yet. But it will be the way you want it, Achille, it will be more wonderful than you ever dreamed it could be, more wonderful than anything you've ever known. Look at the moon.'

"I do, and it almost blinds me. I have never seen it looking more beautiful. It looks human to me then, a goddess of light reaching out her hand to me. I want to cry, not from sadness, but because I'm so happy, fulfilled, like I've made a long journey and can see home just over the hill.

" 'When I leave you,' Mae says, 'wait a few minutes and you'll know what to do. The moon is about to become your mistress, Achille, and if you love her and if you're faithful, she'll give you a life you never thought you could have.'

"She stretches up on her tiptoes and kisses me quickly. 'That's your last kiss as a human being. Good night, loup-garou,' she says.

"She leaves the jar and the bag for me, and I watch her disappear into the darkness. When she's gone I do just like she tells me: I crouch in the grass and wait.

"It happens fast. Suddenly I feel an agony like nothing I've felt on this earth, a pain so bad it drops me to my knees, screaming. Then . . . this is so hard to describe, but . . . the pain is still there, but it's also . . . something besides pain. It's almost as if the pain is a birth-agony, something you have to endure because you'll be changed after it. Since then, I've wondered if caterpillars feel like that, changing into butterflies. I feel like every muscle in my body, every nerve, is being stretched and changed. The ends of my fingers start to tingle and burn as they lengthen. The surface of my skin heats up as the pelt starts to grow. But in the middle of this, I begin to feel a great strength, growing every second. The pain becomes pleasure so intense I can hardly move, and continues for what seems like eternity. I can hear my own voice laughing, crying, gasping for air. The slow, orgasmic intensity builds and builds, stretched out into an unimaginable rapture. You're aware of nothing else; even now, I'm not sure how long it takes to change, in terms of actual time. Then, like a balloon filled too full, it bursts over me in an explosion of power. My senses clear and I feel more alive than I ever have before.

"I am a loup-garou now, in body as well as in spirit. Half-man, half-wolf, more powerful than either, faster, more cunning. I have supernatural powers. I can see for miles in the dark, every little detail comes clear. I can smell a million scents and will learn to differentiate between them all. I can move almost as fast as I can think. And I have a strength that's truly frightening.

"I'm not immortal, but I'll live for hundreds of years, the moon's gift to her lovers.

"And inside my head, precise and clear, I hear the other loups-garous, who know that they have a new brother. They rejoice with me, and welcome me. I hear them in my mind even before I see them coming to join me on that sacred ground which has always been the loups-garous' home since Louisiana was wild and young.

"Ah, Sylvie! At that moment, I realized that my real life had begun! And I've never regretted it, not a minute."

Achille seemed lost in his memories, and Sylvie sat awed, joy and jealousy bubbling together in her soul. Even after this, she had a million questions she burned to ask.

Achille smiled. "So that's the story, 'tite fille. How do you feel about the loup-garou's life?"

The emotions boiling around in Sylvie were too frantic to permit her to form the questions she really wanted to ask.

She grabbed his hand, her voice a tight whisper. "It's the life I *want,* Achille. And the more I stay here, the more I'm sure."

A slight scowl, mixed with an emotion Sylvie couldn't read, passed over him. "Give yourself a little more time, 'tite fille. Time is something you can afford, yes."

They sat in silence for a few minutes, sipping lemonade and enjoying the river breeze.

"That's how you do it?" Sylvie said. "You use this ointment, and somebody gives you a hand job?" She frowned. "Pretty sexist, Achille. So what's an innocent girl to do?"

Achille burst out laughing. "You better ask Mae about that one! She's the Voodoo expert. No, the ritual and the ointment are only . . . well, they're like bicycle training wheels. They ease you into the transformation, make it happen until you learn to control it on your own. It's not like the kiss, where everything happens at once. After a few times, you can transform at will, any night you like. But after the first time, after you're a true loup-garou, you change at the full moon, whether you want to or not. Of course, I can't imagine a loup-garou *not* wanting to, but it's out of our control on those nights."

"You said there were three ways to make a loup-garou. What's the third way?"

Achille grew serious. "It's the worst way, little one, a sin against God and man—and a sin against the werewolves, too. You can become a loup-garou if someone puts a curse on you. It's very rare, but it's pitiful when it happens. You listen to me about this, Sylvie, because it's why we're being so careful with you.

"Your papa is a man of peace, a gentle, religious man who never wanted to do anything but good. And because a bad woman cursed his family, he became a werewolf. It killed his father and it almost killed him. Cursed people don't understand what's happening to them and the physical transformation is a horrible, agonizing experience. They aren't meant for the life, and it's sacrilege for them to be living it.

"They feel only the pain and guilt—to them, the kill is murder. They don't understand our ways, they don't know about justice. They change only at the full moon and they kill because they have to, they can't help it. They refuse the company of other werewolves so they have no one to teach them how a loup-garou should live, and because of that, they die."

"But don't you kill them? Like you kill those people who were bitten?"

Achille shook his head. "We don't have to. They never live very long; they either get themselves killed or they end up suicides."

"But my father didn't die," Sylvie said, a little proudly.

"Because he was persistent and he was lucky. He broke his curse. Nobody's ever done that before, not as long as there have been werewolves in Louisiana. The loups-garous hold your papa in awe, a little. Even if we don't agree with what he did, we do understand why he did it. He wanted another life so badly that he gave up his real freedom for it. Don't believe him entirely when he tells you he hated the loup-garou's life: he might have balked at killing, but there were things about it that were part of him down to his bones. He was a true loup-garou and the Marley curse was only incidental.

"That's why you must be sure you want the life, little one. The thought of passing the curse on to his children was one of your father's most terrible nightmares. His time as a loup-garou was unendurable, so for him to send you to me and Zizi was a supreme act of love. If you choose our ways, it will break your father's heart because he'll never understand it. This is your burden, Sylvie, to show him that, to those truly born to it, a loup-garou's life can be the only one worth living."

17

Three weeks after she had come to stay with them, the loups-garous decided to take their new disciple to Bayou Goula with them. "This is it, little one," Achille told Sylvie. "The loups-garous' *fais do-do*, the werewolves' ball on the bayou. Now, don't you expect to hear no Clifton Chenier music or nothing, no," he said. "Instead of fiddles and accordions, we got howling and moaning."

"Yeah," Gabriel said, "it ain't Tipitina's, but it does sound good to us."

"Let's sit over here under this old tree," Achille said, leading Sylvie to a moss-swagged cypress and spreading a blanket out for her. "We'll get to meet everybody and you'll be comfortable. Now, *'tite fille,* you gonna see some things that might scare you. Or they might not, who knows? But don't you worry because you're perfectly safe. In the first place, you're with me and I'll stay with you for as long as you want to stay. I'm not planning on changing tonight, so anytime you want to go home, you just tell me. In the second place, nobody would do you any harm because you're one of us."

Sylvie laughed. "I'm not scared, Achille! I'm excited!"

Achille hugged her. "That's my little sister. You a good girl, daw'lin."

"Look!" Sylvie said, pointing. "Zizi's ring!" And indeed, many of the gathering loups-garous wore the gold-and-silver symbol of the Krewe of Apollonius.

People were gathering in little crowds, stopping by to speak to Achille and meet Sylvie, catching up on gossip and news. Sylvie was struck by the easy banter of the werewolves, their half-serious sexual teasing, their talk of what the night would

206

bring. Some people were already beginning to disrobe in anticipation of the transformation, stuffing clothes and jewelry into
bags and duffles.

"Aren't they concerned about their stuff getting stolen?"
Sylvie worried. This seemed to be the funniest thing Achille
had heard all night. "Daw'lin," he explained, "this is Bayou
Goula. All Louisiana knows what would happen to somebody
who lifted something from a loup-garou. This place is safer
than the vault at the Whitney Bank."

"Why here, Achille? I mean, why is Bayou Goula the loups-
garous' sacred ground?"

"It was sacred ground long before we got here, little one,
before the French colonists. When Iberville traveled down
the Mississippi, the first people he met were the Bayougoula
Indians. This is where the Indians buried their special dead,
their shamans and shape-shifters. When the first loup-garou
came to Louisiana, those spirits guided her here."

"The first one?" Sylvie asked. "I just thought the loups-
garous sort of . . . well, just happened."

"No, little one. Remember what I told you about how other
werewolves are made? There were no loups-garous here until
1722, when Zizi came. She was a loup-garou then, and she
made others. Zizi was the first one; she's the mother of all
Louisiana werewolves. Most of the loups-garous don't know
that, and that's exactly the way she wants it. You know Zizi;
being venerated as some sort of loup-garou goddess is much
too serious for her."

"Why did she tell you?" Sylvie wanted to know. "Was she
after your hot bod, or what?"

Achille pulled back and scowled playfully at her. "Ooo-*wee*!
You sure gettin' into the swing of things, yes! A month ago you
just an innocent little preacher's daughter and now you hanging
out with the loups-garous and talking nasty!"

Sylvie laughed. "Just my real self coming out. It never could
before."

Achille took in the surroundings. "Anyway, loups-garous
sometimes like to come here, not just for the big gatherings
like this, but alone, to listen to those old spirits and think about
what it all means. Yeah, I spent many hours out here, me, when

I was very young, thinking things over. You can sit here all by yourself, under the moon, and get the feeling that all the Indians and the loups-garous that have ever been here have left something for you. I first met your papa out here, yes."

"Really?" Sylvie was surprised. "What was he doing out here? I mean, he wasn't exactly comfortable being a loup-garou, was he?"

"When he first became a loup-garou he went to Mother Pauline for help. She sent him out here, mostly so he could get his head on straight. He was this close to suicide. Pauline was a smart woman, 'tite fille, she knew that what he really needed was to know himself a little better. So he shows up here one night and what does he find? Me. I was out here myself to do a little thinking. I had just changed when I became aware of someone watching me from the shadows, and sure enough, there was your papa looking bewildered. He'd never seen another loup-garou, and he'd sure never seen the change come on like that. You remember, I told you that when a cursed person transforms, it's just plain agony for them."

"Doesn't it hurt, the transformation?"

"Not if you really love being a loup-garou. You welcome the pain and you learn how to use it. But a cursed loup-garou doesn't exactly look forward to his transformations. Well, I didn't recognize your papa right away for what he was, so I charged at him, mad as hell that someone had invaded our grounds." He laughed and shook his head. "Your papa look like he suddenly changed his mind about wanting to die, because he was *scared*—ooo-*wee*!—was he scared! I'm flashin' them teeth and flexin' them claws and hollerin' and growlin' and I guess I look like the Day of Judgment to him. And then all of a sudden I know him." Achille looked a little mystified, even now. "I mean I *really* know him, not just that he's a loup-garou, but everything about him. That had never happened to me before, to bond with someone so completely, so fast. I knew he was a man in the worst kind of pain and I knew why.

"See, 'tite fille, this was your papa's problem: he was a true loup-garou. The curse had nothing to do with it, it was only a coincidence. But Andrew Marley was born a child of the moon, just like me. He'd felt the pull of the moon all his life and never knew what it was. In time, he might have come to us anyway, but when the curse took him, he'd already chosen a life that was completely incompatible with the loup-garou's.

"I tried to get him to accept what he was, I told him that it wasn't too late for him to join us. I knew what he was feeling; when he was changed, he enjoyed it, it was like nothing else in his life had been. And the next morning, confronted by what he'd done in the night, he was devastated. Another thing that happens to a cursed person is that, the next morning, the ghosts of their kills come to accuse them."

Sylvie gasped. The horror of it was unthinkable. "Does that happen . . ."

"No," he said quickly. "Not to us. A kill is just a kill, it isn't murder any more than killing a bird is to a cat. But when someone places a curse, Sylvie, it's so that the cursed person will be in anguish. And, God help his soul, Andrew Marley was certainly an anguished, tormented man. I tried everything I could to convince him that it didn't have to be that way, that if he'd stay with us and learn our ways and accept what he was that his life could have peace.

"The other loups-garous gathered around and tried to persuade him, especially Zizi. That was another case of immediate psychic bonding. Andrew and Zizi were meant to be together, they both knew it instantly. I told you how loups-garous are: once we find a true mate, that's it. As long as we live, there'll never be another one like that. And Andrew felt it, too. Zizi swears this isn't true, and that what they felt wasn't the werewolves' bond, but just an instant understanding of each other, like I'd had with him. But whatever it was, the minute Zizi touched him, he could feel in his bones everything I'd just told him. He could feel the power of the true loup-garou inside him. And he almost surrendered to it and accepted it.

"But at the very last minute, he broke away from us. We were all crushed, because we knew what was going to happen to him, what agony his life was going to be, whether he broke the curse or not. He would always know a little of what it was to be a true loup-garou, and what he had given up was going to haunt him forever.

"The ironic part was that if he had stayed with us, his curse would have been over in an instant. All the bad parts of being a loup-garou would have just gone away. If he'd *liked* being a loup-garou, it wouldn't have been a curse, would it? And he would have learned to control his transformations, to accept his kills for what they were. But by that time, nothing could convince him. He had been absolutely shattered by his experiences as a cursed loup-garou, and he clung to his faith like a dying man clings to hope."

Achille's shoulders slumped as he remembered that time. He looked so lost and so far away that Sylvie, sensing a pain in Achille that he would not name, said nothing.

At last he brightened and tugged playfully on Sylvie's long, red hair. "Hey, what for you make me so profound, eh? This is the loups-garous' ball, *'tite fille,* we here to have some fun!" He looked around at the gathering loups-garous.

The werewolves were gathering in all sorts of ways. Some came by car, although they had to get out and walk a couple of miles. Most arrived in motorboats or skiffs, singly or in groups, and the young daughter of one of the oldest Cajun families in Louisiana piloted a traditional pirogue, a canoe made of a hollowed-out log. Achille and the other loups-garous sent up a hoot of appreciation when she arrived.

"Look at that," Achille told Sylvie, "the pirogue's the most treacherous form of transportation devised by man, and that little ol' gal handles it like she was drivin' a Mercedes down Carrollton Avenue."

Another whoop greeted a noisy vaporetto, imported from Venice especially to tear along the Louisiana waterways without regard to life or limb. This one was filled with a half dozen raucous revelers, some of them without a stitch on. If Sylvie had thought that the gathering of the loups-garous was going to be a solemn occasion marked by secrecy and silence, this group changed her mind at once. Nobody could be as rowdy as Louisiana natives out for a good time.

"Ooo-*wee*! Darryl Dozier, you ol' swamp gator!" Achille greeted the vaporetto's pilot. "You know, you ain't supposed to be naked till you *get* here! What you doin' outside of Baton Rouge, eh?"

"Gettin' away from the legislature for a couple of days," the man said, tying up the boat. "Man, that Billy B's killing me." Billy was an infamous representative who, it was rumored, had gone far beyond the usual permissively corrupt political conventions. Everybody knew of his excesses, but a blue-ribbon committee couldn't seem to find any live witnesses. The man speaking was chairman of that committee. "Now, Achille, you know how it is in Louisiana: nobody minds when a legislator gets a little richer than he's supposed to. But Billy B is just way outta hand. All the funds for that low-income housing just seem to have vanished into thin air, ain't that a coincidence? And besides, nobody likes him. He coulda got away with a hand-slapping if he'd had any personality at all."

"Yeah, you right," Achille agreed, "Billy B sure ain't no Earl Long, I tell ya."

"Well, he must be pretty tasty after all this fattening up at the public's expense."

"Now, Darryl, you know you can't eat Billy B. He's got a whole term to go."

"Yeah, but I can sure as hell scare some information outta him." Darryl's eye settled on Sylvie. "Whoo-*ee*! Now look at this here," he said, kissing Sylvie's hand. "Achille, I believe this is the first time we ever had a Queen of Carnival out here on Bayou Goula. I bet them gentlemen from the School of Design'd just plain shit if they'd known the Queen was a loup-garou." He kissed Sylvie on the cheek. "Sure good to meet you, little sister. I knew your granddaddy real well. Now, don't you eat no registered Democrats tonight, you hear?"

"Holy shit," Sylvie said in an awed voice when Darryl had gone, "wasn't that the lieutenant governor?"

"Ain't life a bitch?" Achille agreed.

Achille and Sylvie moved around, greeting people, introducing Sylvie. One man wore a silver bullet on a chain around his neck. When Sylvie expressed astonishment, he told her, "Some crazy coonass took a shot at me! Can you believe it? He could have killed me! But he was such a bad shot the bullet lodged in a tree. I dug it out and now it wards off evil."

"What happened to the guy who tried to kill you?" Sylvie wanted to know.

The man grinned. "Hey, you only get one shot at a loup-garou, daw'lin."

A petite brunette, stripped down to a peach silk teddy and Maude Frizon shoes, bent over to unhook her baby blue stockings from her garter belt. Achille stepped back to admire the view. "Ooo-*wee*! Evangeline!" he said, impressed. "You hot tonight, babe."

"I came right from the office," she said. "Oh, Achille, I saw another woman on the street wearing a fur coat. At this time of year, can you imagine? Timber wolf!"

The other werewolves groaned in dismay.

"Evangeline has her own 'save the animals' movement," Achille told Sylvie. "So, Evangeline," he said a little louder, "what you do, daw'lin?"

"Well," Evangeline said sweetly, "I'm sure the way she got that coat was to tell her husband that she'd been dying for a fur. And so that night, she did. I took the coat, too, and gave it a decent burial."

The werewolves burst into laughter and murmured approval. "You oughta leave them coats on the steps of the *Times-Picayune* newspaper, for publicity," Achille counseled. "Make people think twice about buying those things."

"Yeah, you right," Evangeline said thoughtfully.

Achille waved to a young couple who had come on the vaporetto with Darryl. The man, Jan, was a tall, blond Dane; his wife was a pretty girl with enormous eyes and an obvious streak of mischief.

"Now, see these two?" Achille said to Sylvie. "Just proves that everybody gets down to the bayous, sooner or later. Jan and Lisa are a pair of visiting Yankees. What's the prob, Jan? You tired of them sushis and lobsters?"

"Nah," Jan said, "we got the urge for spicy food."

"So," Lisa said, giving Achille an arched eyebrow, "we thought we'd eat Creole, if you know what I mean, babes."

"That right?" Darryl Dozier put in, overhearing this. "C'mere. Lemme tell ya how ya can do the state a' Looziana a big favor. Are y'all Democrats?"

Achille moved off to greet other friends, while Sylvie sat back under the tree. It was going to be a long night.

"So what do you think?" Gabriel said, coming to sit with her and pull his shoes off.

"I think the loup-garou vote must be stronger than I ever suspected," Sylvie said, obviously still rattled by the lieutenant governor. She thought a minute. "I don't know yet," she said, "but it seems like what Achille told me is true: a loup-garou kills for justice. Although there seem to be different interpretations of what constitutes justice."

"That's true," Gabriel said, "but remember that we also kill because that's what a loup-garou *does*. It's just the nature of the beast, Sylvie, and we have a hunger that must be fed, some more than others. Some of us kill for sport, too." He paused to pull his Izod shirt over his head and run a hand through his thick, dark hair. "It's like fucking," he said, considering. "Some people just sport-fuck because they love it. And to some of us, me included, the chase and the kill are like that. I try to control myself, but some nights I just can't get enough. I'd like to give you a brighter picture of the noble werewolf who only kills bad people, but I have to be honest. It's part of the life. Sometimes, you're going to kill people who probably don't deserve it, who just happen to be in the wrong place at the wrong time. Nobody will condemn you for it, but it is expected that you'll get wiser and more mature and develop a higher degree of control."

"Do you feel bad about that?"

"No. It's just the way things are. But if you can't live with that, Sylvie, you'll be tormented by your conscience." Gabriel stood up, his clothes under his arm.

"Wait, Gabriel," Sylvie said, catching his arm, "haven't you ever killed for a good reason?"

"Of course. Several times."

"And how did you feel after that?"

Gabriel smiled. "Wonderful. Wonderful enough to wish that every kill was like that. But that doesn't mean I don't enjoy the ones that aren't. Now, kiss me good night and wish me luck. I'm off to find Zizi and Christian."

After he'd gone, Sylvie sat back against the tree to think. What Gabriel told her had disturbed her. This was, she realized, exactly the dilemma her father had faced and had been unable to resolve.

"You're unsure of your place in all this, aren't you?" said a voice behind her.

She turned and there was her mysterious friend, sitting on the opposite side of the tree. Lucien Drago, the composer. Sylvie was confused. Lucien Drago was a loup-garou?

Knowing that Lucien was a loup-garou instantly cleared up several things for Sylvie. This was why she felt she knew him so well, why he had carried her home the night she wandered away from Quentin and her friends. He'd been protecting her.

She noticed him staring intently at her. Then he got up and moved to sit beside her.

"So you've made your way to Bayou Goula," he said pleasantly.

"You're the one Achille told me about," she said slowly, "the one who first felt me calling for help, the one who was trying to come to me."

He only stared at her with those intense green eyes. He looked wonderful. He was dressed in the traditional young conductor's uniform: jeans, Nikes, and a black cotton turtleneck that made his blond hair look all that much lighter. The shirt, Sylvie couldn't help but notice, was a little tight around his biceps and chest, arrogantly so. This was a man who had no doubts about how handsome he was.

Achille, walking back to Sylvie, seemed delighted to see him. "Lucien!" he said as Lucien stood up to embrace him. "Welcome back to Bayou Goula. Do you plan to dance with us?"

"I don't know." He turned to look at Sylvie. "Will you dance with me, Sylvie?"

Sylvie wasn't sure what he meant.

"You know she can't do that," Achille said, a little sternly. "She hasn't decided."

"Sure, she has. Did you really have a choice, Sylvie? Would you go back to your old life now, after what you've learned?

Can you see yourself married to a pillar of the Church, wearing a little white apron, serving cookies and tea to the Altar Guild ladies?" He leaned a little closer to her, and the look in his eyes made her feel confused and disoriented. "Are you really going to be happy sitting in the Rex Room with all the faded ex-Queens of Carnival, reliving every tiny detail of your debut? Do you want to fill your days with shopping and your nights with card parties? Is that the kind of life you want, Sylvie?"

In one quick motion that took her off guard, he pulled Sylvie to her feet and held her close. "Even now," he whispered to her, "you feel the excitement out here on the bayou, the flow of power, the sexual tension that we all feel on nights like this. You can't lie to me. Of all of us here, I know you better than you know yourself."

Without a trace of shyness or reluctance, and oblivious of Achille's slight scowl, he swept Sylvie up into a long, hot kiss that made her dizzy. When he was through, he eased her back to her seat under the tree and smiled.

"The werewolf's kiss," he said, leaning over to brush his lips seductively over her ear as he spoke. "When the time comes, make sure I'm the one."

Zizi ran over and flung her arms around Lucien's neck. "Lucien," she said, kissing him, "*dansez avec moi, mon cher.*" She waggled a finger teasingly at Sylvie. "Now don't you tempt my beautiful *bébé* away, little one!" she said, leading Lucien off.

Sylvie blushed with embarrassment as Achille, with a resigned sigh, sat down beside her. "He's the one you were telling me about," she said, "the one who had to be prevented from giving me the werewolf's kiss."

"That's him," Achille agreed.

"I had no idea he was one of Zizi's boys. I never saw him at the house."

"He's her only boy. Lucien is Zizi's son."

Sylvie looked at the assembled loups-garous with much more curiosity. "Really? She never said a thing! So which one is his father? Christian? He looks a little like Christian."

"Oh my," Achille sighed, falling back against the tree, "you've asked the million-dollar question, daw'lin. We have

no idea. Drago is Zizi's old family name, so that's the name
the boy has. Zizi never talks about Lucien's father, so I guess
she hated him so much that she cut him completely out of her
life—and Lucien's."

"But . . . Zizi's very old, so that would make Lucien . . ."
She stopped, overcome with the sheer volume of numbers.
"Sheesh. How old *is* he?"

"Who can tell? Maybe a couple of hundred years old."

He caught Sylvie's stricken look. "Aw, now, daw'lin . . .
you know enough by now to know that with loups-garous, it
really is how young you look that counts! You'd take Lucien
for twenty-seven or twenty-eight, and so that's what he is.
Hell, that boy don't look a minute over two hundred, two
hundred fifty."

"Oh, just terrific," she said, "I'll be eighteen in a couple of
months, so I guess that catches me up with him."

"So? Honey, with loups-garous there is no chronological
age. And I tell you what, when the werewolf's bond strikes
you, there's no boundary on age or anything else. We're not
tied to that sort of thing, because it all evens out over time.
Now, you just quit worryin' and enjoy the dance."

All around them the loups-garous prepared for the night.
Some talked and joked, happy to see each other; some embraced
old friends; many engaged in sexual teasing, heating each other
to near madness in anticipation of the moon. Sylvie had been
told that the transformation was easier and more exciting when a
loup-garou was sexually aroused. She saw Evangeline lifted off
the ground, her legs wrapped around Darryl Dozier's waist, her
agile tongue darting softly around his ear as he buried his face
between her breasts. Gabriel occupied himself with a statuesque
brunette while Zizi, Lucien, and Christian watched. Christian,
mesmerized by Gabriel and the brunette's virtuoso performance,
nestled Zizi against his chest and stroked her hair.

"Achille," Sylvie said distractedly, "what did Lucien mean
when he asked me to dance?"

"He didn't mean no two-step, *'tite fille*. You just watch; this
is the loups-garous' dance on Bayou Goula."

Then the moon started to rise. The voices hushed and the
werewolves grew still, expectant. Some stood straight and

upright, their faces raised to the sliver of moon; some spread their arms to embrace the silver light. Then a single voice rose in a slight cry, almost inaudible, growing slowly louder. Sylvie could make out the name Hecate in a hundred whispers. There were gasps, like the gasps of lovers caught in expectant ecstasy, as the moon rose.

One by one, the loups-garous began to moan as the transformations began. Each loup-garou changed in his own way, at his own speed; on some the claws grew first, some sprouted hair immediately, for some the bones lengthened and hardened before anything else happened. But the thing that stayed the same was the look of pleasure, as in a prolonged earthshaking orgasm. Some changed alone and some made love as the transformation progressed, some did nothing but hold hands or hold each other in the strongest tie of companionship and trust. For all of them, this moment was what made their lives meaningful, and they reached out in joy and rebirth to their brothers and sisters.

Sylvie watched, mesmerized by the sight. She felt again that old longing, that unfulfilled need that took over her body and her soul. She felt her own body aching to respond to the loups-garous' invitation to transform, to be one with them as they ran in the night. She could almost feel the wind streaming through her hair, the dust clouds rising around her feet as she ran, and she realized that what she was feeling was the collected thoughts of the loups-garous, their anticipation of what the night held for them. The knowledge that she would not really know what they knew, could not truly feel what they felt, smashed her with despair. She became aware of her own tears, her primal, ripping sobs of frustration. Even Achille, holding her like a child and whispering to her, horrified that her reaction had been so painful, failed to reach her in her bitterness.

She thought of her father with fury. If it wasn't for his own prejudices, she would have been one with the loups-garous, would have been, as they were even now, rejoicing in the physical marvels that they became. She felt that he had hurt her, had cheated her out of her own life.

Achille, knowing what was in her mind, comforted her. "No, no, *'tite fille*," he crooned, "your papa only did what he thought was right for you. Your time will come, child, and soon. Don't grieve so."

She lifted her head from his chest, her eyes burning, and tried to find Lucien among the transformed loups-garous. But they were running off now, into the night in pairs or groups or singly, as they had transformed, the moonlight glinting off magnificent bodies covered with shining fur in all shades of the spectrum, their eyes glowing gold and green and blue and black, howling in glorious acceptance of the moon's benevolent gifts.

One of them broke away from the group and ran toward her, stopping several feet away. His green eyes locked with Sylvie's, and he came forward slowly, brushing her tears with a long, translucent claw. They ran down the claw, staining the bright gold fur of his changed hands. He closed his eyes and brought the tear to his lips, then ran swiftly back into the darkness.

Sylvie could hear his voice as clearly as if he had spoken, could still feel the heat when her breasts crushed against his chest as he held her. "When the time comes, make sure I'm the one."

She intended to see that he was.

PART
SIX

†

The Werewolf's Kiss

18

Transformed, Lucien ran through the night, glad to be free.

Because of the demands of his human life, he hadn't had time to change since the last full moon, and the energy had built up in him until it was almost unbearable. He couldn't understand how humans bore the stress of everyday living: being a loup-garou was a natural outlet for the strain of his human life, and without it he would have gone insane.

He reveled in the feel of his changed body, the supernatural speed at which he ran, the wind cutting through his pelt and cooling his skin, the way his excited blood sizzled like electricity.

Driven, he killed three times that night. The first was to ease his hunger, the second to cool his blood. The third was an execution, a rapist who had terrorized the Garden District.

What a fulfilling kill that had been! Executions were always the best. One of the rapist's victims was a follower of Madame Mae. She had asked Mae for vengeance, but that was the kind of thing Mae would not do. Mae refused to do bad work, and she didn't have to. All she did was tell Achille that the request had been made. It was up to him to decide whether the execution would take place and by whom, and Mae never wanted to hear anything about it afterward. The loups-garous never made a mistake in matters of this kind.

An execution had to be handled very carefully. There must be absolutely no shadow of doubt. Finding the accused party was never difficult: in the instance of the rapist, Lucien got the man's scent off the victim's clothes. No, the delicate part was making sure that the suspect actually was guilty and beyond redemption, and whether he was likely to do the same crime—

221

or worse—again. Usually a loup-garou in human form would stalk a suspect for days, picking his or her mind of all the details, large and small, of the crime and everything that led up to it. Several times, the accused had been innocent, or the offense not great enough to warrant the punishment. At other times, the details uncovered by the loup-garou's mind picking were enough to reopen a criminal case or force a confession.

But tonight's victim had been guilty, all right, and Lucien was in just enough of a bad mood to relish what he was going to do.

The rapist worked until midnight at a warehouse down on Tchoupitoulas Street. Some loups-garous hated to kill in the city. They had to exercise more caution and skill not to be discovered. But Lucien rather liked it; he found that it sharpened his wits.

There wasn't a lot of activity down on Tchoupitoulas after midnight, at least, not the kind that's interested in another man's business. There are too many shadows and too much decay. Tom Hardin left the warehouse and walked across the dark stretch of dirt toward his rusty Trans-Am.

He eased himself behind the wheel and turned the key. The ignition caught easily, and Tom smiled. The Trans-Am might not look too great right now while he was restoring the body, but he babied that engine. It was important to have a car he could rely on. He popped a tape into the player and turned up the sound: Jo-El Sonnier singing "Jolie Blonde." He let the engine warm up slowly while he leaned back and lit a joint. Nice night. So nice, in fact, that it made him restless. He thought about it. The night was still young and he didn't feel like going home.

He took a couple more tokes and got a little loose, still thinking. Yeah, that was it. He knew what he wanted to do. He chuckled a little: he knew he was playing a dangerous game, but he liked it. He was good at it, too—wasn't he still a free man? The challenge was half of it.

Tom stubbed out the joint and eased the Trans-Am into gear. He pumped the gas delicately; only assholes blew their valves peeling out.

The wheels made a soft sound, scattering gravel and dirt, but the Trans-Am didn't move. Shit, Tom thought, now what is this crap? He checked to see that he was in first gear and pressed the gas a little harder. The car moved a little forward, but jerked. Tom wasn't going anywhere.

Damn! Just his luck for his rear tires to be sunk in the only mud out here in this dirt. This damned lot never did drain right. Letting the engine idle in neutral, Tom pulled the parking brake and opened the door. It was a little farther to the ground than he thought; the rear of the car seemed higher than the front. What the hell . . . ?

The whole thing was so weird that he was more confused than scared. What the hell was this big guy doing holding up the rear of his car? Shit, he had it a good six inches off the ground, and it didn't even look like a strain. It took Tom a minute to realize what he was seeing, and only the thud of the Trans-Am hitting the ground shook him into action.

He started to scream, but that choked into silence as a huge hand closed around his throat and he was carried, struggling silently, to the shadows toward the river.

Twenty minutes later, the loup-garou was back in the almost-empty parking lot. He cocked his head, listening for dangerous sounds, and heard none. He considered the Trans-Am, its engine still running and the tape still blasting. He reached in through the window and shut off the ignition. Then, on second thought, he reached back in and ejected the tape. He knew it was probably unethical to take it, but Tom wasn't going to use it, and besides—werewolves *really* liked Jo-El Sonnier.

Lucien ran harder, faster, farther. Usually, the transformation drove everything from his mind, the sheer joy of physical strength washing away all the things that usually pressed him. On those nights he let his mind run free also, doing what he wanted to do, or what needed to be done, following the simplest drives. By the time the dawn rose and he changed back, he always felt rejuvenated. He was totally at peace with himself.

This morning was different. After his transformation, he was still restless and upset. The kill hadn't satisfied him or, at least, hadn't satisfied the hunger that was really bothering him.

He sat up and spent awhile just thinking, running his fingers through the wet morning grass.

It was Sylvie he wanted. He had thought it was only pity he felt for her, that her plight had stirred a protectiveness in him that he hadn't realized he possessed. A loup-garou unfulfilled was the saddest thing he could imagine, so it was only natural that he sympathized with her. Lately, though, when he had started to follow her and had gotten to know her, what he started to feel wasn't sympathy at all.

He had been the first one to hear her call, the first of the loups-garous to feel the plaintive longing of one of their kind trapped in confusion and chained to a life that was unnatural for her. He would have gone to her the first time he sensed her, but it was impossible: he was driving to the airport, about to leave for an engagement with the Lyric Opera in Chicago.

By the time he returned, Achille had picked up her signals. The whole community of loups-garous knew. And by that time, Achille had explained the delicacy of the situation to all of them. He knew what was on Lucien's mind and had expressly forbidden him to give her the kiss.

But Achille hadn't forbidden him to touch her senses, to tap into her thoughts when he could, to follow her on those nights when her frustration drove her to reckless wandering. Through all that, he got to know her better than he had allowed himself to know anyone.

Unfortunately for him, he realized that he had also let himself fall in love with her. He hadn't known it until this very moment, but he knew it was true. And it was dangerous for him.

To love a human woman was madness. It led to a bad end almost always. Humans didn't have the loup-garou's strength or endurance, they didn't age as slowly, they didn't have the depth of feeling or instincts, the hot blood. They didn't allow themselves to become engulfed in sexuality, no matter how uninhibited they professed to be. It was the mating of two different species.

To be sure, Achille had been with Mae a long time and had

been happy with her, as far as Lucien knew. Achille owed Mae a great debt, and this had bonded them; if Mae had ever consented to live the loup-garou's life, she and Achille would have been perfectly mated until they died. But, as Achille's several affairs with loups-garous proved, even his love for Mae couldn't prevent him from finding the fulfillment he could have only with another werewolf.

Achille didn't talk about it, but Lucien knew that it caused him great anguish from time to time.

Lucien had loved losing himself in many women, some of them loups-garous, but he had always been a sucker for true love. He had known from the beginning that love would either make him abjectly miserable or exalt him; his werewolf nature and his own romanticism permitted him no in-between emotions. He wished that he had inherited his mother's frivolity: her attitude toward sex was roughly equivalent to that of a kid let loose in a toy shop with her father's charge cards. She would never find a true mate and settle down. Zizi, he thought wryly, simply loved to fuck and was too easily bored.

Whenever he thought about his unknown father—and it was rarely—it was at times like this. Lucien and his mother differed so far in their approaches to love that he assumed that his intensity of feeling must be his father's genes taking precedence. Zizi never talked about his father, wouldn't even consider a discussion of him or tell Lucien his name, but Lucien was sure that it must have been his father who was devastated by love, and Zizi who had, perhaps scornfully, cut him out of her life.

Lucien knew that he was a classic werewolf: when he found a true mate, it would be for life. He had no wish to put himself through the particularly poisonous hell of loving a human woman and watching her grow old and die while he aged one year to her ten.

If he fell in love with Sylvie and she decided the loup-garou's life wasn't for her, there would never be another woman for him. Not like that. He knew that as surely as he'd known anything. The thought of an endless procession of women, delightful as it had been just a few weeks ago, now depressed him.

He sighed and stretched out on the grass. He wished he had someone to talk to about this. Not Achille. Not Zizi. But someone. He watched the sky, just starting to grow light.

It was Sylvie he wanted, and it wasn't talk he needed.

Damn!

Even while he was pulling on his clothes, even while he was mentally making a list of things he should get done today and the places he had to be, he knew where he was going instead.

He headed toward the French Quarter, to his mother's house on Royal Street.

The sun was barely up when Lucien let himself into the courtyard. The whole house was asleep. Zizi and Gabriel and Christian would all be nestled together in Zizi's enormous lace-dripping bed, exhausted from the night's run. Lucien hesitated for a minute, then sniffed the air, immediately sensing the warm, sweet scent of Sylvie's body.

He tapped very lightly on her door, telling himself that he was letting himself in for big trouble. If she doesn't open it, he thought, or she tells me to go away, that's it. It means it wasn't meant to happen and I'll leave.

Sylvie blinked at the unexpected light as she opened the door. She was groggy with sleep, but she smiled when she saw him.

"Lucien?" she said in confusion.

He simply put his arms around her and held her. It felt so good that it was a relief. She pulled him inside, and he knew that if the house fell down around them, if the whole city had suddenly gone up in flames, if the world ended, he couldn't leave until he had felt her beneath him.

"I loved your opera. I loved watching you conduct, the way you moved, the grace of it," Sylvie told Lucien after they had made love.

"Are you talking about the one we just played, or a real piece of music?"

"I meant *La Luna di Streghe*."

He let his lips trail down her throat. "Really? When did you hear it?"

"Oh, a few months ago, in Houston."

"Impossible. I would have known you were there."

"I don't think you knew *anyone* was there but you and the musicians. You completely forget the audience, don't you? You conduct with your whole body. I've never seen another conductor put himself into the music quite like that. It's a very seductive feeling, I would imagine."

He shrugged. "It's exhausting. But yes, exciting."

"I heard that you were in love with the soprano, the one who sang Aradia. That you were going to marry her."

"She was amusing. And amused. Anything more was her publicist's idea."

"She's very beautiful."

He shrugged again. "She's . . ." he hesitated, "she's human. She wasn't for me. How could I have had anything permanent with a human woman?"

Sylvie bowed her head. Her voice was suddenly tiny, broken in shame. "*I'm* human."

Lucien rubbed his cheek against the softness of her breast and smiled. "You're not. You know you're not. You're one of us."

She tangled her fingers in his hair and lifted his head so she could look into his face. "How do you know? How can you be sure?"

"Oh, I'm sure," he said with finality. "Believe me, if I wasn't, I wouldn't be here."

"Achille isn't sure," she said.

"Maybe he is. Maybe he's just waiting for you to be. You do have a choice, Sylvie."

She threw off the covers and paced furiously around the room, her anger flaring so suddenly that it shocked him.

"Everyone keeps *saying* that!" she said in a low, controlled whisper of frustration and fury. "Why do you all assume that my having a choice means that I have to wait, like a child being told that he'll understand everything when he grows up? *You* had a choice, didn't you? Achille did, Zizi did! And no one put you through this hell of waiting. *What*, Lucien, what is it I'm supposed to be waiting for?"

Her anger mystified him. "Knowledge. You have to learn our ways before—"

"Bullshit! That's nice, but not necessary. I know all I need to know right now; I can learn the rest later. Gabriel did. *You* did!"

"Sylvie," he said patiently, getting up to sit on the edge of the bed, "my mother is a loup-garou. I can only assume that my father was."

Her eyes went hard as diamonds, her voice exquisitely even. "In case you've forgotten, so is *my* father."

"It's a different situation entirely," he said, trying to soothe her. "It's because of your father that Achille wants you to be sure it's what you want."

"I'm sure *now*!" she said furiously.

She stood in front of him defiantly. "My father was wrong to turn his back on what he was instead of trying to make his peace with it. Is that my fault?"

He stared at her, confusion making him silent. How could he explain to her what he didn't understand himself? He was completely on her side, always had been. He had never agreed with Achille's policy of delaying what was inevitable.

Sylvie's voice softened a little. "I know about my father. How he had the gift forced on him and he didn't want it. But I wasn't born under a curse like he was; I was born a loup-garou, like you were. I *want* it, I'd *welcome* it. Doesn't that carry any weight at all with any of you?"

She dropped to her knees in front of him, her hands resting lightly on his bare thighs. The fragile warmth of her closeness made him want her again, but her anger held him still.

"Lucien," she said softly, persuasively, "don't let me go on like this. I'm in limbo. I can't go back to my old life, and I'm not allowed to move into a new one. I know Achille meant well, but it was torture for me to go to Bayou Goula, to watch others enjoying the life I was meant to have!"

He couldn't meet her eyes. There was nothing he could say to her. He agreed with her completely, but he knew that to admit it meant only trouble for both of them.

Her hands moved up his body, and he grabbed her wrists. "Don't do it, Sylvie. Don't ask me what I know you want to ask."

"Why not? Don't you think I felt it, the anticipation, the joy, the exhilaration? And I wanted to be with them—*really* with them, not just a voyeur."

Her whispery voice was silky, half-pleading, half-seducing. Still on her knees, she bent forward, and when her breasts touched his legs the shock of it was like electricity.

"Do it, Lucien. Don't make me suffer anymore. Give me what I want, help me to be what I'm really meant to be."

Only vaguely aware he was doing it, he tightened his grip on her hands. She appeared not to notice.

"Don't ask me that again, Sylvie," he said, his voice tight.

"Lucien. You know you want to, and you know I want it."

She was asking for the one thing he'd been wanting for months, what he'd been burning to do. In the night he'd dreamed of it, the dream so vivid and the touch of her delicate skin so real that he'd awakened moaning in pleasure and then had been plunged into frustrated despair. He'd touched her mind as often as he could, hoping that the fragile link with her would appease his own frantic hunger, but it had only made it worse.

"What was it you said? 'When the time comes, make sure I'm the one'? Well, this *is* the time, Lucien, and you *are* the one. You don't want a human woman and I don't want a human life." She stood up and bent her head, her lips brushing his hair, whispering in his ear. "Do it now, Lucien. Give me the kiss."

He held his grip on her wrists, as if concentrating on that one act could give him strength. He knew that if he touched her anywhere else, if he made one move, if he looked into her face, that he would be lost. He *would* do it, and Achille would never forgive him.

He let go of her hands and bolted up from the bed. Grabbing at his clothes, he ran toward the door, terrified to look at her, having no words to explain that what she wanted was perfectly logical, perfectly right, but out of the question.

He started across the courtyard, stark naked, his eyes blind, his head blurred with conflict. He took a deep breath of morning air, hoping to clear his mind. Sitting quickly on a little iron garden bench, he started pulling on his jeans.

He stopped in midmotion.

"Oh, *shit!*" he said softly.

Sylvie was right and Achille was wrong. Lucien had never before questioned anything Achille did, but this time he had let his compassion for Sylvie's father lead him down a completely erroneous path.

Whether he realized it or not, Achille was trying to do the same thing Andrew had done: make Sylvie's decision for her. All this waiting was only driving Sylvie insane.

Well, it was driving Lucien insane, too.

There was no other life for Sylvie. She knew that and so did he. He'd be damned for it, but he was going to do it. Whatever happened with Achille would simply have to be dealt with.

He started back to Sylvie's room, feeling more relieved with each step. It was the right thing to do. The fact that it was decided made him feel a manic happiness.

She was huddled under the covers. When she heard the door open, she raised her head and looked at him.

Her questioning look, the vulnerable spark of hope in her eyes, moved him unbearably.

"I can't fight you, Sylvie," he said, "not when I know you're right."

She caught her breath. Her eyes widened.

"But not now," he said quickly. "I can't. I mean . . . it's a physical impossibility. You can only give the kiss after your transformation begins." He gave her a huge grin and tapped his incisors. "I'm wearing the wrong teeth."

She laughed, and the joy in her eyes only made Lucien feel more positive about what he was doing.

"You won't change your mind?" she said breathlessly, still not quite believing it. "You promise you will?"

"Absolutely," he said firmly. "As soon as the moon rises, as soon as possible. I've never given the kiss before; it should be an experience!"

Suddenly overcome with elation, he jumped on the bed beside her, like a child with a wonderful secret to tell. "Oh, Sylvie, it will be unbelievable! You can't believe how magnificent the loup-garou's life is, the freedom, the strength!"

She laughed again, throwing her arms around his neck. "I can imagine!"

"No, no, you can't imagine it, because nothing that's ever happened to you will be *anything* like it. The most fantastic orgasm you ever had will seem like nothing beside it!"

Now that the pressure of holding himself back was over, he was like a man who had dropped a great weight and was soaring in the air.

"God, Sylvie! When you become a loup-garou, you won't believe what happens to your senses! You'll be able to taste the wind on your tongue, to hear children a mile away whispering secrets after they've been put to bed. When someone touches you—like this"—he lightly touched his finger to her breast—"you'll be able to feel it with your entire body, with your mind."

He took her face in his hands, watching the pleasure light her eyes.

"I can't wait to make love to you when you're a loup-garou," he said.

"Wait a minute! What was wrong with what we just did?"

"Get real," he said impatiently. "Only . . . Sylvie! It'll be so different after tonight!"

"We'd better do it some more, then," she suggested, pulling him down with her into the cool sheets, "if only to have a basis of comparison."

Two hours later, they both fell into an exhausted sleep.

Lucien woke slowly, feeling as if something were holding him underwater. He was more asleep than awake, so he assumed that Sylvie had rolled across his back in her sleep.

He reached out to touch her, but his arm couldn't move.

Then he was completely awake. He heard Sylvie trying to scream, but the sound was strangely quiet.

He started to raise his head and had it shoved back down against the pillow.

A mocking male voice said, "Go back to sleep, loverman!"

He could see enough to realize that he was being held down on the bed by four, maybe five men, one of whom was sitting on his back, crushing his head against the pillow.

Two more men were struggling with Sylvie; one held her arms behind her back while the other pressed something over her mouth and nose. She fought to get free, then went completely limp against the men holding her. The two of them got her into her coat and took her out of the room, supporting her between them.

To anyone on the street, it would look just like a drunk being helped home by friends. And in the French Quarter, who'd think it was strange?

Lucien struggled, but he was outnumbered. God, if it were only nighttime, he'd kill them all, with pleasure, slowly and painfully. He wondered briefly what time it was, if he could stall them until dark.

The pressure on his head was released as one of the men let go of his hair. When he lifted his head, he saw a tall black man, strikingly handsome and completely in control, watching from the doorway. At first, Lucien felt relief; the man was so composed that Lucien was sure he was here to help.

Then he looked into the man's eyes. They were insane.

The man held a gun, but he held it casually, as if it weren't real or even necessary. He looked at Lucien. "Be smart, loup-garou. Don't make me use this." He waved the gun. "Silver bullets. Just to be sure."

"You'd better be an excellent shot," Lucien said furiously, "because if you miss, I'll kill you right here, and your friends, too."

"No, no, no; you don't want to do that," the man said calmly. "How will you know where she is? How will you know someone won't kill her if I don't show up? Don't worry, I certainly don't plan to hurt her. You'll see her again in a few days and she'll be fine—provided you don't do anything silly or heroic. Now, if my friends let you up, will you be calm?"

"Goddammit, I'll find you tonight, you asshole!"

"Then you'll find her body, too." The man sighed, then said calmly and reasonably, "I've told you she's in no danger. I'm not going to tell you any more than that." He looked at one of the men and gestured with the gun. "Give the gentleman a little nap, will you?"

Lucien felt the sting of a needle.

His last conscious act was to inhale deeply, separating the different, distinct scents of the men and storing them in his mind.

When Lucien lay limp on the bed, Papa Lucifer turned to his followers. "Get out of here. Quietly. Don't alert the whole house."

They shut the door gently behind them.

19

It wasn't that Endore was depressed, it was that his life was starting to make an uncomfortable sense. He had been restless for weeks. It had started with the vague awareness that everything he had ever done might possibly have been done wrong, and on that shaky foundation of the past he had built his present.

He wandered around his house for a while, thinking aimless thoughts, picking up books, looking inside, and putting them down again. Finally, he came upon *The Great Gatsby*, one of his favorites, and lost himself in it for an hour.

But something in Gatsby's story was much too close to home. The whole idea of a man so tied to the past that his present and future were only illusory made Endore wince.

Distracted by the thought, he set the book aside, feeling a pang of futile kinship with Gatsby. He looked around his house, thinking that his whole life for as long as he wanted to remember was an effort to re-create a past that was only marginally his own. Like Gatsby, he wanted to do it all again, only he wanted it to come out differently this time, better, with a happy ending. The past Endore was reliving was partly true, partly wishful thinking.

Gatsby was wrong, Endore thought, you *can't* relive the past, if only because what you remember is discolored with what you wish you remembered.

Like this house. It seemed an ancient house, built in the old Roman manner with blank walls on the outside and inside rooms opening on an atrium. There were painted walls, murals of the gods and goddesses, the old familiar stories all fading and peeling in the elegant manner of decaying glory. Statues and busts in appropriate niches had been polychromed in realistic hues over the marble, then the paint partially sanded away.

The house had a feeling of timelessness, the very air seeming to be musty and antique. Considering the house and the aristocratic manner of its occupant, a stranger would have assumed that the house had been in the same family since the days of the Roman Empire.

In point of fact, it was only a few decades old. Endore had had to raze several small buildings to make room for the house and grounds. Some people re-create the houses they were born in: Endore had created the house he *wished* he'd been born in.

It was perfect, complete in its details, as only the house of a historian can be. But there was about it a cold beauty, a feeling of never having been touched, as if the rooms should have been behind museum ropes. Endore often thought that he neglected the house, much the same as one would neglect a dog or a cat, by leaving it alone so much. It never really had the chance to borrow a spark of life from him. Anyone could have lived here.

His own life, too, was untouched. People had passed in and out like shadows, but not one had taken on the substance to stay. It was his own fault and he now had cause to regret it. He had let his learning become his life. He had never been really happy with the arrangement: there were only a few moments when he was merely content. He had succeeded in going through a very long life without major grief, but he had sacrificed joy to avoid pain. At the time, he thought it was a very sound decision; he now saw it as selfish and cowardly.

He wondered if it was too late to learn how to deal with loss. You must take things as they come, he had once read, but he had been afraid to do that. He hadn't wanted to relinquish control and make the emotional concessions that are part of accepting other people.

Endore shook himself and decided to drown all this profundity and malaise in a double chocolate sundae, a nasty, delightful addiction he had picked up—where else?—in America. The feeling wasn't that easy to shake off, but he made an effort to redirect his thinking.

He had just reached for the freezer door when the pain hit him. It was like a scream inside his head, a confused shriek for help, so frantic that it blinded him for a split second. Something bad, very bad, was happening. And it wasn't close by, either; he was picking up the signal from far away. He let himself fall against the enameled freezer door, clutching the handle like a lifeline, to steady himself until the pain passed.

His head cleared and he staggered to the nearest chair, trying to determine the source. He sat there, shaking, and closed his eyes. Who was it? If he knew who, it would tell him where.

Odd. He couldn't pick up the person, but he was starting to get a definite image of the place. That was almost never the case. But he had a flash, an instant snapshot of a scene. That still didn't tell him who had the problem, but he knew where to go to find out. Only one place in the world looked like that.

The pain hit again, this time like a railroad spike driven between his eyes. His fingers convulsively dug into the arms of the chair, and he screamed in pain and surprise. This *never* happened! The messages he got were clear and precise, demanding his attention but never dragging him down into terror like this.

A name flashed across his brain, not the name of the one in pain, but a name cried out in supplication. That told him all he needed to know.

The pain eased down and faded, dying into a tiny cry that he knew would stay with him for hours. But at least it gave him a chance to close himself off from the psychic message.

He didn't bother to pack. He grabbed his wallet, his credit cards, and his passport. Locking the house, he jumped into his car and drove—with a speed and abandon that awed even the Romans—to the airport. His luck held: it was 10:40 A.M. and he could get on the 11:00 A.M. TWA flight to Kennedy. From Kennedy, he could catch a nonstop flight and be in New Orleans by early evening.

The pain didn't return, but it stayed with him just the same, over all those hours and all that distance.

20

The first thing Lucien was conscious of feeling was something cold and wet against his face. Panicked, he opened his eyes and tried to sit up, but someone pushed him down, gently.

"Lie down, *mon cher*," Zizi told him. "You couldn't stand up anyway, not until that stuff they gave you wears off." She moved the ice pack back over his forehead. "*Cochons*," she muttered. "Don't you worry, *bébé;* your mama's going to kill those bastards for you."

"Why, thank you very much," Lucien said.

"Nobody gonna be killing anybody," Achille said. "Not until we find out what happened. Lucien, your mama picked up what was happening and found you in here."

"That's right," Zizi said. "I was sound asleep, I thought I was dreaming. Then all of a sudden I was wide awake and I just knew you were in trouble. Oh, *pauvre bébé,* if only I hadn't been sleeping so soundly!"

Lucien smiled. He didn't believe it was the loup-garou's psychic bond nearly as much as it had been simply Zizi's maternal radar, and he didn't believe that sleeping was what she had been doing that had distracted her.

"So why don't you tell us what we don't know?" Achille said. "Fill in the blanks. No, wait a minute. I want you to tell this whole story to Mae. Just lie still until she gets here."

Lucien sat up. His head felt as though it were filled with rubber cement. "We can't wait, Achille! God knows what they're doing to Sylvie!"

"My question is," Achille said coldly, "what have *you* done to her? Put some clothes on, Lucien."

As Achille left the room, Lucien slumped tiredly and reached for his clothes. Zizi stood by the bed, the ice pack still in one slim hand. "Oh, Lucien," she said softly, "what am I going to do with you?"

"I didn't do it, Mother," he said, pulling on his jeans. "I didn't give her the kiss."

"I know that. But you were going to."

"I was, yes. He's wrong, you know. Sylvie is ready for it, she has been from the first week she came here."

"I know that, too. Oh, Lucien, you just don't understand what Achille and Andrew share. Even *they* don't understand it, but they're two sides of the same coin. Both of them are stubborn men, they won't give an inch in believing that each of them is right and the other is wrong. But I've never seen two men more alike. Achille puts himself in the opposite of Andrew's place. He keeps thinking, What if she was my child? what if she wanted to give up the loup-garou's life, to give up everything I ever wanted for her, the life I'm convinced would make her happy because it's made me happy? He knows exactly what Andrew's feeling about his daughter."

She took Lucien's arm and pulled him down to sit beside her. "You're so impetuous, Lucien. Please try to understand Achille and be patient. He knows Sylvie is ready. But he also knows that her father isn't. Andrew might not be able to accept Sylvie as a loup-garou, and that rift could break them apart forever."

"It's creating a rift between him and me," Lucien said grimly.

"Oh, please, *bébé,* don't say that," Zizi said. "You know he loves you. He's been like a father to you."

"But I love Sylvie. And I just can't stand to see her like this any longer. Achille has to understand that."

"He does, *mon cher.* Please be patient. Now, I think our first priority has to be to get Sylvie back. You concentrate on that and everything else will work itself out."

When Achille returned it was with Mae—and Andrew.

Achille couldn't keep this from him, but telling Andrew that his daughter had been kidnapped while under his protection had been the hardest thing Achille had ever done.

Also, Mae had insisted that Andrew's cooperation was absolutely required to get Sylvie back, so they brought him with them to Zizi's. Andrew sat in the gathering room at Luna, stunned and confused, while Zizi, Mae, Lucien, and Achille decided the best way to handle things. Lucien was in favor of killing Antoine.

"We could sweep down on his place and wipe him and his slimeballs out in one rampage," Lucien said.

"If you tried to do that," Mae said reasonably, "one of those fanatical followers of his might kill Sylvie. You don't know that we could catch them all together. Besides, Antoine needs to be discredited. This kind of group is hard to wipe out; every time some nut wants power, he or she tries to revive *la Reine Blanche*'s black magic cult. Usually, it fades out pretty quickly, but Antoine has managed to become almost as dangerous as *Reine Blanche*."

"Achille," Andrew said desperately, "can't you pick up on him? Get some sort of psychic message and find out where he's got her?"

"*Cher ami*, we know that. He's keeping her in Mother Pauline's old house on Rampart Street. And he isn't going to hurt her, not physically. What he wants is to make her a loup-garou, to use the old Voodoo rituals so that he'll have a loup-garou under his control."

Andrew looked even more confused. "But . . . *isn't* she a werewolf? I don't understand what's going on."

Achille was miserable. He had made a terrible mistake; he should have simply given the girl the kiss—or let Lucien do it—and let her get on with her life. He had been too cautious, too unsure of Sylvie, which he shouldn't have been, and now he had let this happen. He knew Antoine was devious and unhinged by his craving for power; he should have foreseen this development long ago. He'd never forget this, and if anything happened to Sylvie, he'd never forgive himself, either.

"What Antoine wants," Mae told them all, "is to make a great show of power, to put on a flashy act. That way, he can attract more followers and impress the ones he already has. My guess is that he'll intimidate Sylvie somehow and he'll force her to transform during one of his black magic ceremonies."

"Performing like a Bourbon Street stripper," Lucien said furiously.

"Once he does that," Mae continued, "Sylvie will owe him an obligation, a kill. And the word will spread that Antoine is the most powerful Voodoo in New Orleans. Antoine doesn't want to practice the old religion, he wants to form a cult, and he already has a good toehold."

"Sylvie would never agree to something like that!" Andrew said.

"Not of her own accord, no," Achille said, "but Antoine's got more power than he can handle. He's using some nasty black stone heart that he says he got from *la Reine Blanche,* and I don't have to tell you that it's bad magic. We don't know what he's gonna do to force her. He's capable of anything."

Andrew went pale and still at the name, not so much from fear as from rage. "The man's insane," he said finally. "He can't know what he's doing."

"I agree," Mae said. "Remember, I know Antoine. His having that heart is like giving a thermonuclear device to a five-year-old. Antoine's own power was always mild, his self-control almost nonexistent. That stone is everything that the White Queen was: concentrated malevolence. It's not only the stone, it's what he had to do to get it that empowers it. I have the feeling that the damned power is controlling him, not the other way around. Antoine was always arrogant and ambitious, but he was never the type willing to commit murder." Mae's voice caught a little. She had never hated Antoine; she had known him since they were kids. Now it was as if the real Antoine was dead. If she thought of him that way, the corruption that had eaten away at him was easier to face.

"Whatever he does, he'll do tonight," Mae said. "Now that he has Sylvie, he's sure to put on a spectacular ceremony to show her off, and he can't afford to wait. The longer he keeps her, the more chances he has to make any little mistake, and he knows that the loups-garous are just waiting for an unguarded moment to kill him. Sylvie's his body armor right now."

Mae tapped her fingers on the back of a chair, thinking. "I've got to go there," she said after a few minutes. "I'm going to break him if it kills me. He just can't be allowed to continue this way."

"This isn't one of your better ideas, Mae," Zizi said, frowning.

"If you think I'm going to let you go there alone," Achille told her, "you done lost your mind, girl."

But Mae was unruffled. "I'm not going alone. I'm taking the bishop here with me."

"Me?" Andrew said, surprised. "Of course I'll go with you. I'll do anything you say, Mae. But I don't understand how I can help you; I'm not exactly Dirty Harry."

"Andrew," Mae said, smiling, "the loups-garous may be scary, but you've got something they don't have—and it isn't religion. You'll see. I'll explain everything to you."

"You walk in that house, Mae," Achille said firmly, "and I'm gonna be right behind you. You're going nowhere near that maniac alone. I apologize, Andrew, but you're no match for some sleazy little Hitler with his devil-worshiping Nazis. Mae can be as charitable as she wants to about poor possessed Antoine, but I'm gonna eat the son of a bitch, and I'm gonna do it *real* slow."

Mae sighed. "Just this *once*, white boy," she said firmly, "do things my way."

Achille didn't mention it to Mae, but both of them knew what was uppermost in his mind and driving him crazy with fear. They had to stop Antoine, not only for Sylvie's sake and to get rid of a dangerous maniac, but because the kill Antoine would ask for—and that Sylvie would not be able to refuse—would be Mae.

If it had been left to Andrew, they would have rushed straight to Antoine's and confronted the bastard that minute. Achille was in complete agreement. But Mae, with her controlled rage, insisted that every step had to be taken with the utmost caution. She wasn't about to let her anger overpower what she knew had to be done.

"Bishop," she told Andrew, "if you were going to do an exorcism, would you just go in and confront that demon? No, you would not. The church has set up all kinds of rituals you

have to do first, to protect yourself. It's no different with the
Voodoos. First, we're going to talk with the spirits here, for
protection to keep us safe and to give us strength to fight this
madman. Then, you're going to go to the cathedral, pray harder
than you ever did, and put on the most impressive stuff you've
got. What do you call those things?"

Andrew couldn't help but smile. "Vestments."

"Fine," Mae said. "When Antoine sets eyes on you, I want
you to look like the right hand of God."

"I know just what you want, Mae," Andrew said, catching
on, "but the particular vestments I need are at—" He stopped,
his breath choked in his throat. "Oh, my God! Angela! She
doesn't know . . . I haven't told her a thing. I came right from
the church to Zizi's and I never even called her!"

He looked so distraught that Mae patted his arm. "We'll both
tell her. It'll be easier that way."

It was only a few minutes' drive to Andrew's house off St.
Charles. When Andrew started to put his key in the lock, the
front door swung open.

He and Mae had the same feeling at the same instant, a
cold ball of fear deep in the stomach. "Oh . . . no!" Andrew
whispered.

Andrew dashed through the empty house, calling for Angela,
calling for Walter and Georgiana.

Mae stood very still and took in the living room. Angela's
pretty wicker-and-brocade sewing box lay on its side on the
floor, spools of thread spilling out in a tangle of colors. The
rosewood coffee table was askew, pushed aside so violently
that one leg had broken.

She moved to the crumpled pile of gold-and-white brocade
on the floor, picked it up, and shook it out: Andrew's vestments, so magnificent that they almost shone with their own
lights. A needle and thread still hung from an unfinished hem.
Mae touched the shining satin and felt a shudder of psychic
fear: near the hem, on the white lining, was a definite stain of
blood, so fresh that it hadn't even begun to dry.

21

This was the first time Antoine had used the trick lighting, the constructed costume, the smoky special effects. Of course the crowd would see through the effects, but it was the lingering impression that counted. If engineering could make gods out of gangly rock stars, it could make Antoine a Voodoo king.

Most of Papa Lucifer's followers were high when they got to the meeting. Papa was very strict about drug use on the premises, and even one infraction brought consequences that most of them didn't want to think about. All your hair and teeth could fall out overnight, your body could break out in stinking boils, you could become impotent for as long as Papa Lucifer wished, or you could just get a thorough beating and a couple of broken bones from Papa's henchmen. Since junkies are never very prudent, each of them knew at least one person who had been punished this way.

One of the things you could do at Papa Lucifer's was drink, and it wasn't only permitted, it was encouraged. By the time the lights dimmed and the ominous brass gong heralded Papa's entrance, most of them were glassy eyed and pliant, easily intimidated and easily aroused to anything, exactly the way Papa liked them.

At the first of the three gongs, they all looked expectantly at the end of the room opposite the altar, where Papa would appear and start his procession.

As the last gong died out, a hidden drum started a wild, demonic beat. Out of the darkness a half-naked man leaped, wearing the beads and feathers of the bamboula dancer, prancing and gyrating among the crowd, working them up into mindless riot.

From his concealed place in the anteroom, Antoine watched through a peephole set into the black matte doors. The bamboula dancer was good. Not as good as he himself had been, but good enough. Antoine watched the crowd as they hooted and imitated the dancer's lewder movements, a familiar wave of contempt passing through him. Junkies and drunks, simple-minded robots; this was what made up the bulk of his crowd. It was good enough to get him started, to begin cementing his reputation and get people talking about him with fear and astonishment, but he wanted better. He wanted the devout Voodoos that followed Mae, real worshipers of the old gods and spirits, people who didn't have to be coerced or bribed with drugs, people who would look at him with the same respect that Mae commanded.

The only thing that worried him was the power. He didn't have it: *it* had *him*. The black magic wasn't entirely of his own design; it was as if he were working in a dream when he put together the temple. It was certainly nothing he would have come up with on his own. And most of the rituals also weren't his. In fact, during some of them, he blanked out. Oh, it was his body performing the ceremonies, intoning the words, making the sacrifices, but it was as if he were standing there limp while someone else pulled his strings. It was out of his control. He wasn't sure anymore what he had devised or what had been devised *for* him.

The only things he was doing on his own were the old, familiar rituals that any Voodoo of moderate gifts could do: making conjure balls, mixing powders for spells, removing mild hexes. He couldn't heal the sick or calm the insane. He couldn't talk with the spirits. He couldn't see the future or read the hidden present from the past, or look beyond the limits of time and space. He couldn't call upon the gods or bring the storms. Mae could do all of it and more. He was sure that the only reason he was still alive now was that Mae refused to do bad work. She was certainly powerful enough to kill him.

Sometimes, though, when the moon rose, he fully expected to confront the loup-garou, come for vengeance on Mae's behalf. If he had any qualms about what he had to do, the thought of the loup-garou banished them. He had to strike first.

Antoine took a weary breath, trying to summon the enthusiasm he needed to continue. He thought of how very special tonight was going to be, his moment of glory leading to yet many more moments. He had the girl, and before the night was over, he would have his loup-garou. True, she hadn't consented to the transformation, but she would. He had insurance for it.

Thinking about the future pumped him up. However, the future depended on the present. Antoine lifted his arms and crossed them in front of his head so that the elaborate batwings of his cape, attached to metal extensions, would look all the more impressive for the dramatic moment when he would swoop them out to encompass the room, the hidden red spotlight making him glow crimson.

The drums stopped. The bamboula dancer had finished the preliminaries, and now the company wanted the main event.

The drums started again, a slower, more dramatic beat. All the lights dimmed as the dry-ice smoke started to fume around the floor. The red spotlight flashed and the smoke became churning, vaporous blood clouds. Antoine appeared right in the middle of the smoke. As the crowd screamed and moaned, he quickly spread his batwings, the black and red satin billowing out with the sharp snap of real wings, as if they could actually let him fly. Antoine was a tall man, but the sweep of the wings over his head and out from his arms made him look superhuman.

He closed the wings slightly, so that he could move, and started slowly down the platform stairs, toward the other end of the room, the satin billowing behind him now, the red-lit smoke trailing along the floor, following him. When he passed the stained-glass pentagram, it burst into light.

When he reached the altar, another crimson spotlight hit it, and the entire congregation could see what had previously been hidden.

Sylvie, fastened tight to an X-shaped cross before the altar, held by the wrists with black steel chains. She was wearing a white sacrificial robe, her long red hair loose and flowing over her chest like heart's blood.

Antoine stood in front of her, watching her tearstained face. He touched her hair with his long, gold-tipped nails and ran his hands over her body, leaving sharp trails over the thin fabric. He was genuinely amazed at what he knew would happen to this body in just a few minutes. She tried to twist away, straining against the manacles. The sight seemed to amuse the crowd.

"You sorry bastard!" she spat at him.

He drew back slightly, then slapped her so hard her head turned. The crowd gasped and laughed. A red handprint was already starting to show on her cheek by the time she looked defiantly back into his eyes. He could tell that physical abuse wouldn't break her; very much the contrary. The only thing it would accomplish here would be to titillate the crowd, and this wasn't the night for that sort of thing. Sex during rituals was something that Antoine, personally, viewed with mild distaste, but it was unfailingly good for working the crowd.

He stepped closer to her and whispered in her ear. "Straighten up, Sylvie. Try to remember what's at stake, and who else we have here." He grabbed her hair and turned her face toward a little curtained alcove to the right of the altar. Only Antoine and Sylvie could see what was concealed there: Walt and Georgiana, their faces white and terrified, tied back to back and huddled on the floor. Beside them was Angela, her face bruised and one eye starting to swell. Only Angela was gagged.

In spite of the pain it must have caused her, Angela glared at Antoine with such savagery that he still felt a shiver of apprehension. The kids had been easy, just a little chloroform. But Angela had fought like a warrior; at one point she'd grabbed her sewing scissors and tried to stab him in the chest. If one of his men hadn't caught her arm at the last minute, she might have killed him. As it was, it was only a superficial wound, but it bled like hell. It took three of his men to hold her down and slip her the needle.

Sylvie sobbed and was considerably more subdued.

"Be good," Antoine told her, "and nothing will happen to them. Humiliate me in front of this crowd and I'll hurt them. Badly. Come on, Sylvie; nothing's going to happen to you that you didn't want to happen in the first place. You wanted to be

a loup-garou . . . well, you will be. We'll both be satisfied. And
as long as you cooperate with me, your family won't be in any
danger. I know you're thinking of killing me afterward, but it
wouldn't do any good." He opened his own robe slightly so
she could see the gun tucked in his waistband. "Silver bullets.
I'm not taking any chances that you'll turn on me. I want
to keep you around, Sylvie, but all I really need is for this
crowd to watch you transform. I can make another loup-garou
if I have to. Or two." He gestured meaningfully toward Walt
and Georgiana. "And I could always let your mother wear my
pretty necklace." He stroked the obsidian heart.

Sylvie closed her eyes to blot out this whole nightmare, but
the tears wouldn't stop.

"I need your consent, Sylvie, and I'm waiting."

"All right!" she hissed at him. "Just do it. Do it and get it
over with!"

Antoine smiled and turned to the altar. He took a chased
silver jar and held it out toward her. Sylvie could see a golden
yellow ointment, like honey, only thicker, glazing the inside.
This was the same kind of ointment Achille had told her about,
the kind Mae had used to make him a loup-garou.

She couldn't help it. She thought about Lucien and the
werewolf's kiss and she began to cry again.

Antoine dipped his fingers into the ointment. It gleamed on
his fingertips. "You remember what you'll owe me?"

"Yes."

"You owe me a kill, and I want your first one. Can you
guess who it will be?"

"I don't know, I don't care. One of your sleazy drug pushers,
I suppose."

He laughed softly. "No, nothing like that. I want you to kill
Mae Charteris, dear."

The shock stopped Sylvie's tears. "You can*not* make me do
that! I won't!"

"You have no choice."

"Achille won't let you!"

"He has no choice, either."

"Oh, God . . ." Sylvie sobbed hopelessly. She knew she
couldn't stop herself when the time came. She only hoped

that Achille would intercept her and kill her before she could kill Mae.

"Lift your head!" Antoine's voice had become harsh. He was obviously tired of fencing with her.

Sylvie lifted her head. With a swift motion, Antoine opened her robe down the front. This was to allow him to anoint her heart, but the crowd murmured in a drunken, drugged lust to see Sylvie exposed and humiliated. She heard Antoine start the magic chant, invoking the names of the spirits; she felt the first touch of the ointment on her forehead.

Sylvie was only barely aware of the sound of the huge black double doors slamming open and hitting the walls with an earsplitting bang.

Antoine swung around in fury. Sylvie opened her eyes.

Mae stood on the platform, tall and silent, staring straight at Antoine. She looked magnificent in a crimson silk dress she used for her most important Voodoo rituals. She gleamed with all her arcane finery, including an elaborate silk shawl that used to belong to Marie Laveau and a gold ring that Mother Pauline had given her. Crowning her black hair was a silver tiara set with a moonstone pentacle, a gift from the high priestess of a Witches' coven. Fine gold chains set with diamonds and rubies dangled through her hair, throwing rainbow shimmers around the room.

But it was her air of command that was so overwhelming. Even the most die-hard of Antoine's followers grew a little unsure. Mae's superb confidence reminded them that they were not dealing with some inconsequential fortune-teller: that this was, after all, the Queen of the Voodoos. Even Antoine looked uncertain.

Andrew looked just as impressive in the heavy gold vestments and jeweled bishop's miter. He carried the crook, the staff of his office, like a chieftain's spear. Mae didn't need to look at him to know that Andrew's face wore the expression of an avenging angel, the Archangel Michael come to do battle with the Devil. As he stood hand in hand with Mae, the powers of Voodoo and of the Church Militant were very much in evidence.

Mae took in the room and almost snorted in derision. The

whole thing was a cheap horror-movie set, designed to impress the gullible. Where'd Antoine get this junk? From an old Hammer Film warehouse? Nothing was done with any real commitment on Antoine's part: it was all a show, all props.

Even Antoine's robes. Black silk with the devil-headed pentagram on the back and dramatic batwing sleeves lined in scarlet. A black, high-backed cape. Jee*zus*, Mae thought, he looks like a Disney villainess.

Mae's incipient laughter stopped in her throat. The most frightening thing in the room was Sylvie bound to that cross.

She felt Andrew's hand go icy cold and clammy with sweat, but she had to hand it to him: his expression didn't change.

The longer Mae stood there, without a word, the more uneasy the crowd grew, fidgeting, clearing throats, shuffling slightly, looking from Mae to Antoine and not knowing quite what to do. Several of them had been Mae's followers, and they knew her power; suddenly, they weren't too sure of Antoine's.

Mae's eyes took in the room, her expression scornful. "And what is all this, Antoine? A traveling tent show?" Her voice was exquisitely sarcastic, unutterably bored.

There were little gasps from the crowd.

"I had no idea that it required all of . . . *this*"—she waved her hand to disparage the surroundings—"just to do simple stage magic. Or *whatever* it is that you do these days."

She looked toward Sylvie. "At any rate, I've come for my young loup-garou, whom you stole from me. Don't make me elaborate on what happens to those who anger me, just hand her over before any real harm comes to you."

Antoine felt rage bubble like boiling acid in him. He inadvertently raised his hand to his chest and felt the glassy slickness of *la Reine Blanche*'s obsidian heart. He smiled and unhooked it from around his neck, dangling it in his outstretched hand so that everyone in the room could see it.

"Before harm comes to *me*?" Antoine sneered. "I don't receive harm . . . I *create* it! I have my power direct from the great *la Reine Blanche*!"

Mae tried to maintain her bored demeanor, but her heart pounded. Good God, he really did have it. It really was the

White Queen's cursed heart. Whatever power Antoine had came from it, his newly found ability to influence so many people to so much evil. Murder, drug addiction, debauchery, the knowledge to create mindless zombies. All of that stemmed from the obsidian. Mae knew that Antoine had traded his soul for it, and that was precisely what gave it its power. It emitted damnation like a poison gas.

The thing, now, was to keep up a good front. "*La Reine Blanche,* eh?" Mae said, giving a stellar performance. "If she's all that great, how come she's still dead? I'm getting very impatient, Antoine, and I want that girl back."

The obsidian, caught full in the red spotlight, flashed fire. The gleam from the heart grew, pulsated, its own malevolent light finally overpowering the theatrical trick lighting until the entire room was enveloped in a glowing black veil.

The temperature suddenly dropped several degrees, causing the Voodoos to gasp. A slight breeze stirred, moaned, swelled into a wind, then a gale, a chilling storm wind that howled as if the fiends of Hell screamed in frustration. Many of the Voodoos cried, some held their hands over their ears to blot out the nerve-wracking shriek of the wind.

With a great force of effort, Mae closed her eyes and called on her most powerful spirits for protection. She held out her hand and felt another hand take it in a firm grip: Mistress Erzulie was guiding her. Erzulie whispered in her ear and Mae burst into laughter. She prodded Andrew to do the same, and it was if the sound of her scorn calmed the wind. It died away quicker than it came.

"It's nothing!" she announced. "Another of Antoine's stage tricks, a fake!"

Antoine stepped forward, still dangling the stone. He motioned to a man standing close to the altar, and the man moved toward him, terrified but more terrified to refuse. Antoine forced the man's hand out, palm up.

The man jumped back, but Antoine's two henchmen caught him and dragged him forward, forcing his arm out. The man grew hysterical. "Please, Papa . . . you know I love you! Don't make me touch it!"

"You really love me, Jimmy?" Antoine purred calmly.

"Yes, Papa!"

"And will you die for me, Jimmy?"

Jimmy screamed as Antoine dropped the stone into his hand and wrapped the chain around his wrist.

For a few heartbeats, nothing happened. Then Jimmy's arm shivered slightly. It got worse: the shivering turned to a convulsion that traveled from his arm to his entire body, wracking him, shaking him.

The henchmen dropped their grip on him, as if they might die by contamination. The stone fell to the floor.

Mae rushed to Jimmy and took both his hands in hers. He fell to his knees, his distorted face turning bruise purple as his eyes swelled and rolled back. A putrid, stinking sweat burst over him like sudden rain, turning pink, then red with blood. Mae sank to her knees beside him.

"You're not going to die," she told him, "I won't let you." Mae closed her eyes and called the spirits of the dead, of Baron Samedi. She felt the old, familiar energy start to build, but stronger now, coming with a faster rush. The energy seemed to come in through her forehead, bursting through her like golden bolts of lightning, sending sizzling energy all over her body and out through her hands, into the shivering man.

He fell forward on his hands, his forehead touching the floor. Mae jerked him back up, still holding tightly to his hands. "I tell you," she whispered to him, "you *will not die*!"

At those words, his skin started to regain its color. His eyes shrank back to normal size. He took a great gasp of air, then started to breathe.

He collapsed against Mae, panting heavily, but no longer making those strangling gasps. It was obvious that he was far from well, but he wasn't going to die. He looked up at Mae and said weakly, "Madame . . . thank you, Madame!"

"Jimmy Greene," she said sternly, "you get out of here and get home. Just what do you think you're doing playing around with evil stuff like this?"

"Yes, Madame . . . you right. . . ."

Mae stood up regally and stared at Antoine in a direct challenge. She could see that he was in such a fury that he couldn't speak. Now was the time to take advantage of his hesitation.

"Bishop," she said, pointing toward the heart, which still lay on the floor, "would you get rid of that thing? It's caused far too much trouble."

Andrew started toward the heart. He brushed by Sylvie on the altar but appeared to take no notice of her. Mae had to admire his cool demeanor; even under these ghoulish circumstances, she thought, you can't beat a WASP for aristocratic detachment.

He bent down toward the heart.

"Daddy, *don't*!" Sylvie pleaded.

"Well, well," Antoine said, smiling grimly, "your God can't protect you from this, Bishop Marley. Are you ready to die? Is your soul all clean and confessed of its sins?"

"I won't die," Andrew said casually. "Madame Mae promised to protect me, and what she promises, she has the power to deliver."

"Then pick it up, holy man."

Andrew did. He held it in the palm of his hand, balanced there for everyone to see. The cold wind began again, grew louder and stronger, and it seemed that the cries of rushing air carried the discordant voices of the lost dead. Only Andrew, Mae, and Antoine stood rocklike and unshakable among the panicking Voodoos, each sealed in a bubble of determined antagonism.

Antoine broke first, the shrieking in his ears suddenly becoming familiar, the same nightmarish sound that had assaulted him when he first held the stone, when the demon had ravished his soul. He tore off the batwing cape and covered his ears with his arms.

"You know what that sound is, Antoine?" Andrew asked him. "It's the song of the damned souls, the music the Devil sings as he comes for you, to claim your unrepentant body and soul."

Antoine paled. The bishop might have been bluffing, but Antoine knew how true that statement was.

"Give up, Antoine!" Mae commanded. "Save yourself! All I have to do is let the bishop crush the stone. Shall I do it? Will you stop all this nonsense and return to your grandmother's faith? Just take my hand and swear, Antoine!"

His eyes were completely mad as he lifted his head. Mae knew from that look that Antoine had gone too far, had been used beyond his capacity. Even now, in his agony of fear, he couldn't back down.

"Antoine!" Mae whispered. "Please! It's not too late!" She said it because she wanted to believe it.

In all the confusion, no one noticed Sylvie. No one saw the hands that clamped briefly over her mouth to stifle her startled outcry, that loosened the chains. Lucien, half-changed and silent, eased Sylvie to the floor. He only had time to whisper very softly, close to her ear so that she could hear, "The werewolf's kiss, my love. Didn't I promise you?"

And as he lowered his head to her heart, she felt the first sting of pain as his fangs broke the skin.

The wind and cold still swept the room, but Sylvie didn't feel it.

Andrew closed his hand around the heart. Earlier, Mae had reminded him of what everyone else had forgotten; twenty years ago, by vanquishing *la Reine Blanche* and thereby breaking the Marley curse, Andrew had also vanquished her power over him. Nothing of hers could hurt a Marley anymore. In his hands, the heart was as insubstantial as hollow glass. He squeezed his hand around the crystal, crushing the fine gold wires of its cage, and felt it crack into powder.

The wind and the screams subsided until the only sound in the room was the murmur of the awed Voodoos.

"I seem to be fine," Andrew said, letting the black ash run through his fingers.

Unfortunately, the room grew too still too quickly. Everyone heard Sylvie's ecstatic moan as Lucien raised his head, his eyes closed in delight and triumph.

"What the hell is going on?" Antoine demanded.

He saw the trickle of blood run over Sylvie's breast, staining the white robe.

"You son of a bitch!" he screamed hysterically at Lucien. "You've killed her!" He drew his pistol and fired a single silver bullet.

Mae and Andrew watched in horror as the blood bloomed across Lucien's chest. Lucien stood there for one long minute, as if he didn't even feel the pain. He touched his fingers to the wound in disbelief, looked wonderingly at the blood, then fell forward.

Mae screamed and covered her face. Antoine stared at the gun as if he had never seen it before, and didn't even react when Andrew wrenched it out of his hand, almost breaking Antoine's fingers.

Stars were exploding behind Sylvie's closed eyes. She felt her body sizzle with excitement, a tingling hum as her blood raced. It seemed to her that her muscles were expanding, contracting; her bones were growing in all directions. What should have been a terrible pain was only producing pleasure, a marvelous experience—sexual, to be sure, but beyond the simple physical sensations. It was, she thought with delight, like having an endless orgasm over her entire body and brain; she was blind and deaf to anything else. Just when it subsided, it began again, coming in waves, each one cresting higher until, with a crescendo of energy and power, Sylvie felt the entire sun explode inside her. She opened her eyes and jumped to her feet, surprised again as she saw that everyone else looked so small. She was looking down at the room from a height much more than her five feet, eight inches. This was more like eight, ten feet tall!

Her nostrils were assaulted by scents, so many that they made her nose itch suddenly.

She waved her hand in front of her face and saw the flame-colored fur, the long, black claws strong and sharp as daggers. Lucien had kept his promise! She threw back her head to laugh, and found that what erupted from her was a magnificent howl of glory.

She turned her head and saw Walt and Geo. Geo looked terrified, but Walt's eyes were enormous, not frightened at all. With her new hearing, she heard his awestruck whisper to his sister: "This is *so* cool!"

She saw her mother crumple in sorrow, her tears drenching her face. It hurt Sylvie, but she was through living her parents' ideas of what her life should be.

Sylvie picked up Lucien's scent, but something was wrong with it. She looked around in confusion. Where was he? Her ability to locate people by scent had the halting uncertainty of the child taking a first wavering step. Her new height threw her sense of direction off a little, and her new eyes were slightly unfocused.

At the shot, half the Louisiana loup-garou community had burst through the doors. Changed and terrifying, they stormed into the room like the sound of Gabriel's trumpet, fangs bared and slavering, their angry howls shaking the walls and making the chandeliers tremble. The red glass shades shattered against the floor. Sylvie recognized the jet black loup-garou as Achille and the golden one as Zizi by their scents. But where was Lucien?

The Voodoos started to scatter, screaming in terror, trampling each other trying to get out. Some made their way to Mae, begging forgiveness, vowing eternal loyalty if she would only call off the loups-garous.

Achille snatched Antoine up like a toy teddy bear, hauling him off his feet and into the air above his head in one swift motion.

"I'm not gonna kill you right away, you fucker!" Achille growled. "I'm gonna rip your skin off, inch by inch. I'm gonna eat your eyes. I might keep you around for *days*!"

Sylvie closed her eyes and concentrated on Lucien's scent. It was so weak! She crouched down to track it, and touched flesh. Her scream, combined with a howl of grief-struck agony, stopped the loups-garous in midmotion. In all the commotion, none of them, even with the werewolves' bond, had known what had happened to Lucien. Only Mae and Andrew had actually seen it, but Sylvie knew immediately who was responsible.

Before he could even register shock, Achille felt Sylvie's changed body slam against him as she snatched Antoine away. "Mine!" she screamed, her loup-garou's voice still indistinct to all but the other werewolves. "You're *mine*!"

Sylvie could hear Zizi begin to keen in agony.

As Antoine screamed, Sylvie ripped his chest open with one swift, savage slash of her claws. He was still alive and screaming when she ripped out his heart, dripping and warm. She twisted off his head and flung him across the room.

The heart shone like some enormous, evil flower. Sylvie flung it at Mae's feet. "The heart of your enemy, Madame Mae," she cried, her voice choked with tears. "Gris-gris to keep wickedness from you forever."

The room was cleared now of the Voodoos. Only the loups-garous, Mae, and Andrew remained. Andrew rushed to his wife and children, freeing them and crushing them close. He gently touched Angela's hair, and she buried her bruised face against his chest.

The loups-garous gathered around Lucien's body, transformed in death back to human form.

Zizi cradled her son in her arms. She had regained her human form, with the loup-garou's sureness that intense grief can best be expressed by the human body. She seemed not to notice that his blood stained her skin, the bright red streaks clotting in her hair where it had brushed the wound in Lucien's chest. The horrible part was that Zizi, after her first cry when she saw the body, had not made one sound. She was silent now, her eyes stark and uncomprehending. She touched her fingers lightly to the blood still seeping from Lucien's chest, then looked at her bloodstained hands in confusion.

Achille dropped to his knees beside her, too paralyzed by shock to transform. Achille felt as if his own life had run out of him. Lucien's sea green eyes, still opened, seemed to stare at his soul. Achille gently closed them.

"Zizi?" he said, putting his arm around her shoulders. "Come on, Zizi; we have to get out of here. We'll take him home."

She looked at him as if she didn't know him or understand what he was saying.

"Please, *chérie,* we can't stay here."

But she wouldn't move. She wouldn't let go of Lucien's body.

Andrew sat beside her. "Zizi? Would you like me to give him extreme unction? Then we can move him out of this awful place. You don't want to leave him here any longer."

But Zizi wouldn't respond.

A hand extended to Zizi, a totally unfamiliar hand.

To the loups-garous he was a stranger. The man was very tall, with a gentle dignity in his face. At first there was nothing particularly remarkable about him; he was dressed casually, his salt-and-pepper hair slightly rumpled, but it seemed to the assembled loups-garous that the man radiated a glow of his own, a lucent aura barely noticeable, but definitely there. His dark eyes were very sad, and very kind, and Zizi's first impulse was to rush to him, like a child in pain, and bury her sorrows in his strength. But she only took his hand and let herself be pulled away from Lucien.

"Marie-Thérèse," Endore said in his deep, musical voice, "you should have called me before things got this bad."

"After all these years and all this distance," she replied softly, "I didn't know I could. I didn't know how."

"Didn't I tell you that I'd always be here when you needed me? I heard the girl's call"—he nodded toward Sylvie—"and I waited for yours."

She was very still.

Endore reached out and put his hand on Achille's shoulder. "Achille. Good to see you again. I'm so sorry it had to be under these circumstances."

Achille nodded slowly, seemingly in a trance himself.

Endore took both Zizi's hands in his and looked into her face. "I can feel your grief. And you know that I'll do whatever I can for you. Didn't I once tell you that I'd refuse you nothing? But you have to let us take the boy out of here. You understand that, don't you?"

Zizi lifted her head and looked into his eyes for a long moment.

Then she drew back her hand and slapped him across the face, so hard that the crack of it echoed in the room.

The werewolves were stunned into complete stillness. Achille looked stricken.

"Don't you *ever* talk down to me like that again!" she said in fury. "You don't know me at all. You have no idea about the things I've been through in the last centuries or how they've changed me. You'd refuse me nothing? Oh, Apollonius, you've refused me my *life*. You refused me your love, your company, your comfort, your laughter. We were meant to have those things together, we were meant to be happy. But you didn't want to take the chance that you'd be hurt, and I was the one who suffered for it. All I had was my son. He was the only thing you gave me that I could keep close to me."

The werewolves exchanged looks but said nothing. The double shock of actually seeing Apollonius of Tyana—whom most of them knew only as legend—and discovering the secret that Zizi had kept for almost three centuries was too much for them.

Apollonius was very still, his eyes enormous. After a few minutes he said, "Marie-Thérèse, why didn't you tell me we had a child? Didn't you think it would have changed things for me?"

"No, I don't think it would have. All the things you know, Apollonius, all your arcane wisdom, and you didn't know this. The simple subtleties of the heart completely escape you. But I'll tell you now, the time has come for you to make good your promise. You said you'd refuse me nothing? Well, this is all I want. I want you to bring our son back."

A paroxysm of pain passed through his eyes. "Marie-Thérèse, I told you before, and I thought you understood how important this is. I can't interfere with destiny. The consequences could be disastrous."

"I can't believe you're going to refuse to do this! Good God, Apollonius! Have you lost every shred of your humanity? Are you going to sacrifice that along with your son?"

"Ask me anything else, Marie-Thérèse. This is wrong."

"No. What's *wrong* is a young man being murdered in a burst of anger from a madman. You believe in justice, Apollonius? Then see that justice is done. For once, just this once, will you try to choose love over rationality?"

Apollonius walked slowly over to Lucien and knelt beside the body for a few long minutes, staring at the boy's face as if he were memorizing it. His most horrible memory flashed back to him: the resurrected daughter of the consul, butchering her children because of his meddling with death. He could still see the look in her eyes.

He gently pushed the thick blond hair back from Lucien's face, his hand lingering for just a moment on Lucien's forehead.

It didn't always have to be so inflexible, did it? Wouldn't the sword of destiny cut both ways? Perhaps Lucien was supposed to live and provide the world with the beauty of his music and the sweetness of his charm. Perhaps his murderer was the one who had altered the future for the worse, usurping the power of the gods over matters of life and death.

Apollonius couldn't be sure that he wasn't here to put things right, that this wasn't his chance to atone for the four children and their mother.

Drawing back, he slowly put his hand to his throat, pulling the collar of his shirt up. He undressed quickly, with no wasted motions, never taking his eyes off Lucien.

He put his hand over Lucien's wounded heart and held very still, breathing deeply and slowly. Each breath took longer and longer, became shallower as he changed his own brain waves into a trance state.

His back was to the loups-garous, but they watched as Apollonius, in this totally quiet and dreamlike state, passed silently through his transformation and changed into a wonderful silver-and-ebony werewolf. It had taken only a few seconds.

With a long, hooked claw, he reached into the wound and withdrew the silver bullet, now coated red. He lifted the body like a father lifts a small sleeping child, and bent his head over Lucien's heart, his powerful fangs closing over the wound. For several minutes, there was no sound at all. Apollonius lifted his head, and the loups-garous saw the small bite over Lucien's breast.

Lucien's eyes opened. One hand touched the rapidly healing gunshot wound in the same astonished manner he had taken when the shot had first gone in. He drew several deep breaths and stared up in confusion at the werewolf who held him.

They stood like that for a few minutes, the terrible wound healing faster and faster, closing itself, the skin sealing over, the bright red of raw flesh fading to pink, then fading away, even faster than a loup-garou's wounds usually healed.

"Are you well?" Apollonius asked Lucien. Even in his changed state, his voice was clear and strong, his diction distinct, with the same authoritative timbre of his human voice.

Lucien looked around, trying to orient himself, then back

at Apollonius. "Yes," he said, trying to place the face, "yes, I'm fine."

Zizi lowered her face into her hands and sobbed.

"Good," Apollonius declared, "you're ungodly heavy." And he set Lucien on his feet. Lucien wobbled a little, but Apollonius put his arms around Lucien's shoulders to support him.

Achille grasped Apollonius's hand, the enormous silver-shot paw dwarfing his own black one. "I don't even know how to thank you. All I can offer you is our company and a place in our community. Stay with us awhile, Apollonius."

Lucien looked at the strange loup-garou in wonder. "Apollonius?" he whispered.

Apollonius looked doubtful.

"You've been alone for so long," Achille said. "End it now. Stay with us, with the people who love you and need your guidance."

Apollonius's dark eyes, heavy with sorrow even in his changed state, seemed to brighten a little as he looked around at the expectant faces of the werewolves. Achille, Zizi, Christian, Gabriel, Evangeline, Darryl, and the others. Lucien and the new young one. He felt the ties of blood and affection between them all, bonds so strong that they would sacrifice everything for each other. How long, he wondered, how many centuries since he had had the company of his own people, had enjoyed the special delights of running with the pack, of sharing the transformation, had felt the simple joy of companionship? He felt a sharp stab of longing.

"Listen to me," Zizi said, touching his face, "you don't want to live like this anymore. The solitude and the sorrow are killing you, and all your defenses have become weights around your neck. Stay, Apollonius. You have a son, and you don't even know him. How can it be too late when you have all of time ahead of you?"

He took her face gently between his hands, then held her in a close embrace that seemed to relieve him of years of despair.

"You once told me you'd teach me to love," he whispered to her. "I'm not sure I can. But I *am* sure that if I don't try, I'll be lost."

The loups-garous rushed forward to welcome him home.

*   *   *

Changed back to human form and clutching the stained white robe around her, Sylvie stood looking at Andrew, touching his mind, trying to make him understand. But she knew that it was beyond him; his own dreams for her future were irretrievably lost and he couldn't understand how complete and how right her new life felt to her.

She watched Georgiana look at her warily, knowing that Geo wouldn't hate her, but that, like their father, she would never understand Sylvie's choice and would never feel close to her sister again. It seemed to Sylvie then that she understood everything that Achille had told her about the special pain of the loup-garou.

"We've got to go, Sylvie," Andrew told her as he gathered Angela, Walt, and Geo close. "Please, don't feel that you can't see us. Don't abandon your family."

"Never," she said.

"Dad?" Walt said hesitantly. "Do I have to go?"

"What do you mean?" Andrew said.

"I want," he said quietly but firmly, "to stay with Sylvie. I want to be what she is."

Sylvie hugged him fiercely. "Not now," she said. "You think about it. Hard. And when you're lots older, we'll talk. Hey, it's not like I'm *dead* or anything, okay? If you want me, I'm only over on Royal Street. You promise to come by? Both of you?"

Walt nodded enthusiastically. Geo only looked down at her hands, and Sylvie felt a hollowness at the back of her throat.

"Well, good, then," she said, kissing all of them good-bye. Geo flinched at her touch. Angela looked at Sylvie with sympathy, and she could see that her mother understood everything, including how difficult Sylvie's decision had been. Her mother, a woman of independent spirit if ever there was one, knew all about paying the price to have what you want.

Angela held her for a few minutes. "Don't worry, baby," Angela whispered, "everything will be all right, in time."

Lucien held out his hand to Sylvie and they left the house. Andrew, standing in the door with his family, lost sight of the two of them, but in the distance, very faintly, with the

sensitive hearing that had never quite left him, just as the old,
dull longing had never left him, heard the first joyous howls
of freedom as Sylvie and Lucien danced together in the warm
Louisiana night.

Author's Note on Dates

I've taken some license with some of the dates used in *The Werewolf's Kiss*. The Marquis de Sade wasn't born until 1740, but I think he'd have been intrigued to be included here. The date of A.D. 61 for the Emperor Domitian's confrontation with Apollonius of Tyana is arbitrary, since scholars disagree. However, as Apollonius was thought to be immortal, perhaps he'll come forward with the correct information.

420